John Wingate

St. Martin's Press
New York

Library of Congress Cataloging in Publication Data

Wingate, John.
  Go deep.

  1. World War, 1939-1945—Fiction.   I. Title.
PR6073.I53G6   1985   823'.914   85-25112
ISBN 0-312-33062-6

First published in Great Britain by George Weidenfeld and Nicolson Ltd.

First U.S. Edition

10 9 8 7 6 5 4 3 2 1

How would posterity and the youth of Britain remember my men who had died in such a desperate battle? Unless they were told the story they would have nothing to remember.

In the main it was the youth who pulled us from the desperate mire of 1939–42.

Rear-Admiral G. W. G. Simpson, CB, CBE; Captain of the Tenth Submarine Flotilla. Malta, 1941–1943.

(From *Periscope View*, Macmillan)

Acknowledgements

Inevitably, *Go Deep* records only a fragment of the saga which was 'our' Siege of Malta, the ordeal we shared with the Maltese people from 1940–43. This novel is the story of a fictional submarine during the third phase in the life of this unique submarine flotilla, the Tenth, which was based on Manoel Island and was in existence for only three years.

The relentless achievements of these submarines were greatly responsible for cutting Rommel's supply lines and bringing his Panzers to a halt. That these few submarines achieved what they did while operating under savage siege conditions and suffering grievous losses, is a measure of the inspiration given by their leader, Captain George Simpson, RN – 'Shrimp' to everyone who served with him.

Go Deep records the life of those submariners. But without the help of those who returned from patrol this novel would never have seen the light of day. I regret that it is impossible for my gratitude to reach them all.

My thanks are due to John Rapa who contacted me from distant America; the *Times of Malta*; the Curator for the Hydrographer of the Navy, Taunton; and, especially, to Victor Coppini for his help, friendship and enthusiasm.

I have been privileged to have received unstinted encouragement and aid from so many friends in the Submarine Service, and in particular from those who served in the Tenth. I realize acutely how inadequate is my gratitude to them.

I must emphasize that the encouragement and contributions so freely given by the surviving Submarine Commanding Officers, their officers and men have provided the impetus for this book. I extend my deep gratitude to them:

Commander P. C. Chapman, DSO, OBE, DSC*	*Upstart*
Captain M. L. C. Crawford, DSC*, RN	*Unseen*
Anthony Daniell, Esq, DSO, DSC	*Unison*

Captain G. E. Hunt, DSO*, DSC*	*Ultor*
Captain Michael Lumby, DSO, DSC, RN	*Saracen*
Captain C. P. Norman, CBE, DSO, DSC, RN	*Una*
Vice-Admiral Sir John Roxburgh, KCB, CBE, DSO, DSC*	*United*
Commander P. R. G. Smith, DSC	C.O.P.P. (Canoe M.E.I)
Commander E. T. Stanley, DSO, DSC	*Unbending*
Captain John Stevens, DSO, DSC, RN	*Unruffled*
Commander J. Whitton, DSC, RN	*Unshaken*
Mr C. H. A. Balls	*United*
Lord Hardinge of Penshurst: Secretary to Captain S10	
Mr J. Richards	*Unseen*

The defiant courage of the people of Malta, GC, will evoke admiration for all time. The heroism of the island equates with that of the defenders of Stalingrad; the Battle of Britain pilots; those involved in the evacuation of Crete; the Desert Rats of Alamein; Guadacanal; and Midway.

That Malta could endure three terrible years of murderous bombardment and siege was due, not only to the unique character of its people, but also to the unequivocal and inspired leadership of its two outstanding Governors and its Church leaders. Among those who served General Dobbie and Lord Gort was Mr Wingrave Tench, OBE, and I am immensely indebted to him and his family for their friendship, and for their contribution – offered with typical modesty. As a Civil Administrator and then Director of the Communal Feeding Department, he lived through the whole Siege. His organization ensured that everyone, from the Governor downwards, rich and poor, was on identical rations. His home was open house to Captain Simpson and the submariners; relaxing with 'Gravy' Tench and Greta, Shrimp was able to unwind from the awful responsibilities he shouldered. If Shrimp had faltered, so would his men. Much therefore is owed to Gravy and his wife, Greta.

I acknowledge with immense gratitude the indispensable support provided by the Director and Staff of the Royal Navy Submarine Museum at Gosport.

To Commander Richard Compton-Hall, MBE, RN (Retd) and Mr Gus Britton I extend my sincere thanks.

Go Deep tells the story of one of the submarines during those unforgotten years.

John Wingate
November 1984

Glossary

Asdic (sonar):	The device by which submarines are detected. Submarines are also fitted with this device, when it is used as a hydrophone.
Baron:	A wealthy VIP.
Bearing:	The direction of an object.
Blowers:	Machines with which to blow out the water in the tanks by using low-pressure air.
Blue:	Local brand name for beer ration.
'Bunts' (bunting tosser):	The signalman.
Cable:	Two hundred yards.
Chiakking:	Bantering, teasing.
Chariot:	Two-man human torpedo.
Corticene:	A type of heavy linoleum used to cover the steel deck.
Crack:	To open a valve quickly, and to shut it again immediately.
Desert Rats:	The Eighth Army.
DSEA:	Davis Escape Apparatus.
ETA:	Expected Time of Arrival.
Fish:	Torpedo.
Free Flood:	The open holes in the casing and tanks through which the water enters and drains.
Fruit Machine:	The calculating machine into which all relevant attack data is fed, and from which the necessary information is extracted to carry out an attack.
Focke-Wulf:	German long-range reconnaissance aircraft.
Gens:	General Service in the Royal Navy.

Group Down:	Low speed on the main electric motors, thus using up little electric power.
Group Up:	High speed on the main electric motors, thus using up the battery power rapidly.
HA:	High Angle.
HE:	Hydrophone Effect, i.e. propeller noise.
HE:	High Explosive.
Heat:	Slang for the situation when a submarine is at the receiving end of a severe depth-charge attack.
HP:	High Pressure.
HSD:	Higher Submarine Detector – the rank of a skilled Asdic operator.
Hydrophone:	Underwater listening device.
Incendiary run:	Semi-organized, evening forays ashore to put out fires caused by incendiaries.
Jimmy-the-One (or Jimmy, Jim):	Slang for First Lieutenant.
Jolly Roger:	Skull-and-crossbones flag, upon which the emblems of sinkings are sewn. Flown to denote success.
Ki:	Naval cocoa.
Layer:	As its name implies, when two different densities adjoin in the water, a horizontal curtain (the layer) divides the two. Asdic (sonar) pulses, like light, are reflected and cannot penetrate this layer to find contact with the target; this phenomenon is exploited by submariners to escape detection, particularly during the summer months when layers exist in abundance.
Main Ballast Kingston:	Water into the internal tanks amidships is allowed to enter through the large Kingston valves.
Main Ballast Tanks:	The tank which gives the submarine its buoyancy. All are fitted with main vents, numbers 1 and 6 being external, the remainder internal.
Main Vents:	The large mushroom valves on top of the Main Ballast tanks. When the main vents

are open, water will rush into the tanks; but, if the main vents are shut, the air cannot escape when the Main Ballast tanks are blown, because the 'blow' is at the top of the tank and the free-flood holes are at the bottom. Water is therefore forced out through the holes in the bottom of the tank, HP air taking its place.

Messerschmitt: ME109 – single-seater German fighter.

Oggin: The sea.

Outside ERA: The Engine Room Artificer whose duty is at the panel in the Control Room, and who is therefore 'outside' the Engine Room. Also known as the 'Outside Wrecker'.

Panel: The conglomeration of valves and blows centralized in one central position on the starboard side of the Control Room.

Perisher: Slang for Commanding Officers' Qualifying Course.

Pusser: The Paymaster: the naval authority responsible for pay, stores, etc.

Q Tank: The emergency tank for quick diving. When flooded, the tank makes the submarine ten tons heavier than her normal dived trim. After diving, this extra water is blown out of Q tank by high-pressure air. If this tank is required to be flooded when dived, its vent has merely to be opened to allow the air in the tank to be vented either inboard or outboard, and the sea will rush into Q. In wartime, Q tank is always kept flooded when the submarine is on the surface.

Scorps: Gibraltarians.

Scran: Slang for food.

Slow One: Slow speed on one propeller.

Slow together: Slow speed on both propellers.

Snotty: Midshipman.

Stick: Slang for periscope.

Swain: Coxswain, Cox'n: the submarine's Senior

	Rating.
Ticklers:	Naval cigarette tobacco.
Torpoil:	Special torpedo oil.
*U*s:	British *U*-class submarines.
U-boat:	Enemy submarine.
Uckers:	Naval version of 'Ludo' game.
Ursula suit:	Waterproof overalls in general use, designed by the Commanding Officer of HM Submarine *Ursula*.
Woolworth carrier:	A merchant ship which has been converted to become a small aircraft carrier.
Wop:	Slang for Italian.
Wrecker (Outside):	The Outside ERA.

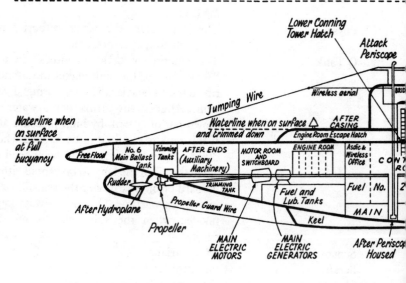

HIS MAJESTY'S SUBMARINE URGENT

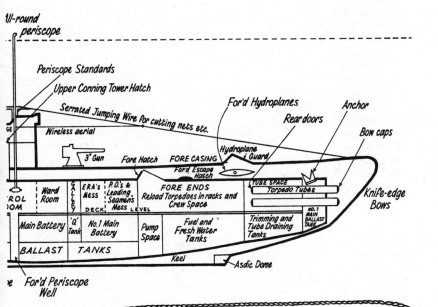

Length 196 ft.   Beam 11 ft.

Surface displacement.. 600 Tons   Max. surface speed .... 10 Knots
Dived displacement .... 800 Tons   Max. dived speed ..... 7 Knots

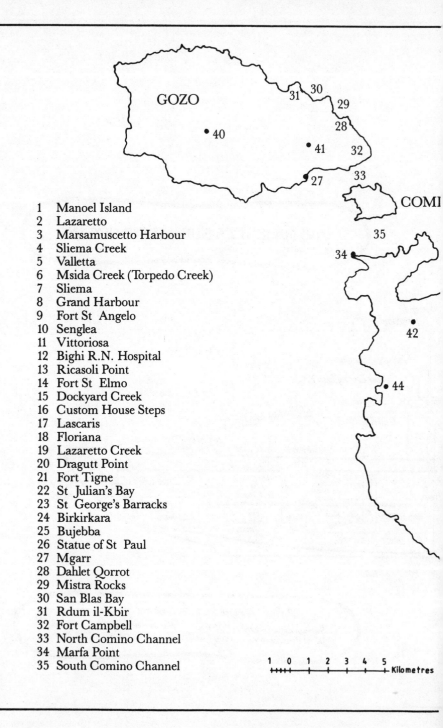

GOZO

31 30
29
28
40
41 32
27 33

COMI

35

34

42

44

1 0 1 2 3 4 5
Kilometres

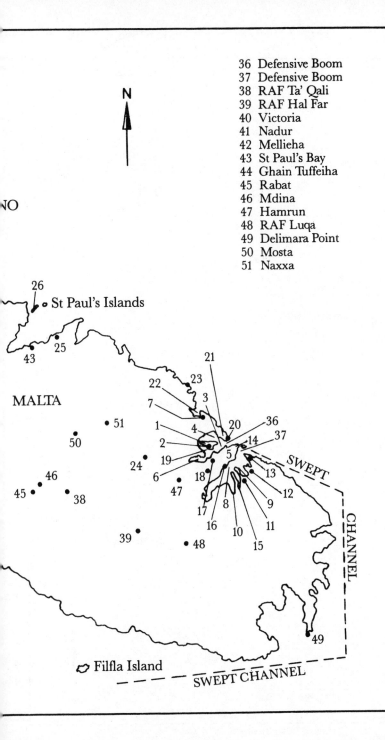

36 Defensive Boom
37 Defensive Boom
38 RAF Ta' Qali
39 RAF Hal Far
40 Victoria
41 Nadur
42 Mellieha
43 St Paul's Bay
44 Ghain Tuffeiha
45 Rabat
46 Mdina
47 Hamrun
48 RAF Luqa
49 Delimara Point
50 Mosta
51 Naxxa

N

NO

26
● St Paul's Islands

25
43

MALTA

21
22 23
7 3
1 4 20 36
2 14 37
51 5
50 19 SWEPT
24 13
6 18 12
46 47 9
45 38 8 17 16 10 11 15 CHANNEL

39 48

49

Filfla Island
SWEPT CHANNEL

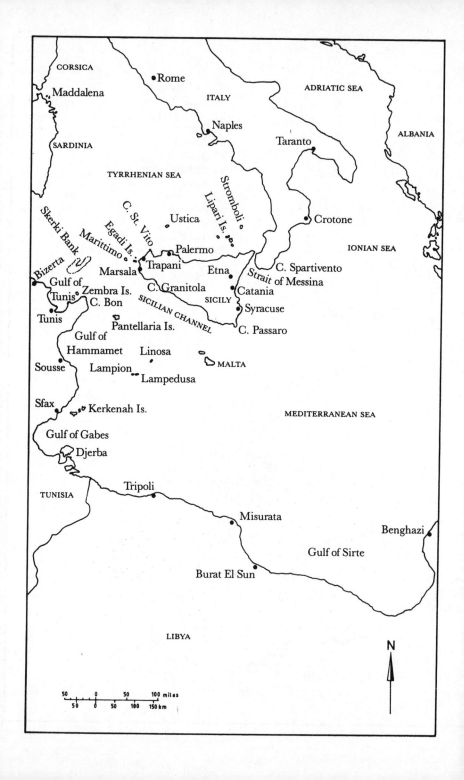

CHAPTER ONE

Pierhead Jump

'Jump in, sir!'

The naval lieutenant slung down his kitbag. He grabbed the RAF corporal's outstretched arm and scrambled down into the boat. The corporal nodded to his bowman and the launch swung clear from the Mountbatten jetty. The throttle opened and as the launch headed for the Catalina flying boat tugging at its buoy in Plymouth Sound, Lieutenant John Carbis glanced over his shoulder.

'Just made it,' the other passenger murmured, a lieutenant-colonel by the pips on the shoulder of his battle-dress. 'Wonder when we'll see the red cliffs again?'

'I've only a single ticket, sir,' Carbis replied, gazing at the Devon coast running westwards on the far side of the Sound.

The army officer cupped his hand to his ear: 'Sorry?' he bellowed above the clatter of the engine. 'You for Gib too?'

'Malta eventually!' Carbis shouted, in no mood for conversation. The PBY2 flying boat was singled-up and swinging to the tide. One of its crew was crouched in the port doorway and leaning out to take the launch's painter. Fendered down her length, the boat rounded up, eased alongside. The colonel scrambled through the aperture and, as the RN lieutenant followed him, the RAF flight-sergeant grinned:

'Third class for you, sir: on the mail bags.'

The passengers' gear was bundled through the opening and, when the door was clipped shut, the flying boat's two engines, one after the other, coughed into life. Carbis lay spread-eagled across the mail bags, his face on a level with the port window. PBY2 409 slipped from her mooring, floated back on the tide. The starboard motor roared, the bows paid off; the port engine synchronized and, heading for Cawsand Bay, the Catalina opened up to full power. Carbis felt her acceleration, the buffeting of the wavelets upon the hull.

He could see the outer breakwater; the RAF Mountbatten Base

flashing past, seagulls wheeling clear of the big bird. The pounding grew to a crescendo and then, imperceptibly lifting her nose, the amphibian was airborne. Gaining height slowly, the Catalina levelled off at three hundred feet, then banked gently to port to head south-westwards. Through the starboard window, John Carbis snatched his last glimpse of England as the pyramid point of Rame Head slid swiftly aft. A few minutes later, the pepperpot of Eddystone reared below them, a white circlet swirling at its rocky base. To the eastward, twilight merged into darkness, while to starboard the crimson sun sank behind the hills. His final memory of Cornwall through the starboard window would remain with him for a long time: gentle, tranquil, very English. He found himself asking the same question as the colonel: when would he see this rolling country of the west again?

It was dark by the time the Lizard came abeam. The wavelets flecked white in the darkness below them as, at five hundred feet, the Catalina headed south for the Bay of Biscay, Portugal and Gibraltar. The colonel was already asleep in the seat in front of the mail bags. The only light came from the luminous glow of the instrument panel in the cockpit where the pilot and his navigator were concentrating upon their flying. Brave men, these, thought Carbis. As lonely a job as any: flying at five hundred feet through the night, within reach of enemy fighters from Brest, they carried out their vital ferrying week-in and week-out, whatever the losses. The preceding flight had never arrived at Gib. The one before that, from Gib to Malta, had landed by error in Sicily.

Carbis' lanky frame did not mould itself easily across the mail bags. His angular face with the protruding cheek bones gave him a gaunt, laconic image; his hair was dark, but had a russet tinge about it. Beneath the bushy, dark eyebrows his lively, deep-set eyes were spaced widely, divided by a long, high-bridged nose. There was a distinctly Cornish look about him. His mind roamed, the pressures of the past few days taking their revenge. At last, he was on his way to Malta. In his pocket he carried the passport they had given him with the photo of him in plain clothes: a civil servant on His Britannic Majesty's Service. The visa was to be used if the aircraft was brought down and he found himself in Spain or Portugal.

The engine droned; the rear-gunner slipped down from his nacelle, clambered past the mail bags; below them, the short seas of the English Channel seemed another world, those long nights and days of flogging the 'oggin' . . .

For twenty months, as a sub and then a lieutenant, he had commanded his little chasseur, the ex-French submarine-chaser, in the Channel. Anti-German invasion patrols in '40; the Channel convoys . . . and now, after many vicissitudes and only weeks before the Dieppe raid, he'd been press-ganged into submarines. It was difficult to credit that the bombshell had struck only seven weeks ago . . . and now, of his own volition, he was one of the four from the Blyth training class to be on his way to join the hard-pressed Tenth Submarine Flotilla at Malta.

He'd never volunteered for anything before: to choose Malta was crazy – but only he knew the reason for his choice. After Pam's traumatic break with him, he was miserable and his pride had taken a hammering. The Tenth seemed a good way out, for that was where the action was . . . his mind jerked back to the present when one of the Catalina's crew handed him a mug of coffee.

'We shan't need the rear-gunner again until Ushant,' the aircraftsman shouted. 'We'll try not to wake you.'

Brest would be the most dangerous bit, Carbis thought. A night interception would be difficult, but the captain was taking no risks – the rear-gunner could sleep all day at Gib if he wanted . . .

The thought that he had been selected for a job which was totally offensive in this damnable war gave Carbis a certain satisfaction. This struggle to the death with the Nazis and Fascists was so delicately balanced at the moment. We couldn't survive another six months like these which had just passed . . . there was even talk of continuing the fight from America and Canada. Oh God! Surely not? Two and a half years on our own had dragged by already – two bitter years of defeats and unprepared landings; of ever swifter evacuations of the army by the navy: we were paying dearly for the locust years . . . 1940 was the black year: the Norwegian landings and withdrawal; Dunkirk and the French collapse; Mussolini's declaration of war on 10 June . . .

Carbis could still feel the despair which the British nation felt eight months ago at the year's end of 1941. On 7 December, the Japs treacherously sank the American Pacific Fleet at Pearl Harbor. Three days later, as a preliminary to their attack on our vital Singapore base, Japanese bombers sent our 'unsinkable' battleship, *Prince of Wales*, and her attendant old battle-cruiser, *Repulse*, to the bottom of the sea. In the Mediterranean, whither John Carbis was now bound, disaster followed calamity. During November 1941, *Ark Royal* was torpedoed and sunk. *Illustrious* and *Formidable*, both damaged, were refitting in the States; *Indomitable* had grounded at Kingston, Jamaica. No armoured deck-carrier was available for Admiral Cunningham's Med Fleet. By 19 December the fortunes of the fleet were at their lowest ebb: the Mediterranean fleet virtually ceased to exist.

Only our Desert Rats (General Auchinleck's 8th Army) now barred Rommel's advance upon Alexandria to link up with the Japanese across India. And this was the month when the German bombing forced the survivors of the Tenth Submarine Flotilla to quit Malta for Alexandria and Beirut; this, the moment when ABC relinquished command of his Mediterranean fleet for his appointment to Washington; and this the instant too, a month later, when Gort relieved Dobbie as Governor of Malta.

But, six weeks later, on the day when Carbis received his appointment to HMS *Talbot*, the name of the submarine base at Malta, the four surviving submarines of the Tenth Flotilla were leaving Beirut to return to their home at Lazaretto in Malta . . . John Carbis grunted, turned on his side, trying to find sleep: in ten days, if *Clyde*, the large store-carrying submarine, could get him there, he'd be joining *Urgent*, the boat to which he had been appointed.

'Ushant should be abeam,' the rear-gunner shouted. 'Regular bus service, aren't we, sir?' He passed a sandwich across the mail bags.

Carbis disliked flying. These airmen had guts; as if flying for hours in darkness, five hundred feet above the sea, on Dead Reckoning navigation, wasn't enough. The Dorniers, Focke-Wulfs and the twin-engined night fighters weren't far off . . .

The submarine course into which he had been pitched had been a welcome break at Blyth in Northumberland. The course members, except for the three other RN officers, had all been RNVR. The North Sea air seemed to have had a remarkable effect on the Wrens, so the seven weeks' training had been a wild affair: and in the semi-darkness John Carbis smiled to himself at the memories.

The intensity of the submarine training at Blyth, combined with the fun of being ashore after two and a half years of war at sea, had set him on his feet, concentrated his mind after the shock of Pam. It was the suddenness of the break with her which had hurt. When she'd disappeared from his life, she hadn't written . . .

It had probably been a rebound affair, anyway, after his love for Anna Seguna: he'd lost her too. To hell with women! He wasn't the world's most successful lover . . . Lofty Small, a contemporary, had been one of the other three RN officers in the course – and he was engaged to Anna now . . .

Lofty and he had been senior midshipmen in *Warspite*, ABC's flagship, when the French had visited Malta just before the outbreak of war. During the At Home in honour of the French C-in-C, Admiral Ollive, Lofty and John had battened on to one of the Maltese families invited to meet the French visitors. For midshipmen of two years' standing, choosing the right 'baron' had developed into a practised skill: choice depended upon one's interest. The most senior midshipmen of the gunroom made a bee-line for the fathers with the pretty daughters, leaving the parents owning boats or tennis courts to the junior 'snotties' . . . and on that hot summer evening of '39, with the strains of the Royal Marine band thumping at the after end of *Warspite*'s quarterdeck, Midshipmen Small and Carbis were concentrating upon the de Marco family and the girl with them, Miss Anna Seguna.

He had beaten Lofty to it. While the cocktail party was at its peak, he had succeeded in inveigling Anna up to the spotting-top to view the fleet lying at anchor in the blue waters of Grand Harbour beneath the battlements of Valetta. There, with the lights of the ships and the shore emerging like glowworms in the stillness of the evening, he had shared his first real kiss with the girl – even now he could feel the softness of her lips, the thrill which had passed between them; he had loved her from that moment. She had taken his hand and led him back to the ladder, back to the thinning crowd on the quarterdeck which had jolted them both back to reality.

But it was Lofty who carried off the prize: the de Marcos had disapproved of their young charge's absence from the quarterdeck with Midshipman Carbis; it was Midshipman Small whom they invited back to dinner at their home in Sliema. Anna Seguna, who was a nurse in the Bighi naval hospital, lodged with them when she was off-duty . . . and Lieutenant Carbis drifted into sleep.

'That's Corunna,' the navigator was shouting to his captain. The Catalina banked to a new course parallel to the lights fringing the Portuguese coast. In four hours they'd be off Cape St Vincent: the worst was over, the roving JU 88s left far behind them . . . John eased his cramped legs across the mail bags . . .

Gunroom rules were ruthless regarding women: all *was* fair in love and gunroom jungle warfare. Lofty had certainly won the first round, though John continued to pester Anna with letters which she ignored. Then the war exploded; Lofty was one term senior to Carbis, so he finished his sub-lieutenant's course three months earlier. Small went

5

to command a trawler in the North Sea, Carbis to his chasseur in the Channel.

It was not until they met coincidentally on the same submarine course at Blyth that Carbis learned of Lofty's engagement to Anna. She had followed him to England but, on the outbreak of war, had returned to Malta by travelling across France to Marseilles; she boarded one of the last ships to Malta before Mussolini declared war on 10 June 1940. So she was back in the island now . . . and with this comforting thought and the droning of the flying boat, the weary Carbis dropped off into a fitful sleep.

'Alarm port!'

The shout and the violent banking of the aircraft jerked Carbis back to wakefulness. Behind him the rear-gunner was cursing as he swung his guns to the bearing. A rush of cold air swept through the Catalina. Through the port, John glimpsed the shadowy outlines of two aircraft swinging down upon them from the brightening eastern sky.

'Hudsons!' the gunner yelled.

The familiar silhouettes swung past to take up their escorting positions on either quarter. The colonel's laugh was brittle as ahead the welcome shape of Gibraltar loomed from out of the dawn twilight. Like a lion *couchant*, the enduring Rock guarded the western entry into the Mediterranean and while it stood sentinel there was hope. As the Catalina banked round Europa Point, Carbis glimpsed the great dockyard, the grey ships strung like water beetles along the moles, but he could not identify *Clyde*. Banking to port again, the Catalina flew around the eastern flank of the great Rock, its huge slabs of water catchments gleaming white in the breaking dawn.

'Brace yourselves for the landing,' the pilot called out as the amphibian started its approach run beneath the vertical north face looming above them. The wheels were down and through the window Carbis glimpsed the figures of watching men flashing past. The roar of the engines died. There was a bump, a lurch, and a violent juddering as the brakes came on – and then the fluttering of the slowly revolving propellers as the wheels burnt off their rubber to halt the amphibian at the end of the runway only twenty yards from the black waters of the harbour.

'All change,' the flight-sergeant called out; he moved towards the door while the aircraft taxied towards the Nissen hut on the edge of the airstrip. The first leg of Carbis' voyage to Malta was over.

'Thanks,' he murmured. 'I didn't have to use my passport after all.'

CHAPTER TWO

Lifeline

It was 30 May 1942 when John Carbis joined his first operational submarine at Gibraltar. The RAF gave him breakfast in the Nissen hut and, when the army truck came to fetch its lieutenant-colonel, Carbis hitched a lift to the dockyard gates. Leaving his kitbag with the police, he squared off his rumpled No 5 suit and strode along the South Mole. It was four minutes to nine when he reached the brow spanning the gap between the mole and the submarine. Compared to the training boat, *L26* at Blyth, *Clyde* seemed a monster. He stood for a moment gazing down at her, the heat of the mole already scorching beneath his feet.

Below him, with two lighters alongside her, lay the giant who was to transport him to Malta. With a dived displacement of almost three thousand tons, *Clyde* and her sister ship, *Severn* (*Thames* was mined off Norway in July, two years ago), were the largest boats in our submarine fleet. Designed as a fleet submarine, her surface speed was 21 knots; but her size (she was three hundred and forty-five feet overall), though cumbersome for offensive operations in the clear waters of the Mediterranean, made her suitable for her role of supplying Malta with the vital stores to keep the island and its submarine base alive. Once a month, loaded with machinery spares, torpedoes, petrol and stores, she made the passage through the Sicilian minefields.

Dockyard maties were already swarming over her, while a chain of sailors handed crate after crate from the lighters through *Clyde*'s fore and after hatches. The position of her bridge and gun, further forward than in other classes, gave her a pugnacious look, though, it was said, this siting gave her a better turning circle when dived. The sentry had spotted him and an officer was detaching himself from the working party. The sentry loped up the brow and took Carbis' 'pusser's grip'. 'Lieutenant Carbis, sir?'

'That's me.'

'The first lieutenant is expecting you.'

At the bottom of the brow, Carbis half-turned to salute the ensign hanging limply from its staff. The first lieutenant introduced himself:

'Welcome on board the Malta bus.' He led the way towards the after hatch, taking care not to interrupt the loading chain of sailors. 'The captain's just finished breakfast.'

Carbis shinned down the vertical ladder. The sunlight dimmed above his head and then he was threading his way past the line of men passing boxes from hand to hand along the passage-way. He recognized the smell he was already beginning to associate with submarines: a mixture of torpoil, diesel and humanity. The control room was a mass of gear and stores; green circular smoke canisters were already lashed along the passage. A leading stoker, who was dipping the tanks, stood up to allow the officers room to pass through to the wardroom. Two lieutenants were seated at the table perusing the day's signal log, while a seaman cleared away the remnants of breakfast. The older of the two, a stocky, fair-haired man with brown, humorous eyes, got up and held out his hand. Entering the wardroom, Carbis removed his cap.

'Lieutenant Carbis, sir. Reporting on board to join.'

'Sit down, Carbis. Had a good trip?'

'Uneventful, sir. Glad to be with you, though.'

'Brookie' Brookes smiled. 'The other passengers have already joined from *Eagle* and I thought you'd be missing my bus.' He swept his hand towards the busy passageway. 'Number One's got a bunk for you, but we're pretty busy on last-minute storing. Sling your hammock and make yourself at home.' He glanced at his first lieutenant. 'You've booked the table at The Rock, Number One?'

'Thirteen hundred, sir. I'll fix another place.'

Brookie nodded. 'Join us, Carbis. We're meeting at the Victoria for a final pre-prandial before sailing.'

'Thank you, sir. I'd like to.'

'You won't get much to eat at Lazaretto, so you might as well make the most of a good meal.' He smiled; 'One of the advantages of being a store-carrier. Hammer Hawkes is your CO, isn't he? *Urgent*?'

'That's what they told me at Northways, sir.'

'Hammer's Jimmy is due for his perisher, I believe: he's on my future passenger lists.' Carbis felt Brookie watching him intently. 'D'you know Hammer?'

'No, sir.'

'He was our Third Hand when I was Number One of *H43*. You'll not be bored,' Brookie grinned. 'You'll get along fine. See you at the Victoria.' He turned to the wardroom flunky who was squaring-off the green baize tablecloth. 'Ask the signalman to bring me yesterday's log,' he said, and sat down again to continue with the day's work.

The first lieutenant led the way for'd and showed Carbis to his bunk, the lower one of the three, tucked against the boat's side. 'I'll leave you to settle in.'

'What's the rig?' Carbis asked. 'It's hot ashore.'

'You can stow away your blues,' Number One said. 'Whites: tropical shirt and shorts for Gib, but you won't be wearing them again for a long time. They'll kit you up like the pongos, in khaki, when you reach Malta.'

John Carbis was on his own, one amongst seventy-five men. In silence he began to sort out his gear, spreading it along his bunk while the endless chain of hands filed past him. He felt lonelier than he had for a long time.

'*Harbour stations . . .*'

Carbis, the only officer passenger, sat by himself in *Clyde*'s wardroom as her ship's company bustled to their stations for leaving harbour. The captain was climbing up the conning tower to the bridge, while the wires were being singled-up.

'*Shift to night lighting.*'

He could sense the added tension as *Clyde* prepared to sail for her second store-carrying trip under her new captain, for Brookes had only recently taken over from his predecessor. The flunky had shipped red bulbs instead of white and Carbis was left alone with his thoughts. The bustle had changed to a restrained murmur of voices as systems were checked, while lookouts donned their Ursula suits to protect them from the weather. It took twenty minutes for a man's eyes to adapt to full night vision and changing to red lighting reduced the waiting time.

'*Obey telegraphs . . .*'

The coxswain was on the wheel, the engine room ready. Up top, they'd be slipping the springs at any moment . . .

He had been made to feel part of the team, even though he was only a passenger and more in the way than being of any use. The run- ashore had been fun, and lunch at The Rock Hotel, after a bout with the fruit machine, had been a rollicking affair. Number One's natural reserve had been more than off-set by Brookie's tomfoolery, a role he enjoyed immensely but which concealed a decisive and ruthless character when circumstances demanded. After lunch, while the others got their heads down under the shade of the bougainvilleas, Carbis had made his excuses to take a last look at the bustling high street of Gibraltar.

Wars came and went, but Gib never changed: he'd been here five years ago when he'd been a 'mid' in *Esk*, one of our destroyers which shared the Nyons Patrol with the French, in an attempt to protect our shipping from Axis submarine attacks during the Spanish civil war. The main street still smelled the same; the locals, the 'Scorps', were still irrepressibly jovial; the juke-boxes jingled and the tiny pianos continued to tinkle from behind the beaded curtains of the bars.

For old times' sake, he rode in a gharrie, its flea-bitten pony picking its way through the bustling main street where children played and fowls squawked. But at sunset, as he drove back to the dockyard, the tap was abruptly turned off. No longer did the twinkling lights spatter Gibraltar's flanks like glowworms on a summer night. The blackout cast the great Rock into massive relief against the indigo of the twilight sky. By night, in contrast to the gaiety of daylight, Gib was at war: the dark alleyways brooded upon the secret town, the shutters of the houses clasping hands across the deserted street to shut out the immensity of the universe above.

The first lieutenant had moved *Clyde* back to her depot ship, *Maidstone*, where Carbis located her after his brief visit to the town. A couple of *U*s and an *S* boat lay in one trot alongside their mother ship; *Clyde* was berthed aft of them, ready for sailing. She seemed much smaller there than she had appeared at her berth on the mole: looking down upon her for the last time from the height of the depot ship's quarter-deck, it was hard to realize that, at this critical moment during the siege of Malta, *Clyde* was vital for the island's survival: the surviving merchant ships from the convoys being fought through from either end of the Mediterranean were being bombed to bits in harbour, before their cargoes could be unloaded. The fast minelayers, *Manxman* and *Welshman*, were dashing at 40 knots through to the island but, to fool enemy intelligence, their runs had to be spaced irregularly. But *Olympus*, another store-carrying submarine, with part of the crews from *P39* and *P36*, had just been mined off St Elmo Light, six miles from Malta. Of her ninety-eight complement, which included passengers returning to Gib, only twelve survived to reach shore.

Under the command of Brookie's predecessor, *Clyde* had been refitted for her present role. Her forward battery was taken out, her reload torpedoes and most of her gun ammunition landed. She made a passage to Malta in April with stores, benzine, kerosene and ammunition but, on sailing for her return to Gib, her fore-planes failed. She put back to Malta, but the intensity of the bombing and the destruction of the dockyard made repair impossible.

With the defective hydroplanes lashed amidships, she again began her return passage to Gibraltar. Using only her after-planes for control while dived by day, all went well until, within two days of reaching The Rock, the lashings parted. She was lucky to reach port safely because, to avoid catastrophe, she was forced to proceed on the surface at only 8 knots.

Carbis glanced at the clock in the corner: 1950. She would be carrying out her trim dive at any moment, in the safe waters of Algeciras Bay. Soon, when he became Number One of *Urgent*, *he*'d be experiencing the anxiety of his first trim dive, but that would be nothing in comparison to the worries of *Clyde*'s first lieutenant. The weight and position of every store, torpedo, smoke float and passenger; the adjustments to be made for the different densities of the dangerous fuels being carried in the tanks – all these had to be calculated and compensated for. Too heavy, and she could hurtle to the bottom; too light, and she'd never get down; yes, an anxious moment for *Clyde*'s Number One . . .

'Diving stations in five minutes' time . . .'

The announcement was repeated throughout the boat; the diesels stopped; in the silence while she shifted to her main electric motors, Carbis watched the hands in the control room as they waited for the order to open main vents; this was to be a careful, controlled dive, without klaxon.

'*Open main vents* . . .'

The vents clunked open above his head as the Outside ERA pulled at the levers on his diving panel; the boat slowly took on a bow-down angle and half a minute later he heard the shout which he was to hear so often during the months ahead: '*First clip on!*'

And so the old lady (she was now eight years of age) carried out her trim dive. The process took over half an hour, because the next time she dived she would be on her own in a hostile sea. She must settle at periscope depth in neutral buoyancy, in perfect trim. With stores and torpedoes lashed along the passageway, she could not risk taking on a steep angle: a Mark 8 torpedo weighed a ton and a half . . .

'Lookouts in the tower. Stand by to surface . . .'

Two minutes later they were on the surface again. Carbis sensed the tension easing when the diesels began thumping, back-aft in the engine room. The fresh air streamed through the boat.

'Carry on smoking.'

The watches were set for patrol routine; men turned into their hammocks in the fore-ends; the boat began its zig-zag on approaching Europa Point, because the moon was almost full. *Clyde*, even though trimmed down, was a sizeable target for a lurking enemy U-boat.

Carbis heard the captain climbing down through the lower hatch. He had discarded his Ursula suit and, entering the wardroom, was placing his binoculars on his settee when the diving klaxon blared. Brookes jerked round and moved swiftly back into the control room as the first lookout scrambled down the lower conning tower ladder. Carbis watched events as the vents opened and the boat took on her bow-down angle.

'Shut off for depth-charging!'

And then Carbis listened to the familiar drill with which he was to become familiar: 'One clip on! Group up: one hundred and twenty feet: blow Q! Lower lid shut and clipped . . .'

There was a clang! Then another, not so close.

The officer of the watch was standing next to the captain: a lone bomber – a JU 88 – had attacked from up-moon, keeping low, invisible against the Rock's foreshore.

'Unfriendly brute,' Brookie murmured. 'I'll give him fifteen minutes, then we'll be on our way.'

At 2040 *Clyde* surfaced once more and set course for the Sicilian Channel south of the Egadi Islands; then she would thread through the minefields at one hundred and twenty feet, three miles from the enemy's coastline. Stacked with gleaming blue-coated torpedoes, green smoke-screen canisters, her tanks full of 100 per cent octane for the RAF's fighters, this explosive machine with its seventy-five men should be surfacing off Filfla, the islet at the south-east corner of Malta, on the morning of the ninth day. A brusque start to operational submarining, Carbis thought to himself. Looking at his messmates beneath the sombre red lighting, it was difficult to believe that this was normal routine for them: Malta depended upon *Clyde* and they'd been doing this Piccadilly Run for months. He turned in early to his bunk and keeping his imagination from working, fell immediately to sleep.

CHAPTER THREE

Return of the Vandals

Even before Luigi Grima felt the pressure of his father's hand on his shoulder, the clamminess of the rock cave had woken him to a drowsy half-sleep. He grunted, knowing he could not put off the moment any longer. Father liked to start his fishing early, for the bombers had been droning overhead all night and the all-clear hadn't yet sounded from the sirens of Victoria. The danger from marauding fighters was less when fishing off the snags of the Mistra Rocks than in the open waters of the Comino Channel; here, in the shelter of San Blas bay, the little *Santa Maria*, his father's deep-prowed boat, could be hauled up the beach overnight. The small port in the adjoining bay at Dahlet Qorrot was crowded with craft and too much of a target for the elder Grima's liking.

'Come on, son, put your back into it . . .'

The sharp gravel scrunched beneath the boat's keel and then she was afloat, a violet silhouette against the crimson sun which was rising abruptly from the eastern horizon. The older man glanced at his watch: five o'clock on the morning of 12 February 1942.

'Shove me off,' he told his son. 'I'll be back for dinner. Don't get into trouble.'

Up to his knees now in the cold sea, Luigi leaned against the boat; half turning her, he thrust her out as his father leaned forward against the oars. The son waved, then turned slowly back to the beach and the foot of the valley. The Rapas had a fire going already, but he had been cautioned by his father not to accept anything they might offer him to eat: rations were short and they had been over-generous already. A small boy was running half-naked towards him.

'Hey, Luigi, Grandfather says you're to have breakfast with us.'

'I've work to do for my father.' He rumpled the child's black curls. 'Thank Grandfather, all the same.'

Luigi hurried past the Rapas' caves which the grandfather had with uncanny foresight hewn out of the cliff. There was ample space for their own living quarters and for the goats. To avoid the crowded public shelters in the village of Nadur, the Rapa family moved down here for a night's sleep while the bombers lumbered overhead. They were kind people and ever since the tragedy had invited the survivors of the Grima family to share their shelter. Luigi waved to the old man beckoning at the entrance to the cave, then hurried onwards up the track towards the village. Even now he could not dispel the memories of that terrible night.

The bomb had been a direct hit, when the whole family were together for Christmas Eve. His mother, his elder sister and both his grandparents had been killed: he could still remember the terror of being pinned by the wooden beam which had saved him, of the shouts of the Protection Officer and his men as they battled feverishly to clear the rubble. Miraculously, his father and Theresa, Luigi's fourteen-year-old sister had been chatting with the neighbours and so had also survived.

Father still walked about like a drunken man. Only the comfort of the priest and his own faith had saved his reason, though the kindness of the Rapas was now bringing him back to some sort of life, unreasonable and fractious though he still was. Little Theresa was safe with the sisters and was settling down to convent life. If it had not been for his father's need of his son at this dreadful moment, he would have departed for Valletta to join up with the forces. He was eighteen but the Gozitans needed their young men. Father Michael had told Luigi: 'Stay with us until your father is well again.' And the priests, if not always right, were best heeded . . .

And so Luigi had remained, frustrated, as were so many of his own age-group. Always on the edge of trouble, they longed to get into the fray, angry at what they saw and heard: until the massacre of his family, this siege and war had been a game for Luigi. Not so now . . . They said that Valletta, the dockyard, and the heavy concentrations of population in the suburbs had suffered infinitely worse than Gozo and its inhabitants. The churches they loved, their theatres, their magnificent and cherished public buildings, all had suffered as badly as each other; a heap of stones in jumbled confusion looked much the same, whatever its origin . . .

'Ow! Luigi!'

He smiled. They weren't to be bored today, for Joe was organizing a trip across the water. He'd been secretive: an ominous sign. The gang knew he was in with a bunch of hoodlums in Rabat, but they did not ask questions when playing the black market. It was early for all nine of them to be here; they were signalling for him to join them at their secret base, a broken-down triangle of stone walls overlooking the cliffs of Rdum il-Kbir. When he reached the gang, there was little left of the one shared cigarette someone had scrounged.

'Not fishing, then?' Joe asked. 'Coming with us?'

'Yeah. I'll get father's dinner first. Meet you at M'garr.' He glanced at their leader: 'How'll we get across?'

'If there's no ferry, we'll borrow a boat.' The guffaw evaporated as Joe shot his arm towards the sea. 'Look out! *Messerschmitts!*'

They flattened themselves against the wall, their heads just above it while they watched the two ME 109s swooping towards Nadur. As the aircraft levelled out, the Bofors at the fort began pumping away. Though the rounds were bursting short, they were close enough to make the fighters shy off. They banked to the right and hugging the coastline skimmed towards the cliffs on which the gang lay concealed. A couple of hundred yards short, they separated, the leader banking sharply for the village. The rear fighter came hurtling onwards, parallel with the cliff and on a level with the cliff-top.

The wing tip could have been no further than thirty feet clear when the gang leapt to its feet. Following Joe's lead, swearing and yelling they shook their fists at the pilot. The grin inside the leather helmet vanished abruptly when the German gave his international two-finger salute. The plane banked steeply to the left and roared up the valley towards Nadur.

'We could have got it if we'd had stones ready,' someone said. They began scrambling for suitably shaped missiles when Grandfather Rapa and the boy, John, walked up to them from the coastal path. Joe and Luigi were competing with their stones for accuracy and range when the old man spoke:

'You'd better clear off,' he said bluntly. 'The pilot must have been lost. If you chuck stones at him, it'll only draw his fire on the village. He'll shoot you up. Go on, clear off.'

'Grandad,' the little boy shouted. 'Listen! He's coming back.'

They all heard the sound they could identify so accurately, the staccato roar of a Messerschmitt 109, growing louder at each second.

'Take cover, you fools!' the old man shouted as, pulling the child down beside him, he shoved his charge between his own body and the wall. Luigi and the gang flattened themselves on the track as the yellow-snouted fighter hurtled straight for them. At the last moment, having spotted his target, the pilot pulled to the right to skim parallel with the cliff-top as he had done before.

'Now!' yelled Joe, leaping to his feet and hurling his stone at the disappearing tail. A hail of missiles flew through the air.

'Some *must* have hit,' Luigi said. 'We couldn't miss, he was so close.'

Fascinated, they watched the fighter pull up sharply, bank, turn again.

'He's coming back!'

But now the pilot was trying to reach them from a wider angle, and Grandfather Rapa and his grandson were hiding behind the other side of the wall. The machine guns chattered; the puffs of smoke trailed; the bullets whined and spattered against the walls.

'The bastard!' The hail of stones flew through the air.

'Got him!' someone yelled.

Thrice more the German dived, each time from another direction; three times the youths hurled their stones. Zooming vertically above their heads, the fighter hung momentarily. Then, instead of diving again upon them, it swooped straight towards the sea.

'God!' someone yelled. 'He's going for the boat!'

They sprang up, mesmerized; the fighter was diving, its guns blazing; a hail of bullets was threshing in the water, the line of spurting spray creeping towards the *Santa Maria*.

'Father, *father*!' Luigi screamed helplessly. 'Jump over the side!'

They could see, even from here, the shocked face of the fisherman when he saw the danger. For an instant he stood upright in his boat, holding his net. The splashes in the sea kicked viciously, smothering the boat. The spray cleared. Across the gunwale slumped a twitching body, its head in the water.

Luigi began running, the voices of the others echoing behind him. As the fighter turned again, he took no notice of the flying bullets when they whined over his head to plump into the cliff. Crazy with rage and fear, he plunged into the cold water and began threshing his way towards the *Santa Maria*.

This was the second time in two months that he'd walked out through the iron gates of the cemetery. But this time, with his sister beside him, Luigi had not wept. Head up, an implacable hatred was churning inside him. One of the Carmelite nuns gently took Theresa's arm. He let his sister go, watched them walk away through the departing crowd which had come to support them in this familiar ritual of death. Grandfather Rapa appeared at his side.

'We can leave now,' he said, taking Luigi's arm. 'It's over.'

'What can I do?' the youth asked hopelessly.

'We can mend the boat. You'll lodge with us.'

The old priest had overtaken them. 'Thank you, Father,' Luigi muttered briefly.

'You can go now,' Father Michael said. The leathery face with the sad eyes seemed used to these realities. 'God be with you.'

'What'd you mean, Father?'

'You can leave Gozo, now. You've done your duty.'

For a long moment, Luigi stood staring towards the south where a column of black smoke hung over Valletta.

'He knew I wanted to leave,' he said quietly. ' "It's got to be the navy," father said. "Not the RMA." '

Grandfather Rapa led the way back to his house in the village. 'I was at St Angelo when I was a matelot,' he said. 'They'll make a man of you there.'

The priest shook his silvery head while he watched youth and old age departing together towards the village.

'The boy's a man already,' he murmured, crossing himself, 'like so many of them. Take care of him, Lord.'

The customary knot of Maltese sailors and workmen stood on the shattered first floor which had once been the officers' bathroom. There was neither roof nor wall now, but a couple of chipped enamel baths still stood bravely defying wind and weather.

Routine had relaxed since the last of the flotilla had left four weeks ago. The skeleton ship's company were caretakers now, keeping things going here at Lazaretto and preparing for the submarines' return. No-one had ever faltered, whatever further horrors Kesselring and his Fleigerkorps II perpetrated upon defiant, battered Malta. A month was a long time and events altered daily, especially with the arrival of the new Governor, General Lord Gort, VC, five days before *P35*, the last surviving submarine, had sailed for Alexandria. There was a new spirit of hope, a fresh defiance; a stubborn reaction to the continuous bombing, the threat of imminent invasion, the dwindling stocks of petrol for the RAF, and the lack of basic rations to keep the lifeblood coursing through the beleaguered island.

'If you still want to volunteer for the sweepers,' the Regulating Chief Petty Officer said in an aside to the ordinary seaman standing amongst the onlookers, 'see me before dinner time. Make up your mind; I've a long list already.'

'As soon as *Clyde* is berthed,' Ordinary Seaman Grima replied, 'Thanks, Chief.'

The Chief was squinting to where Fort St Elmo cut off the view to the east. 'There she is now.'

Grima could not sight her at first, not knowing what to look for, unlike the experienced old Chief. Then Luigi spotted her: *Clyde* looked so insignificant among the waves curling towards the black buoys of the boom which was opened to allow entry to Marsamuscetto Harbour. Here on Manoel Island, which was joined to Gzira and Sliema by a narrow causeway, stood Lazaretto, the ancient leper hospital, its buildings now serving as the base for the absent Tenth Submarine Flotilla. As Luigi watched the submarine growing larger at each minute, he felt a surge of pride. He was, through circumstances not of his choosing, at last free to make his own life.

He was serving this renowned, depleted flotilla which, with its small submarines, had been dealing such lethal blows upon the enemy. Among the Maltese, these *U*s were regarded, as they sailed and returned from patrol with their Jolly Rogers flying, with a proprietary pride. These boats were *theirs*, the only weapon with which they could avenge the terrible destruction Malta was suffering day and night. Small and handy, these boats could get in close to the enemy shore, attack its harbours, put commandos ashore, land spies. Luigi Grima was now part of this élite band. At last he had an objective: to serve this flotilla was the best way he knew to avenge the murders of his mother, father and sister . . .

His gaze took in his new home, the base in which he lived. Behind the broken masonry on which he stood reared the massive, sloping walls of the fort after which Manoel Island was named. It stood squarely in the centre of the harbour, bounded on the north side by Sliema Creek in which the peacetime destroyer flotillas used to lie at their buoys, and on the south by the deep-water harbour formed by the vertical battlements of Valletta; a few hundred yards to the south-west was Msida Creek where the torpedo depot, run by the Torpedo Gunner, Mr Warne, had miraculously survived the bombing; the northern shore of Lazaretto Creek was the causeway joining Manoel Island to the mainland of Sliema.

For the first time in his life, Luigi felt an upsurge of pride. To hasten the return of the surviving boats of the flotilla from Alexandria, he'd volunteer this forenoon temporarily to man the minesweepers. It was the nightly laying of mines by enemy aircraft and E-boats in the swept channels which had caused the recent losses. Once these channels were cleared, the flotilla could return to reconstitute itself again under their leader, the officer about whom Luigi Grima had heard so much. 'Shrimp', the officers and men of the flotilla called him: Captain George Simpson, Royal Navy.

It was he who had built up the flotilla from scratch, inspired it since the Italians had first attacked on 11 June 1940 – two years ago, two long years of agony for Luigi's people, two years of accepting the leadership of their first extraordinary Governor, Sir William Dobbie. The Maltese revered Sir William because of his faith in God and because of his comradeship with their Archbishop, Dom Maurus Caruana. Unlikely allies, together they had inspired the Maltese people to endure the agony of bombing, the pangs of starvation . . . this was what Luigi's father had told him, and now Grima was sharing the struggle, was taking part in the fight to the death for what the Maltese people believed in . . .

Clyde was yawing, the following sea surging white across the break in her long after-ends. In minutes she would be clear of the threat of mines, the lethal, sinister weapon which in one awful instant had blown so many of our submarines to bits . . . Only five weeks ago, *Urge*, one of the five survivors, had left Lazaretto for Beirut, only to be destroyed by a mine in the unswept channel – unswept because the Spitfires were too few to protect the sweepers . . . *Urge*'s captain, the Chief had told Luigi, was 'Tommo' Tomkinson, second only to David Wanklyn, Tommo's best friend and skipper of *Upholder*. Wanklyn had been awarded the VC for his company and himself; but only a fortnight before *Urge* was lost, *Upholder* too was destroyed, depth-charged by a torpedo-boat off Tripoli.

'She's almost through the boom. Look, Grima,' someone said, 'she's on main motors now . . .' Men were scrambling up through the gun-tower to extricate the wires and fenders from the casing. At Harbour Stations, her hands were fallen in on the fore-casing, in white sweaters and blue trousers, as smart as during peacetime. Her captain could just be seen, his head peering above the rounded coachroof of *Clyde*'s bridge. He was waving his cap in acknowledgment of the cheers from the crowd on the breakwater of St Elmo Point.

Lines of women and children dotted the long breakwater, like icing on a cake. Yelling and screaming; laughing, weeping and waving, they bellowed out their lungs to welcome in, at this most critical moment in the long siege, yet another life-giving British submarine. They had spotted *Clyde* as soon as she had showed as a smudge on the horizon. To them – these hungry watchers living in the caves below Laskaris, up most of the night as with their children they cowered from the bombs – the big submarine meant petrol for the Spitfires and Hurricanes; to these knots of waving figures the blue-painted whale wallowing through the boom represented their only chance to hit back at the hated enemy. *Clyde*, they knew, carried torpedoes for the *U*s who would send them speeding and bubbling to their targets: Rommel's supply ships. To Luigi's countrymen, *Clyde* spelt revenge, a speedier end to their anguish. As Grima turned to follow the berthing party down the steps, he too felt for the first time that he belonged to this close band of submariners; however humble a part he was to play as a seaman and officer's servant, he would be helping to make those submariners' lives in harbour just a little easier.

The berthing party waited on the petrol lighter, ready to take *Clyde*'s lines. She was turning at rest, the waters of Lazaretto Creek churning brown as she manoeuvred on her electric motors. Lieutenant-Commander Masham, temporarily in command of the base while Captain Simpson and his staff were running the flotilla from Beirut, stood returning the submarine captain's salute while *Clyde* edged gently alongside.

'Brought your gin and beer,' her captain, a cheerful, fair-haired lieutenant called down to Masham. 'Nice quiet reception, thanks to the Spits.'

'All part of the service,' Masham laughed up at him. 'Don't know how long it'll last.'

The hoses were already being passed across and coupled up. Twelve minutes later the pipework jumped and pulsated as the precious aviation spirit poured into the queue of army tankers. Then each was off, away in dusty clouds and bumping through the potholes, to whisk the priceless lifeblood to secret tanks at the edge of the airfields. Only when the last drop had been squeezed from her tanks did *Clyde* proceed to Torpedo Creek, as Msida Creek was known. There she would unload all her precious 'fish' and most of her smoke canisters, the residue being held to screen Lazaretto for when the next air raid occurred.

By nightfall, her company and all hands at the base had completed the unloading. Only then did they relax, tired and hungry, the job done: everything delivered – spare machinery parts for the submarines when they returned, ammunition, medical stores. As soon as she could, to avoid being bombed alongside the base, she would sail again with stores and passengers for Gibraltar. Not a large contribution, thought Luigi, for Malta and its starving thousands, though her unglorious role was more than justified: no offensive naval force remained at Malta (Force K had been decimated last December) but her people knew that they were not abandoned while *Clyde* ran. There was still hope – and this fact was what made her undramatic, dangerous role so vital for the morale of Luigi's people.

CHAPTER FOUR

An Extraordinary People

It was four days later, after *Clyde* sailed for her return trip to Gibraltar, that Carbis began to realize what the people of Malta were enduring. His servant, Ordinary Seaman Grima, had produced a morning cup of tea. The young Maltese placed a can of hot water on the stone floor of Carbis' cabin.

'Seven o'clock, sair.'

'What's happened to you, Luigi?'

'Busy night, sair. Got caught in the Manoel Bar when the shop next door was hit.'

The Maltese sailor's cheek was swollen from a fall: he and others in the bar had tried to save the shop-owners next door from the fire caused by the explosion. The man lingered, wanting to talk to his new officer who had just arrived from another world. Propped on his elbow, Carbis sipped the black brew sweetened with a drop of condensed milk. Luxury indeed, but rations were easier now that there were no submarines to care for. Luigi was talking of his recent time in the minesweepers.

'We've swept over two hundred mines in the channel, sair.' A broad grin spread across his puffed face. ' "The boats will soon be back," the Chief said.' Grima looked serious. 'Is he right, sair?'

John Carbis shook his head. 'Wish I knew. But I'm joining *Urgent* tomorrow, Luigi, which is what matters to me.' He rolled out of bed, picked up the can of water and grabbed a towel. He had to go easy on the razor blades for they were almost unobtainable. As for toothpaste, he was becoming used to cleaning his teeth with a frothy toothbrush – so long as the soap held out. He walked along the first-floor balcony, past the cos' empty cabins and Captain 'Shrimp' Simpson's quarters. The names of the submarines were painted on boards fixed to the doors of the empty cabins, name boards which were removed as the battle progressed: haunting, ghostly . . . 'co *Urgent*': behind the board's anonymity was the character who would be holding in his hands John Carbis' life and those of 32 others. Carbis reached the end of the balcony and, turning left, found the wash place; it was open to the skies, its wrecked walls too unstable to carry even a roof of corrugated sheeting. He plunged his face into the basin of cold water then, grateful for Grima's lukewarm shaving-water, began scraping at his face with his blunt blade.

The cracked mirror was slung by a length of codline from the angle-bar holding up the roof. He hoped that the face staring back at him did not seem too young, if he was to be pitch-forked into this Jimmy's job. Dammit, Pam was right, then: those *were* grey hairs flecking the black hair above his ears. As he tried to work up a lather with his shaving-brush, he leaned closer to the mirror to take a better look at J. Carbis . . .

Yes, his nose was unusually long; but thin and aquiline with its high bridge. His brown eyes (patient, like a spaniel's, Dad once chided) saved him from looking too imperious, too haughty: he knew he *could* be intolerant of wanton carelessness or stupidity. The stubborn streak in him was betrayed by his wide mouth which would clamp shut like a trap when he was stressed or when trying to quell his quick temper.

But he was glad to notice that there were faint crescent lines of humour at the corners of his lips. He enjoyed dry wit and perhaps the slightly humorous expression of his mouth offset the impression of severity which the face he was trying to lather presented to the world: not too bad, he hoped. Pleasant enough, with an air of cheerfulness about it . . .

It was strange to be here, in this empty base, void of all operational officers except for one other: Ashton, a sub-lieutenant who had been waiting for weeks for his boat to return. It was this waiting which was aggravating, but tonight he was going ashore with the sub for a sort of 'incendiary run', like they used to do in Gosport in '40. They might even be able to find a beer among the bars of Sliema.

He went back to his cabin, shifted into his khaki tropical rig of shirt, shorts and sandals then returned along the balcony to the steps leading down to ground level where the arches edged the deep water of Marsamuscetto Harbour. He halted to peer at the sandstone crests bordering each step. They'd been carved by the crews of the submarines, silent memorials for some of them now. The tower and crossed battle-axes of *Usk*, mined off Cape Bon in '41. The kneeling man with the world upheld on his shoulders: the renowned *Upholder*'s crest, lost only a few weeks ago. And *Urge*'s; she was lost only a fortnight after Wanklyn's *Upholder*. There, also, were the badges of *Unbeaten* (Britannia with her shield and trident) who, with damaged tubes, had returned safely to Britain; Pat Norman's *Una*, now operating temporarily from Beirut; the cock and weather-vane of Dick Cayley's *Utmost* who was back in Britain for refit; the three trees of *Upright*, also in Britain refitting after losing a battery through bombing while in the Malta dockyard.

Those grim days were only a few weeks past. Boats were remaining on patrol rather than being sunk in the harbour. They were being forced to dive by day in Lazaretto Creek and Marsamuscetto Harbour, surfacing at night for maintenance and preparation for the next patrol. In three weeks, half the men in the Tenth had been killed. And, gazing in silence at those stone crests, John wondered how many of those badges would still be survivors when, in a year's time, he hoped to be going home. He walked down to the arches: there, opposite him, two hundred yards across the blue water, two large gashes disfigured the yellow sandstone of Valletta's battlements. These were the uncompleted entrances to the intended submarine pens upon which work had begun eight years ago. Shelter for six submarines, their crews and facilities was to have been provided under those two hundred feet of rock. But the politicians stopped the project: too expensive at £350,000, the cost of one submarine. In disgust, Carbis walked on to the opening on his right, the courtyard which led into the tin-roofed wardroom.

He was ready for his breakfast in this deserted hall. Afterwards, he would finish his tour of the base, see the engineering workshop, the periscope-servicing room and the shelters which Captain Simpson, using the skilled efforts of the Maltese masons and his own sailors, had burrowed into the sandstone. He would try to find the piggery which, under Pat Norman's and Pop Giddings'* management, had saved the base from starvation.

Though the ship's company's pig farm had got off to a shaky start, there was helpful advice from some of the Maltese ship's company who were ex-pig farmers. In spite of the engineer commander's doubts (Commander Sam MacGregor: 'I can't help noticing that both sows are twelve cylinder jobs . . . what happens if they give birth to fourteen pistons?') the pigs proved a great morale booster, the men taking a keen proprietary interest in their farming. Regrettably the

*A retired lieutenant-commander and first lieutenant of the base.

24

current herd of pigs had been massacred during one particularly vicious bombing raid on the base. But the earlier porkers which the ship's company had raised and subsequently slaughtered, had been prudently stored in the dockyard's cold storage.

Carbis failed to complete his tour of the base: the red alert was flying for the rest of the afternoon and evening, so he was compelled to take to the undergound shelters. The drill was rigidly enforced because too many submariners had been killed while goofing at the bombers, instead of playing safe.

Twilight no longer merged into a night of semi-darkness as it once did in peace-time: then, the stars remained invisible unless one reached for them through the glow from the lights of the towns. But now, thought John Carbis, as he strolled with Ashton, the sub, across the causeway for Sliema, now a suffocating shroud fell upon the island when twilight ended. Like Britain, no light showed; like his home in summer, the interiors of the houses, those which remained standing, were unbearably stuffy: the drawn curtains behind the closed shutters allowed no chink of light to escape, nor air to enter. There was no moon and it was very dark by the time the two men reached Tower Road which skirted the rocky coast of Sliema. Though they had shifted into 'whites', it was good to feel the breeze from the sea. The glow from a lighted match flared suddenly ahead.

'*Put out that light, you bloody fool!*' an angry Maltese voice roared in the darkness.

'We might be up the Smoke,' Ashton murmured.

The sub was right, thought Carbis, though London could have been on another planet.

The all-clear had whined only half an hour earlier, so they had little time to wander through what was left of Sliema to find a suitable bar. They saw the flats which the submarines' crews had used; they identified the remains of the apartment which *Sokol*'s Polish captain had rented. Retrieving from the rubble the priceless medal which General Sikorski had taken from his own breast to pin on Boris Karnicki's chest, *Sokol*'s captain had scaled a ladder to reach his piano balanced on the swaying floor above him. There he had thumped out the Polish Grand March, *fortissimo* . . . already these cos were legendary, these captains from the first phase of the Tenth Flotilla's life.

Few blocks of flats remained intact, but miraculously the sailors' syndicated apartments had suffered no casualties. The worst day had been during last February when the officers' eastern end of Lazaretto had been hit. The captain and all the officers of the Greek boat, *Glaukos*, were killed through not taking cover promptly in the shelters burrowed out of the rock.

'Let's try the Eight Bells,' Ashton said as they were approaching the stretch of shore north of Tigné Fort. But as they neared the bar, the sirens began wailing again. Dark figures emerged, scuttling from the pub as the guns began hammering away from St George's, close to the barracks.

'We'd better join them in their shelter,' Carbis said. They broke into a run, when they noticed a group of men gathering on Sliema Point. As Ashton and Carbis reached them, the Bofors battery behind them began pumping away, while the beams of a dozen searchlights started weaving through the night sky.

An elderly Maltese was speaking his thoughts aloud:

'They're our new radar-controlled searchlights. Listen . . .' and in the silence, even above the wavelets lapping the beach, Carbis heard the drone of the enemy bombers, a throbbing note different from that of our own Beaufighters which were lurking up there at 15,000 feet.

'Making for the dockyard,' the man said. 'They're over Pieta . . .'

The overhead throbbing had drawn across the watchers when someone yelled:

'Four of them! Look – the searchlights are locking on . . .' and then, when the rest of the probing blue-white pencil beams switched off, Carbis spotted the silvery bomber bathed in light, a tiny dot over Pieta. An instant later, two other beams locked on to this leading bomber which was now caught in a concentrated cone of light.

'*Got him*,' the old man croaked. 'Won't be long now . . .'

Carbis sensed the anticipation shared by the mesmerized onlookers on the point. Their necks craning upwards at the condemned bomber, they watched while a Beaufighter plunged down from the night . . . a long burst of cannon, the flicker of tracer, flying sparks but, uncannily, no sound: all they could hear was the throbbing drone of the invaders plodding towards their target. Suddenly, another attack from the rear by the Beaufighter; more sparks, flashes of fire. A rumble of explosions erupted from the Floriana direction; spurts of flames and yellow flashes shot above the dark outline of the city.

'They're jettisoning . . . Ah!' The sound from the small band of onlookers was a sigh. '*There*! The parachutes . . .'

Carbis counted the white mushrooms drifting down so slowly across the city . . . one, two . . . three, four. The bomber was struggling on gamely, the pilot apparently still flying his machine.

'The bastard!'

Then there was a shout when the Beaufighter circled, dived for the *coup-de-grâce*. A final burst was pumped into the lone machine. Orange flames licked along the fuselage. Slowly, like a falling leaf, the plane began plunging to earth, a hellish catherine-wheel of leaping fire and smoke. Another yellow glow was added to the horizon to the west of Pieta.

In the abrupt silence, Carbis could hear the cheering echoing through the night: from as far as Valletta; from Juliana, from Pieta, he heard them, the exultation borne on the breeze, the cheers being taken up from one suburb to the next, until all Sliema was rejoicing in its shout of vengeance. The remaining three vandals might have escaped: but the fourth would never again attack this island and its stubborn people . . . silently the group on the point began melting away. Carbis and Ashton started to make for the bar.

Suddenly there was a violent *swish!* of air. *Wheeee! Phee-ew!* Six times, directly overhead . . . Every man in sight flung himself to the ground. There was the usual *whoosh!* of air which announced the near-miss . . . and then the night erupted into an inferno of crimson, yellow and violet light. A stick of six bombs, plunging into the crowded sector of Sliema, one after the other . . . For a few seconds, utter stillness . . . then, the crackling of flames and the screaming of the stricken shattering the night.

The prostrate figures detached themselves warily from the dusty pavement: dazed, unsure whether they were alive. They started to run, crouching, limping, one after the other, towards the flames and the cries.

'You had better come home with me.'

The man spoke with a calm authority as he helped the half-conscious naval lieutenant to his feet. The officer's companion, a sub-lieutenant, had been carried off to Birkirkara Hospital with the other casualties. The tall, powerfully built Maltese was peering at the blackened face. 'I've seen you before, haven't I?'

'Carbis,' the officer mumbled. 'Lazaretto. Thanks.'

'Toni de Marco,' the Maltese introduced himself. 'Protection Officer for Sliema. My house is off Balluta Bay, about half a mile. It's quicker to walk until they clear up the shambles. Think you can make it?'

The lieutenant spoke not a word as the Protection Officer, a man in his early thirties, led the way down Howard Street. De Marco understood; he had witnessed many frightful nights, but he'd never experienced such a shocking incident as this.

The tunnel had been stuffed full of women, children and babies, crammed, as usual, in rows along the walls. The blast killed everyone outright along the first fifteen yards. When the first men of his team had forced their way inside, they thought that the people were all alive, sitting silently with their eyes open. Those further back in the tunnel were panicking, when the inner blast wall also collapsed to trap all the survivors at the far end. It was nearly two in the morning now and the few survivors had only just been extricated. A ghastly night which he, a hardened Protection Officer, would never be able to wipe from his mind.

What effect would the horror have on this young officer, fresh from England, whatever similar savage scenes he may have seen back home? The chap had done his bit, helped until the final, crushed little body had been taken off to the morgue. Carbis was showing only the normal reactions to shock and there was nothing which a stiff gin couldn't put right. My Dotty, Toni thought to himself, has a soft spot for submariners. She'll cope, even though it's two in the morning.

When they arrived at his house, the door was opened before they reached it. 'My wife, Dorothy,' Toni de Marco introduced. 'We'll let the rest of the family go on sleeping, but make yourself comfortable.' He went to the cupboard and extracted the gin bottle. He felt exhaustion overcoming him: the symptoms of hunger, he knew. On 800 calories a day, he could not even shave for long without having to rest his hand for a while. The Armed Services were rationed to 2,000 calories a day (3,000 was normal in peace-time) and even they were feeling the pinch, apparently . . . He glanced at the angular Englishman flopping into the chair, waited for the gulp of raw spirit to do its work. Carbis could not be more than twenty-two or three, but he looked years older, as so many of them did.

'Better?'

Carbis' mouth curled at the corners into a tired smile. 'Miles better . . . and thank you, sir.' He was peering quizzically at his host. 'De Marco, did you say?'

Dotty broke in, a smile of recognition in her dark eyes as she perched like a bird on the edge of the sofa.

'You were a midshipman just before the war. We met at the Commander-in-Chief's cocktail party for the French. *Warspite* . . . d'you remember?'

The lieutenant in the grubby whites stiffened: 'Of course. And . . .'

'Anna was with us, Anna Seguna. She'd remember you. She became engaged to a friend of yours.'

'Lofty,' Carbis replied. Toni caught the shadow of wariness in Carbis' eyes. 'Lofty Small. We were in the same submarine training class a couple of months ago.'

'She still lodges with us,' Toni went on, 'when she can't get home to Mdina for a break. It's a small world . . .'

Another couple of gins and it could have been a pre-dinner session. De Marco warmed to this laconic lieutenant, let him talk and unwind. He could be an amusing cove, with a dry sense of humour: the sort whom Toni liked. There was a trustworthy look about Carbis; but behind those brown eyes with their level gaze, Toni would warrant there lurked a swift temper. Then Toni de Marco talked about himself, since the chap seemed interested.

'The Central Region Protection Officer is my boss: Wingrave Tench. Amazing man. He's also organized the island's feeding: the toughest of jobs there is. He makes sure that, from the Governor downwards to the poorest civilian, we all get the same rations: he's the Director of the Communal Feeding Department. With three thousand helpers, he runs the Victory Kitchens.'

'How's he do that, with practically no food?' asked Carbis.

'The Services have built us soup kitchens in every town and village: we burn wood, paraffin, diesel, even sawdust. Crude but it works. Everyone gets his fair share.'

'What goes into the soup?'

'Horses, anything edible. The soup looks much the same whatever's in it. We don't ask questions and no-one has starved. We try to help the dockers when a ship gets through: unloading flat-out is tough work.'

'A black market?' Carbis asked.

'Almost stamped out since the middle man was controlled by ration tickets. You can't get rid of it completely: the problem had to be solved swiftly.'

'How d'you mean?'

'The last ship to reach us had a cargo of a hundred thousand tins of peas. How d'you divide *that* between two hundred and fifty thousand people?' de Marco laughed shortly. 'But we've managed it. Speed of unloading is the key. We've had too many ships sunk in harbour with their cargoes. Sickening, after they've been fought through the Med to relieve us. Transport is vital to us and the army provides it. Without the phones, which they keep going too, we'd be lost.'

'Petrol?'

'Priority is for the RAF's tanks around the airfields. The rest goes to the army and for vital transport. No taxis now, no cars. We've bikes – a motor-bike, if privileged; bicycles and your flat feet, otherwise, but there's a daily bus service running once a day throughout the island. The Grand Harbour and Valletta–Sliema ferries keep going.'

Carbis did not speak for a long moment. 'You make us feel very humble,' he said quietly. '*We* are the privileged; our rations are more than double, I'm told.'

'We don't resent that,' Toni said. 'We know you've got a job to do. When you're out there,' and he inclined his head towards the sound of the waves lapping the beach, 'we think of you. Every ship of Rommel's you sink, every German and Italian you drown balances the books a bit.' De Marco paused, then added, 'We're expecting invasion. Any moment . . .'

'What makes you think so? They've waited long enough.'

'My boss. He's in at the top; he has to know what's going on if he's to eke out the rations.'

'How long before they run out?'

'That's the most guarded of secrets. The priests say ten to fifteen days. There're rumours of a convoy coming from each end of the Med soon.' He shrugged his shoulders. 'They'll never *capture* the island. But *starvation* . . . ?'

'How long can the people go on?' Carbis asked. 'It's frightful to see the kids with all those sores.'

'Scurvy. They've sent us a shipload of dehydrated cabbage. Rotten, most of it. I don't know what we'd have done without Gravy. I'd like you to meet him. His house is open to you submariners. His wife, Greta, asks nothing better than for Shrimp and his COS to feel that Pembroke House, Gravy's home, is a sort of oasis when boats get in from patrol.'

Carbis was trying to stifle a yawn, but his eyelids were drooping.

'Bed,' de Marco announced. 'Dotty's got one made up for you.' He walked across and hauled Carbis from the chair.

'Thanks, sir. I shan't forget tonight.'

Dotty pecked him on the cheek. 'I'll let you sleep on,' she said, 'Toni's got a meeting with Gravy and we won't wake you.'

'Shake me, too, please,' John Carbis said. 'My submarine's due in tomorrow. I don't want to miss her arrival.'

CHAPTER FIVE

Strange New World

Carbis felt sure that the wind was freshening. *Urgent* took another 'green' sea, the solid water sluicing along her fore-casing before butting against the bridge. He ducked with the two lookouts as the spray drenched them all. He tugged at the towel encircling his neck beneath the Ursula jacket, felt the cold trickling down his chest. He tried for the umpteenth time to dry the lenses of his binoculars with the sodden periscope paper from his pocket.

'Keep your eyes skinned,' he told the lookouts. The moon had set and it was pitch dark; even the phosphorescence of the swirling seas was failing to give that extra light which it did sometimes on a rotten night. Should he call the captain now that visibility was down to zero? While considering the question, a call came up the voice-pipe:

'Permission for relief lookout on the bridge, sir.'

'Lookout on the bridge.'

The relieving lookout, who had been acclimatizing his eyes in the conning tower, emerged through the upper-hatch to take over his watch. After a muttered turn-over, the off-going lookout disappeared below, having completed his hour's trick: an hour was the custom in submarines, the strain being intense and concentration vital. The men with the best eyesight were used as lookouts, whatever their job – seaman or stoker. Two hours was the officer of the watch's stint, unlike that in surface ships where a four-hour watch was kept.

'Yours is the dangerous sector, Smith.' Carbis had got to know the able-seaman in the tube space during an attack during the last patrol. The man was grunting from the folds of his Ursula suit as he ducked from another sea. A surly individual, Smith came from Tooting; he had moaned throughout the whole attack to the ginger-bearded TI, Petty Officer Bolder. Carbis had sensed that Smith resented an 'odd' new officer watching over them all in the tube space. The crew had been told that Lieutenant Carbis would be taking over as first lieutenant when the present incumbent, Giffard, left the boat to go home for his 'perisher', the Commanding Officer's Qualifying Course. And John Carbis, alone with his thoughts on the dripping bridge of *Urgent*, was thankful that at last his understudying of Giffard was almost finished. Neither he nor Giffard were enjoying the long-drawn-out business of the hand-over: four patrols were more than enough.

The captain, 'Hammer' Hawke, had stopped the zig-zag: *Urgent* was plugging into the seas to take them head-on. She was virtually hove-to, her diesels coughing fitfully from aft as her stern plunged into the troughs. Another hour and the charge would be right up and, with luck, the captain would dive to make life more comfortable. 'You can never tell with Hammer,' Giffard had said, barely concealing his relief at being sent home. It was clear to Carbis that both of them, captain and first lieutenant, were very different personalities.

Hammer was volatile, a jolly extrovert, never happier than when he was up to some prank. His favourite trick in the Lazaretto mess was to engage his victim in conversation while reading a newspaper. Hammer would surreptitiously empty the fuel of his cigarette lighter on to the lower end of the paper. He would then offer the reader a cigarette and ask for a light. He was a dab hand on his pocket concertina which he played with rhythmic gusto whenever the mood took him, whatever company he was in. Wherever he was, he made things zing. 'All right in small doses,' Giffard had complained, 'but trying to live with . . .' There was only one – no, two – driving forces motivating Hammer: getting at the Hun and chasing the women. A bachelor, when in harbour he would leave the boat to Giffard for days while he disappeared into the anonymity of Maltese homes. Giffard, shy and somewhat morose, appreciated being left to get on with his job but found that trying to keep up with his captain ashore and in the mess was beyond him.

Carbis wondered how *he* would match up . . . the idiosyncrasies of captains had to be humoured, he knew. He'd been in command himself, and still resented being pitchforked into this novel existence. He could admit only to himself that he found these submariners – at least the few he'd met so far – though delightful people, enjoyed that effortless superiority inbred amongst this élite branch of the Service. They were groomed to feel that they were the *crème de la crème*: hadn't Max Horton, Flag Officer, Submarines, ordained that, submarine cos being our most precious asset, were to be treated as Derby winners?

Three months ago, on returning from patrol and within two miles of Marsamuscetto boom, Dick Cayley in *Utmost* had been shot up by an ME 109. Since then, Shrimp had ordered that no captain was to be on his submarine's bridge when entering harbour, until the boat was through the boom. But, yes, Carbis admitted to himself, Horton *was* right: these ten COs were a prime target for the enemy. These captains were critical to our hitting back at Rommel, to preventing our Eighth Army from being over-run.

But, he, Carbis, still felt an outsider, still sensed that being a 'pressed man' left him outside the tribe. Provided Hawke did not ride him roughshod as being an inexperienced and green Number One, he'd try to control his own quick temper . . .

He ducked again from another 'green' one roaring down upon them. Was the weather deteriorating? He'd better play safe and tell the Old Man. He held on to the bridge rail and leant over the voice-pipe:

'Bridge to control room.'

'Control room – Bridge . . .' a somnolent voice answered from the snug world below.

Carbis was hunched over the acrid brass voice-pipe, his eyes ranging across the port side of the bridge. Was he having hallucinations? Less than fifty yards away, threshing through the breaking seas, the lean upper deck of a destroyer was lunging past. It was so close, this section abaft the break in her fo'c'sle, that the ship's bridge was already invisible. And as she was rolling towards him, he spotted her two torpedo mountings, each with triple tubes; her twin gun-mounting right aft. Water sluiced across her quarterdeck as she lurched away, rolling to port. There was her creaming wake . . . and the spectre had vanished.

Carbis' fingers were groping for the diving alarm. His thumb found the push and shoved:

'*Dive! dive! dive!*'

The lookouts were already tumbling down the upper hatch. Carbis leaned down, yanked at the voice-pipe cock, then jumped after the lookouts. He had dived the boat on his own only twice, but he knew that *Urgent* could, in decent weather, get down in sixteen seconds. As he pulled at the upper hatch's handle, he realized also that in this sea she could take longer; he snapped on the clip of the longer handle, felt a snatch of relief as in the semi-darkness he yelled downwards:

'*First clip on!*'

Then the shorter of the two handles:

'*Second clip on!*'

He slithered down the steel ladder, felt the rim of the lower hatch beneath the soles of his feet, then dropped down the control-room ladder to the corticene deck. The lower hatch was shut and clipped behind him. The calm and warmth of the control room was a pleasant contrast to the turmoil of the seas above. The captain was standing, hands in his pockets, watching his first lieutenant taking *Urgent* down.

'*Blow Q.*'

The high pressure (HP) air hissed as it blew the water from this emergency diving tank holding ten tons of water and which was sited for'd of the boat's centre to get her down quickly; the pointer on the diving gauge was revolving steadily around the glowing dial: forty, forty-five, fifty feet . . .

'*Vent Q inboard.*'

The foul air roared behind Carbis' head while it vented into the submarine. Routine stuff, carried out day-in, day-out on patrol . . . the boat was levelling off as she neared her ordered depth of eighty feet.

'Well, Carbis?'

The captain was watching him intently.

'A destroyer, sir: she passed close down our port side.'

'Did she see us?' Hawke turned towards the first lieutenant who was standing back between the depth gauges, watching, controlling the planesmen.

'Go on down to one hundred and twenty feet, Number One,' Hawke ordered. 'Shut off from depth-charging.'

The command was passed verbally from man to man through the length of the boat. Bulkhead water-tight doors swung shut; clips snapped on. The control room was now a world on its own, shut off from its neighbours.

'*Did she see us?*' the captain snapped.

'She must have, sir. But I saw no-one on deck.'

'What was the weather like'

'Working up to gale force, sir, I reckon.'

Carbis met the long, searching glance as Hawke asked:

'Why wasn't I informed? You read my night orders?'

'I was about to call you, sir, when she slipped past from out of the night.' Carbis knew his explanation sounded wet. He would never have accepted it from his own officers in the Channel . . . He could sense the silent criticism of the listening control-room team.

'All-round sweep completed,' the asdic operator reported. 'HE fading on Red 10.'

'One hundred and twenty feet, sir,' Giffard reported. 'Grouped down, slow ahead on both motors.'

'Very good. Remain at diving stations until we know whether she saw us.' Hawke nodded at Carbis and began leaving the control room. 'I want a word with you.'

Carbis followed the stumpy, crouching figure to the wardroom where Hawke sat down on his settee. Fingers interlaced and palms together, his elbows on the table, his blue eyes stared impassively at Carbis whom he kept standing. A pool of water formed on the deck from the lieutenant's dripping trousers.

'If you're to be my first lieutenant next trip,' Hawke said quietly, so that the man in the passageway could not hear, 'we'd better get things straight.' He paused, weighing his words, while Carbis felt resentment building inside him: he'd erred, but he hadn't wanted unnecessarily to disturb his captain . . .

'I'm the captain of this hooker,' Hawke said. 'From my first lieutenant I expect a hundred-and-one per cent loyalty. My Number One sets the example and must keep me informed of everything, *everything* that's going on in my submarine.' He paused, the hard light softening in his eyes. 'I know you're new to this game, but it's a different way of life to surface ships. I'll give you *one* patrol to settle down as my Jimmy: no longer. The lives of everyone in *Urgent* depend on your efficiency and you being able to get along with me. Understand, Carbis?'

'Yes . . . sir. I'm sorry.'

Hawke smiled bleakly: 'Okay: you'd better get back on watch. I'll surface in a few minutes.'

Carbis shuffled back to the control room. The lookouts glanced at him while they buttoned up the jackets of their suits. Then the asdic operator reported no HE on his all-round sweep.

'Lookouts in the tower.'

The captain was standing behind Carbis: 'Surfacing in five minutes' time. Eighty feet.'

The gale continued all the next day, but eased during the evening.

The hands went to supper early and by the time *Urgent* began preparing to surface for the night's charge, only a long swell remained. The first watch was well advanced when Carbis completed reading the captain's night orders which were kept on the chart table. Number One was on watch in the control room. Before turning in to Giffard's ship's-side bunk at the end of the table, Carbis wanted to enjoy a few minutes of quiet to himself. When he returned to the wardroom, the Third Hand, Sub-lieutenant Danberry, was already snoring in the upper athwartships bunk; Ross, a lieutenant RNR, was asleep on the settee beneath. Carbis eased himself on to the captain's settee, extracted his tobacco pouch from the drawer beneath Giffard's bunk and filled his pipe.

He'd recovered from the captain's rollicking, while Hawke had behaved throughout the day as if nothing had happened. He'd kept the boat deep all day until the weather had moderated enough for a periscope watch. The HSD (High Submarine Detector) and the SD (Submarine Detector) were the ones who suffered, for while the remainder of the boat was able to be at 'Watch Diving', one 'watch-on' in three, the two asdic operators had to be 'watch-and-watch'. But, though positioned to the south of Pantelleria to wait for an expected convoy from Palermo to Tripoli, it had been a blank day. John Carbis had spent his watch in the control room re-reading the sailing orders and catching up on the signal logs.

In September '41, when pleading for reinforcements, ABC* had told the Admiralty: 'Every submarine that can be spared is worth its weight in gold.' And as Carbis flicked through the signals, it was exhilarating to read among the addressees the names of the newly re-constituted Tenth. Shrimp, his staff and the four surviving boats had returned to Malta when the approach channels had been swept clear of mines on 5 July. By 20 July the flotilla was re-forming at Lazaretto – *P41*, *P44*, *Utmost*, *P31*, *P34*, *Una*, *P43* and *P35*; just in time to cover 'Pedestal', the massive and last-chance operation to relieve Malta which was within thirteen days of starvation . . . Carbis rose to his feet, then eased himself to the end of the settee when the captain re-entered the wardroom.

'It's much quieter up top,' Hammer murmured. 'I'll surface now to get in our charge.' He raised his voice and called out to the control room: 'Shift to red lighting!' He extracted his dark glasses from his drawer, donned them. He sat there motionless, while the hands filed

*Admiral Sir Andrew B. Cunningham.

silently down the passage to their diving stations.

After surfacing, Carbis lay on his back in Number One's bunk. In an hour, at 2300, he'd be relieving him on the bridge. The diesels were pounding away, back aft; the captain was on the bridge; some of the hands were smoking and playing uckers, the remainder sleeping. *Urgent* had stopped rolling and was zig-zagging. Carbis crossed his arms beneath his head and tried to sleep . . .

Everyone in *Urgent* was itching to return to Malta: how many merchant ships of the 'Pedestal' operation had reached the island safely? he wondered. The Tenth's existence and that of the island depended upon the outcome of this gigantic gamble and, judging by the signal log, the German and Italian Air Forces had flung in everything they had to destroy the convoy. Perhaps this dispersal of Kesselring's air effort had *just* done the trick and relieved the pressure on our Desert Rats who had held fast at a place called El Alamein, only sixty miles west of Alexandria?

Under their new Commander-in-Chief, General Alexander, and their new Commander, General Montgomery, the Eighth Army had reversed the tables. After a three-day battle, they had given the Afrika Korps a bloody nose: Rommel's dream of linking with the Japs across India was fading rapidly.

No-one in The Tenth had really hoisted in the tardy news about the Eighth Army which percolated through to the flotilla at the beginning of July, five weeks ago. Was it because the submarines were so pre-occupied with getting at the enemy again? Not only had the Desert Rats held, but Rommel was on the run westwards with the Eighth Army in hot pursuit – and the invasion threat against Malta was receding daily. Only a few weeks ago the news was at its blackest, Carbis thought to himself as sleep began to claim him: Rostov in Russia had fallen to the Germans; and the Japs were menacing the east coast of South Africa.

Everyone in *Urgent* was fed up with this blank patrol off the Kerkenah Islands; it must be disappointing, too, for the boats to the north of *Urgent*, disposed on a line south of Pantelleria. The Italians were pushing no convoys through while the 'Pedestal' convoy was being fought through. No co enjoyed shallow water, or the mirage effects off North Africa during the mid-summer heat. The humidity in the boat during the daytime was extreme; even at night it was too hot to sleep. Drowsiness was overcoming Carbis and soon he was asleep.

CHAPTER SIX

Rough Cargo

Though Carbis had donned his submarine sweater, the chill of the early morning seeped through to his bones: weariness, perhaps, because he had not got his head down early enough. In half-an-hour Ross would be relieving him and Duggie was never late. Carbis shook his head to clear the drowsiness creeping over him. He jammed the binoculars more firmly into his eye sockets; once more he started sweeping from the starboard quarter and up the starboard side on another all-round sweep.

It was very dark. The new moon was setting and was invisible behind the low cloud hanging like a shroud over this desolate coast. The humidity after the sirocco which had blown itself out yesterday evening had left everyone limp; it was too easy to succumb to this lethargy.

The diesel exhausts snuffled back-aft, the only sound in the night; the charge was floating now and the batteries right up, ready for another day's diving. Down below, the helmsman was altering course regularly to his ordered zig-zag and as the boat, trimmed down with her fore-casing almost awash, slunk slowly through the black sea, the water hissed as it curled along her pressure hull. The shadowy figures of the lookouts on either side of him were silent too as they crooked their elbows on the bridge rail; the captain was dozing in his camping chair which was wedged between the starboard side and the periscope standard. Thank God this was *Urgent*'s final night off these dreary, low-lying banks of the Kerkenah Islands: Hammer disliked this billet with its shallows, but it was a focal point for enemy convoys and there was always the chance of a target. But not on this patrol, apparently . . .

'Got a bit of periscope paper, sir?'

The murmured request came from the starboard lookout, Able Seaman Swinley, and Carbis handed him a tissue. 'Thanks, sir.'

Having cleaned off the lenses, Swinley braced himself, then began to sweep up the port side again. John Carbis took the opposite side, concentrating on the starboard beam and moving for the hundredth time towards the bow. In twenty minutes he'd be sinking a cup of 'ki', the hot, concentrated chocolate brew which for generations had been drunk by night-watchmen. He'd be turning-in to Ross's warm bunk . . .

It must be the tiredness which was playing tricks with his eyes: the darkness seemed even thicker there. He'd cut back slowly across the stern, then start the sweep for'd again. Gradually he drew his right elbow back, letting his forearm slide along the bridge rail. There . . . again, a definite, more opaque blackness: a faint smudge, but certainly visible . . .

'Captain, sir . . . *Alarm*, Green four-five!'

There was a scuffling at the back of the bridge; then Carbis, who had not taken his binoculars from the smudge, felt Hammer alongside him, crouching, lining up his binoculars parallel with those of his officer of the watch.

'Got it . . .! *Sound the night alarm!*'

Carbis yelled the command down the voice-pipe, heard the rattlers insistently summoning all hands to Night Action stations.

'Medium-size ship,' Hawke snapped. 'Keep a look-out for her escort.' He slid to the starboard torpedo sight, began setting his estimates of course and speed.

'*Stop the generators. Group up . . . half-ahead together. Stand by all tubes!*'

'Keep to your sectors,' Carbis told the lookouts. The temptation to concentrate on the target was strong, but an escort could swiftly emerge from this Stygian darkness. The diesels died; as the boat surged ahead, the only sound was the hiss of the sea and the soughing of the breeze from her own way . . .

'Don't lose her, officer of the watch. I've got to get off track.'

Urgent was swinging to starboard: the captain was turning a full circle to gain time . . . the target, a dark mass with a foaming slash at her bows, could not have been at more than a thousand yards.

'*Stop starboard!*'

The boat was swinging rapidly and Carbis had his work cut out to keep the looming silhouette in his field of view . . . The reports were booming up the voice-pipe:

'*All tubes ready . . .*'

Urgent's stern was swinging past the target and Carbis slipped to the other side of the bridge. Hammer was crouched across the torpedo firing sight and adjusting his settings.

'Too bloody close,' he was muttering. 'Slow astern together.' He jerked up his head and glanced at the gyro repeater: 'Meet her! Steady on 290°.'

As the swing eased, the giant bows bearing down on them seemed horribly close: she'd cross only two cables ahead . . .

'Course, sir,' the steady voice of Wescombe, the cox'n, reported up the voice-pipe, '290°.'

Urgent's bows were pointing barely twenty degrees ahead of the looming target. Amazingly the submarine had not yet been sighted . . .

'*Fire one!*' Hawke was crouched motionless over the sighting bar: '*Fire two . . .*'

One slight tremor was followed by another. Carbis spotted the first streak of trailing bubbles: then, as the second pencil line followed the first:

'*Full astern starboard, slow ahead port!*' As the captain yelled down the voice-pipe, a devastating explosion split wide the darkness.

The blast slapped *Urgent*'s bridge like a blow from a giant's fist. The flashes of light, white, orange, and violet blinded the onlookers. There was an ear-splitting roar and a succession of explosions as the ship was blown asunder. Bits of ship were shooting into the sky which was suddenly as bright as day. And as the shocked bridge team picked themselves up, Carbis watched the captain calmly continuing to con his submarine: '*Steady on 090°. Full ahead together.*'

The sea was hissing and suddenly the water around the boat was boiling with splashes.

'Down!' Hawke shouted. 'Take cover.' They flung themselves to the deck, shielded their heads with their arms: all save Swinley who, aghast at the holocaust, stood transfixed in the starboard wing. Carbis heard his cry, then a clang! as something hit the bridge. The boat shivered as a heavy blow struck her somewhere aft. They jumped to their feet: of the ship there was no trace, save the threshing seas where she had been.

Leading Torpedoman Michael Mott stood back from his switchboard and wiped his sweaty hands on the cloth stuck into the curled waistband of his sarong. He watched with satisfaction the progress which his pupil, Able Seaman Joseph Nunn, was making with his switchboard drill. They'd closed up 'at the rush' when the rattlers sounded but Mott arrived only in time for the inevitable command to 'Group up'. It was always an exciting moment, streaming two thousand amps from each battery into the main motors.

Joey had slammed home the massive breakers with commendable speed, one after the other, *slam, slam, slam* . . . but was still too eager. Too swift, and the main motor fuses could blow – and that brought down disaster upon the head of the rating in charge of the motor room: LTO Michael Mott. Joey grinned when they felt the tell-tale tremor through the hull: the first 'fish' had left its tube. They waited.

'Two,' counted Joey. They felt, rather than heard, a violent crack! a difficult sound for Mott to recognize, despite his experience of wartime patrols.

'Can't be a hit,' Nunn said. 'Too close, eh, Hooky?'

Mott noted the anxiety in his junior's voice: and then the world about them split wide. A *whoosh!* of air, a shock, then excruciating pain in his eardrums and blood.

Losing consciousness for a moment, the LTO knew nothing until he felt Nunn struggling to lift him to his feet.

'Hooky, quick . . . Friggin 'ell . . . *Water!*'

And as Mott collected his senses, he smelt the fire, saw the sparks and the spitting, the flames spurting behind the port switchboard. A cloud of smoke and steam blew out as a stream of water cascaded through the deck head.

'Fire in the motor room!' he shouted above the pandemonium. 'Joey – extinguisher . . .'

And as Nunn battled with the mounting fire, the LTO staggered, gasping and coughing, into the engine room. 'Tell 'em on the bridge,' he croaked. 'We're holed in the motor room. Water's pouring in.' He saw the anxiety on the Chief ERA's face: burnt-out motors; salt water on batteries was a submariner's nightmare: chlorine was lethal.

'Look after Mott,' CERA Plumb ordered his second-in-command. A stoker caught the LTO as he crumpled to the plates. Plumb hurried for'd to the control room and pushed his way to the voice-pipe.

'*Blow six main ballast.*'

It was the calm which Hammer displayed in emergency which most impressed John Carbis. Hawke stood there, hands in his shorts' pockets, half-stooping, his shaggy head bent, his face fringed by his red beard: he was silently waiting to see whether emptying the after main ballast tank would bring *Urgent*'s stern sufficiently out of the water. If that gash in the pressure hull remained much longer at water level, the boat was lost. Thank God the wind had abated . . .

The silence was tangible while the after-ends imperceptibly began to cock upwards. Hawke wanted no more water in the for'd ballast tanks if he could help it: the boat was fully trimmed down.

'*Stop blowing.*'

At the after end of the bridge, CERA Plumb, a tall, brawny man with a wry sense of humour, was being roped up with a bowline by the first lieutenant.

'Over you go,' the captain said. Watching them as they picked their way through the jagged wreckage, Hawke called over his shoulder:

'Keep your eyes skinned, Carbis. I never sighted her escorts: probably searching for survivors, poor buggers.'

Hawke didn't express the fear they all shared. If *Urgent* was savaged now, even if they risked diving with wedges half-driven into the gash, there'd be little future for the two men slithering along the after-casing.

The captain moved back to the voice-pipe:

'Bridge – control room . . .'

'Control room . . .'

'Ask the navigating officer for the time twilight starts . . . and the course for Malta.'

'Aye, aye, sir.' The cox'n's voice was imperturbable. CPO Wescombe was the 'father' of the boat; aged thirty-eight, he was eleven years older than the captain. The more tense a situation, the more his attitude denoted 'business as usual'.

Urgent had been struck on the starboard fore-side of the conning tower by a twelve-foot girder which was stuck into the bridge plating. Carbis had surveyed the extent of the immense damage and McVicker, the Outside ERA, Fell, the Second Cox'n, and four stalwarts were already frantically attacking the damage with crowbars, tackles, hack-saws and rope. They had just slid the offending girder across the pressure hull and into the drink. Gawn, the PO Tel, was emulating a trapeze artist and rigging up a jury aerial for the after-end of the bridge.

Both periscopes and their standards were buckled; the for'd jumping wire was hanging like knitting along the casing and inviting entanglement around *Urgent*'s propellers; the W/T mast was smashed and the upper steering and binnacle were wrecked.

Miraculously no-one on the bridge had been killed, but poor old Swinley's shoulder was badly crushed. Carbis lowered him on a heaving-line down the tower, and they turned him into the stoker PO's bunk. Before coming up top, Number One gave him a morphine tablet. Mott's hands were burned and he was in his hammock, half-unconscious from the fumes he had inhaled.

'Control room – bridge.'

'Bridge?' Hawke's ear was over the bent voice-pipe. 'Very good.' Hammer glanced at his watch, turned to Carbis:

'Course for home is 065°. Don't zig,' he ordered, adding quietly: 'Forty minutes to twilight.'

'Aye, aye, sir.' Carbis leaned across the voice-pipe: 'Steer 065°.' He raised his binoculars and concentrated again on his all-round searching.

So, the boat could not dive because of her holed pressure-hull. If there *had* been escorts for the ammunition ship, they could not be more than a mile-and-a-half astern; and *Urgent* was still in the enemy's main convoy route which was patrolled by aircraft. Without periscopes the submarine was blind. She had no binnacle and no W/T communications. Even if the pressure-hull holds watertight at depth, John Carbis thought to himself as he searched slowly round the horizon, Duggie Ross has his work cut out; if the gyro compass fails, we've only got 'Faithful Freddie' by which to navigate and find Malta – and the island, being miles away, will take three days and nights to reach. We'll be able to use our eyes only at night when surfaced . . .

Gawn was clambering over the back of the bridge, the grin on his face showing even in these last moments of darkness.

'Reckon my jury aerial is as good as new, sir,' he reported. 'Should wake them up in Malta.'

'Thanks, PO Tel,' Hammer acknowledged. 'But hold on a bit, for goodness sake. We're too close to the enemy yet!' He was making way for Gawn when the port lookout shouted:

'*Aircraft port quarter!*'

The drone of a low-flying aircraft was growing louder. Hammer pushed Carbis from the voice-pipe, rested his thumb on the diving push. '*Stop hammering!*' he yelled towards the after-casing. Apart from the murmur of the water curling along her hull, the only sound came from the twin engines of an aircraft approaching on a steady bearing from abaft the port beam. 'Don't move,' Hawke murmured.

The drone grew into the roar of engines. For an instant they saw the Cant 52 lumbering towards them, a couple of hundred feet above the sea. As she flew across *Urgent*'s bows, Carbis saw the blue light from the cockpit.

'She may not have seen us,' Hammer murmured. His thumb still on the diving push, they listened for her to bank towards them. The droning diminished, faded to the north-east, then was no more.

'Carry on, Chief.'

The hammering in the darkness began again with renewed frenzy and then Number One shouted aft:

'Another wedge, sir . . .' There was desperation in his call.

'More cotton waste?'

'Just a wedge.'

During those next seven interminable minutes, McVicker's and Fell's working party finished off cutting through the jumping wire which they carefully ditched over the side. No more could be done. They cleared the casing as Carbis saw Giffard bending down to grab the Chief's arm. Then, bringing their saws and hammers with them, they were slithering down the sloping casing. Plumb shouted upwards:

'The best we can do, sir. Take her down slowly.'

'Blow one main ballast,' the captain commanded. 'Stand-by for a controlled dive – no klaxon.' The two exhausted men climbed up the starboard rungs, clambered over the bridge rail. Carbis felt her bows lifting until she was level.

'Stop blowing,' Hammer ordered. 'Clear the bridge. I'm going below. Don't dive her until I tell you.'

Carbis was alone. He stood by the voice-pipe, waiting to shut the cock. In the next few minutes they would know whether they could ever reach the island which meant life for them all.

Giffard was calling up the voice-pipe:

'Come down, officer of the watch. Shut the upper lid.'

Carbis reached down, yanked at the lever, shut the cock. As he crossed to the hatch, his eyes were level with the bridge rail: a sliver of first light was streaking the eastern horizon.

CHAPTER SEVEN

True Valour

Urgent's new first lieutenant felt the hot sandstone through the soles of his shoes. He stood on the dockside to glance at the damaged bridge of the submarine to whom, he felt, he now belonged. The plating was twisted and crumpled, but the damage terminated inches above the brackets supporting her name plate. There it was: *URGENT* . . . His ship; he, now, her first lieutenant. Hammer had told him of his decision just before he and Giffard went ashore, both to Lazaretto: Giffard was joining *Clyde* before she sailed tonight on another return trip to Gib.

URGENT: her capitals stood out from the blue plating of her rusting conning tower: *Urgent*, one of the 'second group' boats now rolling out of Vickers Armstrong's yards at Barrow and from the Tyne. Carbis preferred their sleeker lines to the nine bulbous-bowed boats of the 'first' group. The second group were better boats to handle dived, less liable to break surface in a bad sea, when firing a full salvo of torpedoes. As Carbis squinted against the sun, the sentry on the brow shouted across to him:

'Can you wait a second, sir? Lieutenant Ross is on the phone to the captain.'

John was in no hurry now: the boat was in dockyard hands. He'd given leave to two watches and he was taking the opportunity to visit Bighi Hospital: when *Urgent* had berthed here this forenoon in Dockyard Creek, both Swinley and Mott were taken off by ambulance.

The wedges and cotton waste had held the gash in the pressure-hull: even from the pressure at seventy feet, the inflow had been manageable, and directed into the bilges: *Urgent* had remained at seventy feet during the day and, as the wood swelled, the leak had diminished over the three days' passage back to Malta. It wasn't only Carbis who sighed with relief as, for the last time, they surfaced when sighting *Speedy*, the minesweeper. The RAF must be in the ascendant, because a couple of Spits had been circling overhead for the twenty miles' run-in on the surface to Grand Harbour.

Urgent was secured by 1030. Hammer had left her Jolly Roger flying and even when the fore-hatch was opened, the onlookers from the battlements of Valetta were still waving and cheering. Another detail for Carbis to remember: the pirate flag must be sent up to Carmella's for her nuns to stitch on another emblem: a white bar, the symbol for a supply ship sunk . . .

Douglas Ross was emerging through the fore-hatch. 'Sorry to keep you, Number One. The captain won't be coming back tonight. He wants you to ring him in the morning.' Both men grinned. Hammer would be away tonight, unobtainable: there would be relative calm for a few hours in the boat. 'What time will you be back from Bighi?'

'Shan't be long,' Carbis said. 'I'll take the weight tonight. I've nothing on and a hell of a lot of work.'

'Thanks. Danberry's new to Valetta and I'm showing him the sights.' He grinned 'Not the red light district.'

'Not down the Gut then?' Carbis felt the friendship growing between Ross and himself. For the first time since he'd arrived in the flotilla he sensed that he was becoming less of an outsider.

'Back soon.'

'Thanks, Number One. I hope Mott and Swinley are okay.'

John started to walk up the creek. Smoke was still rising from the buildings hit during yesterday's raid: evidently the Lutwaffe were easing up, in spite of the arrival of the convoy survivors five days ago – only *five* out of the *seventeen* merchant ships, but one of them a tanker, they said. The army had mounted its unloading operation, 'Ceres', as soon as the ships berthed; another couple of days and they should all be discharged. Two more days . . . The enemy knew that Malta's existence depended on these supplies and the next raids must be imminent. John Carbis hurried towards the head of the creek, past the crumpled workshops, the craters and the mounds of debris. He'd follow the creek road round and skirt the Margherita Lines to Vittoriosa and Calcara. He should reach the hospital before they started serving supper. And perhaps . . . ?

Might she still be on duty, Nurse Anna Seguna? He tried to ignore his quickening excitement. He felt a hypocrite; the reason for his visit to the hospital was, *he* knew, more than an interest in the welfare of two of his men. He was seizing this opportunity to visit Anna

Seguna . . .

He could never forget Anna, his first love: the cause, he was sure, of his rebound affair with Pam. Anna, gorgeous Anna with the dark mysterious eyes; he could see her so vividly, standing with him up in *Warspite*'s upper bridge – *three* years ago now? In her naval nurse's uniform now and twenty-one years old, would she still be so attractive, that delicious girl with the red, inviting lips, the rounded figure and marvellous legs? Anyway, though she *was* engaged to Lofty Small, there was no harm in keeping up old friendships, was there?

Calcara Creek opened before him, the massive bastion of Fort St Angelo rearing above the turquoise deeps of Grand Harbour. He paused momentarily, moved by the spirit of defiance those battered walls proclaimed. Then he spotted the tanker.

Her gunwales flush with the water, a string of fenders along her sides, a bevy of tugs and a salvage vessel fussed about her; they were evidently trying to keep her afloat as she discharged her life-saving cargo into the lighters lashed alongside. She must be the tanker which the dockyard maties were talking about: *Ohio*, they called her. She *must* stay afloat, they said, six hours longer for the remainder of her uncontaminated high-octane spirit, oil fuel and kerosene to be pumped from her. Carbis regarded her with amazement.

Ohio's hull was buckled and streaked red with rust: her grey super-structure was blackened and twisted where the bombs had struck; her two HA guns, for'd and aft, still stuck defiantly skywards; for'd of her funnel, a cruel wound dented her starboard side and jagged, dark caverns pierced her upper deck. Judging by the evident frenzied efforts to provide her with more buoyancy, this was a desperate fight to pump the fuel out of her before she settled on the bottom of the harbour.

Carbis knew, as they all did, that without that precious fuel the Spitfires, whose numbers had just been augmented by *Eagle*'s and *Furious*' ferrying, could not continue to defend Malta; nor to save the Eighth Army by attacking Rommel's supply ships without which he could not advance on Alexandria. But this vital ship of the 'Pedestal' operation *had* arrived; the battle must have been a bloody business.

He walked on, for the first time seeing with his own eyes the dogged courage of the dockyard workers who were utterly dead-beat: moving lethargically, starvation had reduced them to automatons. For nights and days the soldiers and the dockyard men had continued to unload and to carry out the repair work. The gallantry of our merchant seamen was giving Malta and our Eighth Army the hope of survival and the chance to hit back: the Maltese people, if they died on their feet, were not going to fail them. Also – for the first time – Carbis felt a pride in being out here, in sharing in the fight. He strode onwards towards the point, to the great white hospital with the red crosses painted on its walls.

On that same evening, the Protection Officer for Sliema was standing on the battlements above Custom House jetty. He was tired after the long meeting presided over by Wingrave Tench and the VIPs, and had earned this moment of tranquillity while he waited for Anna.

He'd promised Dotty to escort Anna home after her long spell of duty; she'd take a dhaisa to Grand Harbour if she missed the ferry. This procedure was routine for both of them, whenever he came to Valletta as he had done last Saturday, five days ago: a Saturday he could never, never forget as long as he lived. Until that moment, when first he had sighted the merchant ships edging round the point of Fort Ricasoli, he and the others who were in the know had accepted that the island could hold out for only sixteen days longer. Surrender was inevitable if the population was not to die in their thousands; Britain could never permit such a sacrifice however determined were the stubborn Maltese to continue the fight to the death.

Two days after the arrival of the first four ships of 'Pedestal', de Marco went to Valletta expressly to watch the tanker which was reported to be entering harbour. Praying for her with thousands of others, willing her to succeed, seemed to make things easier. When he first spotted her, she seemed to be stationary, but by closing one eye de Marco had judged her to be just under way. Her upper deck was awash, a line of fenders strung along her sides. Lashed to her starboard side was a destroyer, her pendant number *G77* identifying her as the *Penn*. Towing the tanker from ahead was the *Rye*, one of the island's overworked minesweepers. *Ledbury*, a 'Hunt', was secured astern to control *Ohio*'s heading, while *Bramham*, another 'Hunt', and three other sweepers, *Speedy*, *Hythe* and *Hebe*, formed a close screen about the stricken vessel.

That was three days ago. But now, watching her from the battlements while the last of her fuel was being pumped into the lighters, Toni de Marco knew she had but hours to live. Her tank decks were awash: pumping was barely keeping abreast of the water still flooding into her. But the bulk of her fuel, that precious life blood which she fought so bravely to bring through to save the island, was already in the underground tanks of Malta's airfields. At this afternoon's meeting, the latest count was over 9,000 tons . . . TONS . . . of fuel and aviation spirit. TONS . . . this was a miracle after the drops which the imperturbable store-carrying submarines had been running through the minefields from Gibraltar.

Ohio's arrival *was* miraculous . . . she had been sighted off Ricasoli Point on that sun-drenched Saturday forenoon, the day of the feast of Santa Maria, a sacred day. It was no wonder that the crowds lining Valletta's battlements, the creeks and breakwaters, were convinced that God's hand was at work. Weeping and laughing, cheering and waving ecstatically, they watched her as de Marco did, until at last she came to rest under the protection of the Royal Malta Artillery, those gunners who had made such a name for themselves with their deadly box-barrage . . . Toni squinted across the blue water: was that Anna's ferry rounding St Angelo?

The news of the 'Pedestal' convoy had swept like a bush fire through Valletta: Lord Gort, a natural communicator, had hidden nothing from his people when he had spoken to them on the re-diffusion system.

Out of the seventeen merchant vessels which had passed through the Strait of Gibraltar, only four cargo ships had arrived, two days before *Ohio*: the Commodore's ship, *Port Chalmers*, had survived by a miracle; also the battered and charred *Rochester Castle*; the blistered *Melbourne Star* and, later in the evening, straggling after them, *Brisbane Star*. None of them carried the precious wheat for which the island waited, all the grain-carrying ships having been sunk. On that joyous but terrible Thursday, those in the know were in despair: the tanker upon whom the existence of the island depended had failed to arrive.

Now, after three days, de Marco still sensed an immense feeling of gratitude while his gaze lingered lovingly on the twisted lines of the sinking *Ohio* . . . as he had learned this afternoon, the men of the Navy and the RAF, as well as the unbelievably brave seamen in the sunken merchant ships, had paid an awful price. That grand old lady, *Eagle*, the obsolete carrier who had fought so long in the Med to save Malta, was torpedoed and sunk by a U-boat; *Manchester*, the cruiser, was so badly mauled by two separate E-boat attacks off Cape Bon that she had to be scuttled; *Cairo*, the anti-aircraft cruiser, bombed and sunk; *Nigeria*, the fighter-direction cruiser and the cruiser, *Kenya*, badly damaged; *Indomitable*, an armoured-deck modern carrier, damaged; the destroyer, *Foresight*, sunk. But the Italian battle fleet had not sallied forth to annihilate the stragglers, though enemy cruisers and destroyers *had* steamed southwards.

De Marco had been told that four factors must have affected their gutless efforts: first, they had no stomach for a fight after their two years' experience against ABC's fleet; second, they were desperately short of fuel; third, the RAF from Malta, through Air Vice-Marshal Park's astute bluff, had convinced the enemy that heavy air strikes were on the way; fourth, and fortituously, was the dissuasion caused south of Stromboli by Alistair Mars in *P42* who torpedoed and severely damaged two of the offensively-bound cruisers.

God certainly worked in a mysterious way: at the same moment as this battle was being fought out in the Sicilian Strait, other critical events were happening, it seemed. On the day that the four cargo ships steamed so gallantly into Grand Harbour, a new soldier had taken over command of the Eighth Army at El Alamein, a general called Montgomery. And, on the day when *Ohio* limped in, the valiant 'Auk', who had stood and barred the way so stoutly against Rommel last month, was suddenly relieved by another man about whom the Maltese knew nothing, the General Alexander who had halted the Japanese in Burma. Crazy to alter the High Command at this vital juncture, de Marco mused . . . and he screwed up his eyes against the glare of the setting sun. Yes, that was Anna's ferry, half-way across the harbour. He trotted down the hundreds of steps to Custom House jetty.

Anna looked all-in, despite the freshness of the blue dress which accentuated her trim figure. Her face was grey with tiredness, the pallor accentuated by her black hair and deep-set, dark eyes. She looked older than her twenty-one years which was hardly surprising after all she'd been through: she still refused to talk of the time *Illustrious* came in, of the awful casualties: she'd been on duty for five days and nights without a break.

'Sorry to keep you, Tonio . . . I *am* glad to see you!'

She nipped from the boat, her step springy for all her fatigue. Impulsively she kissed him on the cheek while the other passengers scurried past, hurrying to reach their shelters, or what was left of their homes, before the night bombers came for *Ohio*. She threaded her arm through his: 'Come on. I'm dying to get home.'

As they struggled up the long ascent, up the steps back to Strada

Reale, he *did* feel like a father towards her: she was chattering on about her day, talking of her hopes, asking about Dotty, about 'home' as she termed her lodgings with them. His heart went out to her, this hard-working naval nurse, her youth snatched from her too early, much too early . . .

'Marvellous, isn't it, that they've nearly emptied the petrol out of *Ohio*?' he said.

Her face was serious. 'I was talking to a wounded sailor,' she said. 'He'd had a bad time in Tobruk. "A shambles," he said. Trying to help the army.'

'They don't give us the bad news.'

They were silent while they recovered their breath. But they couldn't waste time or they'd miss the Sliema ferry from Marsamuscetto. She said, urging him upwards again:

'Guess who I saw tonight?'

He thought for a moment. 'Nigel Small? Your Lofty, as they call him? I'd have known if he'd arrived.'

'No – but you're getting warm.'

'His chum, John Carbis?'

She grimaced: 'How d'you guess?'

'I told you that we'd met during that bad night in Sliema. He joined his submarine the next day. I haven't seen him since.' He glanced sideways at her. 'He remembered you.'

'I was just eighteen,' she murmured. 'A lot's happened.'

'Only three years: you, me, Lofty . . .'

'And John . . . John Carbis: he's first lieutenant of *Urgent*. She's being repaired in the dockyard.'

'Badly damaged?'

'He wouldn't say.' Her soft voice had an edge to it. 'They're so damned secretive.'

'So would you be, if your life depended on the enemy not knowing your whereabouts.' They reached the top and halted to recover their breath.

Tonio's comment irritated Anna. What did *he* know of what it was like for a woman to be involved with a submariner? She glared at him peering down on Marsamuscetto harbour where three of the little *U*s lay like sleek blue water beetles in the deep water lapping Manoel Island. What *could* Tonio know of her apprehension, of her feelings? The man to whom she was to join her life might soon be *there* in his submarine, moored up with the others. Tonio seemed so satisfied with himself, standing there in his neatly-ironed, clean khaki shirt and shorts. She stamped her small, sandalled foot in annoyance.

'John did tell me what boat Lofty's in: *P50*.' She snorted in disgust. 'But he wouldn't tell me what flotilla or anything.'

'Must be the Tenth, with that pendant number,' Tonio said. 'They're building up their strength now that the flotilla's back in Lazaretto.' He was looking at her, half-smiling: 'You're very pensive,' he chided. 'Come on: we'll miss the ferry.'

But Anna was not listening. She stood gazing down at the boats for a few moments longer, her thoughts far away. Strange, what petty incidents could affect individuals' lives: if, during that peace-time evening in *Warspite*, the de Marcos had not taken umbrage at John's disappearance with her during the At Home, Tonio would not have unintentionally influenced her parents against John Carbis. She'd been so young and the Segunas were a formidable family.

'They're so different, those two,' she murmured. 'Lofty's so open, bubbling over. John's, well . . .' She hesitated, feeling for the right words.

'A very *complete* sort of chap; keeps himself to himself,' Tonio volunteered. 'I reckon he's got a temper, though. He's different to most of them . . .'

'M'mm . . .' She would not elaborate. But she sensed him glancing sideways at her in the fading light, knew that he'd noted the flush in her cheeks. She took his hand and scurried down the great cutting between the cliffs. Half-running, they had to dodge the busy cave-dwellers who were dossing down before the night murderers from Sicily flew in with the darkness. She was sure there was a new spirit amongst this obstinate and close-knit community: the mommas were singing, the old men chatting, squatting together where the last of the sun still shone; the children were chasing each other between the goats and the squawking fowls.

Though there was no extra food yet from the convoy, there was petrol now for the night fighters.

There was hope.

CHAPTER EIGHT

Burat-el-Sun

Able Seaman George Brawdie was twenty-four years old. He had made the navy his career and worked hard to support his wife, Peg; with the arrival of their little Julie, he had been thankful to put up his first good conduct badge before he'd sailed in *Urgent* for the Med. Leaving them both with her parents in Gosport had lifted a load from his mind, and now all that he wanted was to get this blood-stained war finished.

He'd trained at Whale Island and successfully passed his non-sub rate of seaman gunner, but when he'd put up his gunlayer's badge he hadn't known what he'd let himself in for: here he was, *Urgent*'s gunlayer, responsible with his two trainers, Swinley and Lang, for the efficient working of the submarine's secondary armanent. He liked a quiet life and enjoyed his own company which was why, he supposed, that in a moment of crass stupidity he had volunteered to be the boat's cook . . . a duty undertaken for a spell of three months. He'd rubbed salt further into his self-inflicted wound by volunteering for a second spell, but on one condition: if anyone complained he'd jag in the job.

He switched off the hot plate and tea urn and cleared up the galley, feeling pleased that the skipper had gone to supper early this evening. Pat O'Brien, the wardroom flunky, was squaring off in the wardroom on the other side of the bulkhead: he was a mine of information when things were warming up. Diving stations at seven-thirty had been the last buzz. The squat, dark ordinary seaman, a natural comedian who came from Glasgow, slid round the bulkhead and tumbled the crocks into the sink.

'That's it, then, Banger,' Pat said. 'The Old Man's made up his mind.' He began swilling the plates about the greasy water. Fresh water was a precious commodity and its supply determined the length of the patrol. Personal hygiene was thereby simplified, all unnecessary washing being discouraged. Banger had grown a beard which Peggy

54

hated: he would have to request to continue shaving before returning home.

'When's he going to diving stations?'

'He told the officer of the watch to report at nineteen-thirty,' O'Brien said. His voice lowered and the younger man, an HO (Hostilities Only rating), glanced up at the professional: 'What d'yer reckon, Banger? All right, is it, going in on the surface? Won't they be waiting for us, after us missing the Wop U-boat this morning?'

'The skipper's no idiot,' Banger replied softly. 'Knows what he's up to, mate ' But the gunlayer did not feel the confidence he was pretending. Hammer Hawke was as crazy a captain as any, but how long would his luck hold?

'Gunlayer in the control room.' Bill Dale, the steady, quietly-spoken Stoker Petty Officer, poked his head into the sweltering galley. 'Captain wants a word with you, chef.'

Telling O'Brien to finish off, Banger threw down his cloth and hurried aft. The Old Man was at the for'd periscope and taking bearings for the navigating officer to put on the chart.

'Ah, Gunlayer,' Hawke said, catching sight of Brawdie from the corner of his eye. 'As this is your night, I thought you'd better identify the entrance. Down periscope.'

The all-round periscope slid down into its well as Hawke took Brawdie to the chart table. 'Here's the entrance buoy to the channel. D'you see how the port opens out inside? There should be a lot of coastal shipping on the jetties and the U-boat ought to be alongside the fuelling pier: she looks like a petrol carrier.' Hawke traced *Urgent's* intended track across the plan of Burat-el-Sun Harbour. 'I'll try to get close enough for you to use your gun on her: but you'd better be a better shot than I was with my torpedoes.' He grunted, glanced at the clock above the chart table. 'Take a squint through the high-power periscope.' He nodded at the Stoker PO standing by the lever at the panel: 'Up for'd periscope.'

As the face-piece came level, the captain opened up the two handles, put the lens on the bearing: 'There, you can see the buoy, just to the right of the masts inside the harbour . . .'

Hawke stood back for Brawdie to take over the periscope, but for only ten-second looks; after missing the U-boat this morning when she was turning into the channel, the air and surface patrols must be fully alerted. At each look, Banger was building a picture in his mind of what lay ahead: there was the black buoy rolling in the glassy swell and sticking up above the shimmering horizon. The sea was a dirty yellow-brown and behind, just visible, was a sprinkling of red roofs to the right of a jumble of masts and funnel tops.

'Small ships, sir, most of 'em?'

'Coast-crawling in the shallows. Tunis to Tripoli; to Burat, then on to Benghazi, Tobruk and Mersa Matruh. The Panzers are thirsty beasts. Can you see the lorries yet?'

'No, sir. Just the dust along the road.'

'Down periscope.' Hawke grinned. 'That's the only way I could tell how the war was going. When I saw square helmets behind the steering wheels of trucks going east, I knew that the "Auk" and his Desert Rats were retreating.'

'Which way are they driving now, sir?'

'East, yesterday.' He flicked his fingers and stood back from the well as Dale raised the periscope again. 'I reckon it'll be a miracle to see our round helmets driving west for a long time yet.' Replacing Brawdie, he jammed his forehead against the rubber surrounding the eye-pieces. Brawdie saw the pencil of light streaming into those ice-blue eyes: 'You'll be able to hasten the helmet 'change-round' if you can hit that petrol-carrying U-boat tonight, gunlayer.' Hawke swung round on his heel, checking, always checking, on another all-round look. 'The light's fading.' He slammed the handles upwards, the signal for Dale to lower the periscope. 'What time's the end of twilight, Pilot?'

Ross looked up from his chart table: 1814, sir.'

'That'll do us nicely. We'll catch 'em at their evening meal. Gunlayer, stand-by for gun action at 1930. Gives you time to get yourself organized.'

'Aye, aye, sir.' Brawdie was grinning behind his black beard. 'It's time Big Bertha had a go.' He felt the mounting excitement as he left the control room to shake his gun's crew: the trainer, Swinley, and the range-setter, Lang; Fergus, the three-badgeman and loader; and the cocky Pat O'Brien, ammunition supply. They had to get up the 3-inch shells and stow them along the passage: he'd wait for diving stations before requesting permission from the new Jimmy to open the magazine.

'Take her down slowly, Number One,' the captain ordered. 'Slight bow-down angle. We should touch at seventy-five feet.'

'Aye, aye, sir.'

John Carbis had never bottomed a boat before. And after this morning's humiliating performance when he had almost lost his temper, he wasn't going to make a mess of this. His hand moved to the pump order instrument above his head. A touch from R tank, just a few gallons, into M, along the internal line, should do the trick . . . the indicator glowed its mauve command.

'Crack M,' he ordered, listening to his command being repeated for'd verbally to the leading stoker in the pump space; in his cramped compartment below deck level, the burly and reliable Davies, bent double between his pumping machinery, operated his complex valve-box: a mistake by him and disaster could follow catastrophically swiftly.

'Sixty feet,' he told the second cox'n, 'less dive on the fore-planes.'

The bearded Acting Petty Officer Fell spun his hydroplane wheel half a turn anti-clockwise and as M, the compensating tank for'd, took in its extra water, the pointer on the depth-gauge started to move downwards.

'Check Kingstons shut.' Carbis had at least remembered one basic drill: sand and gravel on the seatings of those large, vital valves would do no good if the boat was forced to go deep or had to shut off from depth-charging . . .

'Stop pumping.'

She was settling down nicely, gaining depth steadily with a gentle bow-down angle. The captain was standing behind him and Carbis sensed that *Urgent's* new Jimmy was on trial as he took her down to the bottom.

'Sixty-five feet, sir,' he reported. 'Seventy . . .'

There was an audible scraping, a scratching noise . . .

'Stop together,' Hawke ordered. 'Nicely done, Number One.'

Urgent was on the bottom in seventy-two feet. He hadn't made a balls of it this time. He'd also pumped a bit out of O, the midship compensating tank; he must remember to flood back the same amount when she expanded again on coming up . . .

'Go to watch diving, Number One: you can prepare for gun action now, with the watch. I'll catch a trim on the way up. Diving stations in half-an-hour's time.'

'Watch diving, Cox'n,' Carbis told the grey-haired Wescombe on the after-planes. 'The gunlayer can open up the magazine. Stand-by for gun action.'

The captain and Ross moved into the wardroom, Carbis remaining with Danberry, the officer of the watch, in the control room. There *must* be minimal noise: a dropped 3-inch shell, a spanner clanging to the deck could alert enemy hydrophones laid across the sandbanks at the entrance to the port.

Ross was returning to take over as oow, so that Danberry could get dressed: as gunnery officer his station was on the bridge to direct the fire. Ross was bent over his chart, re-checking the approach-course track to the buoy. Carbis shoved his hands into his pockets and tried to concentrate on his own part in the coming action.

He still felt sore from the spectacle he had made of himself this morning. After missing the Italian U-boat, when going out to the deep field again, Hawke had ordered watch diving so that the hands could go to dinner and snatch some rest. Carbis had not compensated sufficiently when the hands moved for'd and the boat had gained depth. On correcting, he had allowed her to take on too steep a bow-up angle. She had started to porpoise and only by flooding Q and speeding up had he prevented, by a bee's whisker, a break-surface . . . and only seven miles from Burat.

Hammer Hawke had kept the hands at diving stations. Then he had drilled his new first lieutenant: time and time again, sending the hands for'd, bringing them aft; going deep, settling on an ordered depth; coming up from deep to settle precisely at periscope depth, twenty-eight feet. Not until Carbis had succeeded three times at each drill, when his temper was at explosion point; not until Hammer was satisfied did he dismiss the impatient hands to watch diving – and their spoilt dinners. Carbis had fumed silently, but now, six hours later, he was beginning to simmer down; of course, the Old Man was right. At least, he, Carbis, was beginning to feel more self-confident in his own competence; he held thirty-four men's lives in his hands. Watching the hands quietly preparing for gun action, he knew how vital it was for them to have confidence in their Jimmy: if the captain was killed, the first lieutenant was in command.

Hammer wasn't tackling this entry into Burat without weighing up the dangers. He had succeeded in reaching this position in spite of the high mine risks in these waters. *Usk, Undaunted, P32* and *P33* were all sunk by mines off this coast; *Union, Cachalot, P38* and (only five months ago) Wanklyn's *Upholder,* were all destroyed by depth-charges in the area. And Force K, Malta's only surviving offensive surface force, had been wiped out through mining off Tripoli: the cruiser *Neptune* sank, with only one survivor; *Aurora*, her sister ship, was badly damaged; 'Pepperpot' *Penelope* was damaged; the destroyer *Kandahar* sunk.

This was certainly a dangerous coast, but it was exhilarating to be on patrol again after *Urgent*'s dockyard stint. The deep-dive trial off St Elmo to check the welded repair to her pressure-hull had been satisfactory: a relief for all on board. Watching his chums sailing for patrol to blast Rommel's convoys to hell while *Urgent* was condemned to the dockyard, was making Hammer impossible.

Kipps, the signalman was ready in his sweater, his binoculars slung about his neck and carrying his Vickers light machine-gun.

Carbis glanced at the clock: 1920. 'Shift to red lighting. Diving stations in ten minutes' time.'

The lookouts were dressed, cleaning their glasses and mustering at the base of the ladder. They would enter the tower first, to accustom their eyes to the darkness.

The boat was soon in red lighting, the eerie glow transforming everyone's features, rendering them all like old men. Tom Danberry in his blue sweater, was threading his whistle beneath the straps of his binoculars. The gunlayer, Banger Brawdie, was checking that his 3-inch shells were stowed properly the length of the passageway. As soon as the bridge was manned, the gun's crew would scramble over the bridge rail and down the bridge ladder rungs to their gun; at the same moment, the ammunition supply numbers would scuttle into the conning tower, ready to hand up the bricks to the man on the bridge. Shoving them into the chutes on either side, the shells would slide down to serve the gun, once the ready-use locker was empty.

'Well, Number One, how're we doing?' Hammer was standing beside Carbis, a gleam in his eye.

'Just about there, sir. Five minutes to go before 1930.'

'Good. There's no moon until after midnight. Providing we pick up the buoy, it should be plain sailing.' He glanced at his first lieutenant. 'The troops seem in good heart.'

'Yes, sir. The rum tot at supper helps, but they're itching to get their own back a bit. Brawdie stirs 'em up.'

'Come over to the chart table.'

'Sir?'

They bent over the table, Hammer in the centre, Ross and Carbis on either side.

'I'll take her in between the Hissa Bank and the Zeris Rocks.' Ross pricked off the distance to the entrance buoy: 'Five and-a-half miles to the buoy, sir. Half-an-hour grouped up.'

'I don't want too many up top. Stay below at the chart, Pilot. You can run the echo-sounder once I'm committed to the run-in.' He turned to Carbis. 'If you get no reply from me, having called me twice, you're to take command, Number One.' He paused, then added: 'There'll be no time for the niceties. Get to hell out of it as fast as you can, if anything goes wrong on the bridge. You might be able to con her from down below if there's enough light from the fireworks to use the periscope . . . D'you understand?'

'Yes, sir . . . if, twice, I get no reply from you.'

Hammer glanced at the clock. 'Let's get on with it. It'll be dark up-top now. Go to diving stations.' He raised his voice: *'Stand-by gun action. Lookouts in the tower.'*

Carbis watched the thick-set figure stumping from the control room to don his dark glasses and to dress in the wardroom. Perhaps he, Carbis, was wrong about him, after all? The first lieutenant turned abruptly to take up his station between the gauges. The planesmen were closed up, the control-room crew complete; the motor and engine rooms had rung through; there remained only the TI in the tube space . . .

'Tubes' crew closed up, sir . . .'

'Captain, sir: ready to surface,' Carbis called through to the wardroom. He felt his adrenalin pumping. An all-round HE sweep; catch a quick trim . . . then straight up to the surface from deep. Half-an-hour's run-in on the diesels for a bit of a charge . . .

'Sixty feet,' the captain called from the wardroom. 'Man the tower.'

Urgent was on her way.

CHAPTER NINE

Busy Half-hour

'Stand-by gun action. Man the tower . . .'

The gunlayer climbed through the lower hatch and up the tower ladder to the rung below the upper lid. Holding on with one hand and leaning his back against the wall of the conning tower, he hung there listening to his crew assembling beneath him. 'Gun's crew in the tower,' reported Fergus hoarsely from the darkness below. Fergie, the loader, was the last up, so now Banger Brawdie's team was complete: this waiting was the bit they disliked most.

Banger could see the stars through the dark circle above his balaclavaed head. They swooped in the heavens above him, in rhythm to the rolling of the boat. He twitched up the roll-neck of his sweater, the dark one he always used at night when action would be at close quarters. It was cold here, on the clammy rungs: the brass had its own peculiar, acrid smell. The diesel generators were thumping away down below and drawing in a stream of fresh air for their combustion. When they stopped and the boat changed over to her main electric motors, the moment for action would be imminent. But even though they had exercised this drill innumerable times, he could never prevent his heart pumping like this . . .

Toni's doss-house seemed light-years away; it was in fact only four nights since the fun of that last evening with his mates, chiakking the girls. They always loved it, the lasses who frequented the Britannia Bar, *Urgent*'s drinking haunt. The *ambite* was undrinkable but better than nothing, once Jack had finished his 'blue', the half-pint beer ration issued twice during each rest period. Yes, it had been a lively, last evening: the Black Mamba, the curvaceous queen of Sliema, had cut up rough with the competition she faced from her cronies: the boys had egged the others on – Randy Annie, Lippy Lil and Baggie Aggie, for once, standing up for themselves against the Mamba . . .

He had consigned to his opposite number, the gunlayer of *P31*,

Peggy's present – the lace doily. *P31* was sailing for home and he would post the parcel on arrival: nice to think that she'd be receiving this link with him soon, but how long before he himself was on his way? If he could hit that petrol-carrying U-boat in a few minutes' time, by how many seconds would this flaming war be shortened? Things were going badly for us at the moment, with the German army romping across Russia towards Moscow; and, a few days before *Urgent* sailed, they'd learnt of the Dieppe disaster on 19 August.

The captain had explained why the flotilla was having a disappointing start since its re-birth at Lazaretto: the Germans were transporting overland pre-fabricated sections of their U-boats for assembly in the Balkans. The Hun was equipping the Italians' anti-submarine escorts with modern Asdics and enemy anti-submarine countermeasures had improved dramatically.

Only three weeks ago *Thorn* had been depth-charged and sunk by the Italian destroyer, *Papa*. And *Porpoise*, having laid her mines and sunk two large supply ships, had recently been hammered off Sollum. Her batteries damaged, she had just made Haifa, thanks to two 'Hunts' being sent out to escort her home on the surface because she could not dive . . . and Sollum wasn't far from Burat-el-Sun.

To counter this enemy activity, Hawke had told them, our submarines were being widely dispersed to draw the heat away from Taranto and Sicily, our submarines' principal target areas, which explained *Urgent*'s billet in this God-forsaken part of the Med; *P44* was off Khoms where she'd just sunk a salvage ship and its escorting schooner; *P42* was off Taormina, on a cloak-and-dagger job. Not far north of *Urgent* off Misurata, was *P50*, fresh from England and on her first patrol. Banger was looking forward to meeting her back at Lazaretto, because Knocker White, a fellow *Ganges* boy, was a seaman in her. *P46*, recently from Gib, was playing havoc off Kuriat, having sunk two ships; and all of them, except for *Urgent* up to now – and for obvious reasons – were dumping dummy wooden periscopes whenever they left their billets. These dispersion tactics *ought* to be having an effect, despite our disappointing tally . . .

God! This waiting was getting him down: perhaps the bridge had failed to sight the buoy? Lieutenant Ross had taken a star sight on surfacing, and he was seldom wrong: ex-merchant navy officers made dab-hand navigators. Ross was especially competent, everyone said: he'd lost his brother in the North Sea, machine-gunned in the water by a JU 88 after his trawler had been sunk. A married man, Ross never took unnecessary risks . . .

The hammering of the generators was fading – *Urgent* was on main motors. The rush of air past his ears had ceased: there was silence now in the dark tower.

'*Gun action!*' Paddy Kipps' face appeared in the open circle above Banger's head. 'Up you come, Banger!'

The gunlayer heaved himself through the upper hatch, felt the wind on his face as he straddled the rail over the port side. Groping for the first rung, he shinned down the curved side of the superstructure, until he felt the slippery plating beneath his feet. Grabbing the handrail, he lurched along the walking-platform to the guard-rails encircling his gun. Swinley was hard on his heels and as Brawdie took up his position at his elevating handwheel, he heard Fergie battering at the butterfly nuts of his ready-use stowage.

'Trainer closed up, safety stops off!' Swinley shouted above the wind. The black shape of a buoy swished close down the port side; Brawdie turned his handwheel, saw the barrel elevating and depressing; he checked that his sight was clear, then Fergie and the loading number yelled that they were ready.

'Gun's crew closed up!' the gunlayer shouted up to the bridge. 'Ready for action.'

'*Very good.*' It was Danberry, the sub-lieutenant, standing above the wind baffle on the starboard side of the bridge. '*Load with* HE.'

The breech operator swung off on his lever; the breech block dropped down; Fergie rammed home the first shell. There was no tompion to remember, thank God: the end of the barrel was filled with 'non-floaters', the non-floating grease stuffed into the barrel and over all the working parts.

'Loaded with HE, sir!' Brawdie yelled. 'Ready to open fire!'

He was peering ahead, searching for his target. There! A bunch of small ships, growing larger every second, were strung out at anchor across the small port. The low-lying breakwater was sliding past to port; ahead was a group of flat-roofed buildings . . . then a crane and, on the water-front, a squat building, probably the harbour control's office. On its roof was perched a gun, a vicious-looking thing, and apparently unmanned. The ships were strung out haphazardly, difficult to guess how many. They were darkened, but pinpoints of light were flickering at the head of the harbour. The U-boats' petrol pier?

'For – – – –'s sake, why don't we get on with it?' Swinley was muttering from behind his sight. 'We can blow this sod out of the water.'

'Shut your mouth,' Banger murmured. 'The Old Man doesn't want to rouse them until the last . . .'

'*Target*: second ship to port!' Danberry yelled from the bridge. 'Point-of-aim: ship's side, below her funnel. *Stand-by to open fire* . . .'

Banger felt the mounting swing to port as Swinley wrenched at his wheel. Swinging right again, Brawdie's cross-wire settled on the ship's bridge then steadied on her funnel. He wound down his wheel, watched the sight lower to a point between wind and water.

'Trainer ON.'

'Layer ON.'

Paddy Kipps, the signalman, was opening up with his Vickers, the tracer pouring into the Germans running towards their gun on the harbour office building.

'*Open fire!*'

The gunlayer pressed his firing trigger. The *bang*! drowned the stuttering of the Vickers. The splash of orange fire blinded him when the shell hit.

'The bugger's jammed!' Fergie was wrenching at the breech block, trying to extract the empty shell case.

'Gun's jammed, sir!' Brawdie yelled in exasperation.

'Shift target.' Danberry was directing the signalman's fire to the next ship, looming on the port bow.

'Bore clear,' Fergie shouted.

'Load!' Banger ordered. The breech slammed shut.

'Trainer ON . . .'

Banger squeezed his firing lever, saw the shell bursting into the innards of the ship.

'Shift target,' the gunnery officer shouted. 'Next ship, Red two-o. Open fire.'

'Trainer ON.'

'Gunlayer ON.'

'Fire!' Again the shell crashed home; then another, and another. His team was finding its rhythm, working smoothly, the gun barking regularly.

'Shift target . . .' Banger was enjoying himself: the crashes, the bangs, the Vickers stuttering across the top of their heads. His heart was racing, his crew working like clock-work. From the corner of his eye he could see that the harbour was ablaze, flames jumping and spurting, not only from the panicking ships, but along the installations on the jetties.

'*Check, check, check* . . .!' The gunnery officer's shout was barely audible above the racket. Brawdie lifted his hand from the firing lever and turned towards the bridge.

The captain was peering through his binoculars, his head darting from rail to voice-pipe as he conned his submarine to shave the sides of the merchant vessels. *Urgent* was weaving between them, slicing through the water as the cox'n spun his steering wheel at Hawke's elbow. Unperturbed as ever, Wescombe wove the boat close under an anchor chain, then across to the next trot of ships. The upper deck of a coaster passed within yards, while Hammer searched for his prime target. They were nearing the head of the port and he must find it, now or never . . . Two ships were opening fire on each other, tracer flying between a coaster and what looked like a cable ship. This flashless H.E. was devastating stuff: the enemy had no idea where the fire came from . . .

'Watch out!' Danberry was pointing to the bridge of the ship sliding to starboard of them. Kipps' Vickers stuttered again, its flame-guard glowing red. Bullets spattered against *Urgent*'s forecasing, then ceased abruptly when Kipps riddled the enemy gunner. The harbour was ablaze, night turning into day; above the cacophony Banger heard the captain yelling:

'*There she is*, Sub! Behind that derrick's sheer-legs: *see her*? Starboard ten . . .' His command was like a pistol shot as he conned the cox'n towards the target . . . 'Meet her . . . steady . . . steer for the sheer-legs.'

'I've got her, sir!' Danberry shouted over the rail: '*Target*: submarine on the jetty. Red five. Open fire when your "A" arcs are clear.'

Banger could feel the boat answering to her helm as the captain swung her to clear the jumping wire.

'Trainer ON!'

His heart hammering, Banger depressed seven degrees, watched his horizontal cross-line steadying at the base of the big submarine's conning tower. He squeezed his firing trigger.

A flash sprang to the right of the sheer-legs.

'Left two . . .' Danberry's spotting had always been erratic. Lang, the range-setter, corrected: 'Left two . . .' Swinley yelled: 'Trainer ON . . .'

Banger pressed the firing lever again: he saw the flash, heard the bang when the shell exploded against the pier at the submarine's after-ends.

Urgent's swing was easing to starboard when Danberry bellowed again:

'Right one . . .'

It was difficult for the trainer, Swinley, to allow for *Urgent*'s swinging:

'Trainer ON.'

Brawdie knew that this was his last chance: refusing to be hustled, he waited until his sight crossed the centre-line of the conning tower . . . squeezed again; felt the recoil; heard the crash; saw the flash where the brick struck, this time at the base of the sheer-legs. The Vickers was chattering above his head, so that he missed Danberry's next command. To his surprise, *Urgent* was swinging to port again, weaving through the line of ships, back to the seaward side of the harbour. A couple of coasters were blazing away, their shots flying across *Urgent* and into each other.

The submarine was sliding from sight behind the coasters, when Banger saw the sheer-legs buckling, then keeling over: slowly at first, then crashing across the U-boat's fore-casing. As the enemy submarine was disappearing from sight, an orange explosion burst from her. A shower of sparks, flames and debris hurtled skywards to add to the fireworks. There was a vivid, electric-blue flash and a blast like a hammer blow. Where the submarine had lain there remained only a dark hole in the jetty.

'Shift target: merchant ship. Local control,' the gunnery officer was yelling. Even at his gun, Brawdie detected the glee in Danberry's voice: this was the moment for which every gun's crew yearned. The gun was under the control of the gunlayer.

'Left four, Swin . . . target that one with the tall funnel.' The gun swung to starboard: 'Trainer ON . . .'

Banger fired, fired and fired again until Fergie yelled through the smoke and the brown cordite fumes: 'Ease up, Guns . . . you're ahead of the ammo!'

But while they paused for more bricks, Banger recognized the ship he'd first fired upon when entering harbour. There, a shade to the left, was a white vee; then another to the right of it, cutting through the black water . . . '*E-boats!*' he yelled, pointing across the port quarter. At this moment, Harry Lang crumpled by his dials. Fergie was dropping to his knee and turning over the twitching body. Bullets, flashing like sparklers, were thudding into the bridge plating. Green and red tracer was drifting slowly towards them, then curling away ahead.

'*Check, check, check* . . .' Danberry roared: 'Clear the gun! At the rush!'

Fergie glanced up: 'Harry's a gonner, Guns.'

'Leave him. Get below – *quick*!' Brawdie heard the captain's command above the whistling of the ship's wind. The klaxon was blaring from somewhere far away. Banger yelled upwards to Danberry: 'Lang's hit bad, sir!' He rolled the bleeding body on to its back. The seaman was horribly dead. The shadow of a buoy slid past.

'Clear the gun!' The captain's voice flared with anger. 'I'm *diving*, you fool.'

Brawdie leapt for the handrail as the sea began sluicing along the fore-casing. His feet barely touched the walking-platform; he bounded up the rungs, hand over hand, reached for the captain's out-stretched arms. He heard the water swirling behind him as he scrambled on to the empty bridge, vacant except for the silent Hawke.

Brawdie plunged for the dark abyss, glimpsed the foam of phosphorescent seawater cascading against the after-end of the bridge. He felt the searing pain as the lip of the hatch ripped away his flesh, felt the captain's feet across his knuckles on the upper rung. Water was pouring in a torrent about his head; below, the lower lid was banging shut. In the sudden darkness there was an overwhelming roar, the clang of metal – then, suddenly: *silence*.

'First clip on,' Hawke said. 'We're all right, Guns. Tell 'em to open up below.' And as Brawdie banged on the top of the lower hatch, Hawke's report echoed in the tower: 'Second clip on. Tell the first lieutenant, "Sixty feet and shut off from depth-charging." '

Even above the thudding from the clips which were being freed from the control room, Banger heard the racing of fast-running propellers reverberating in the tower. And even as he dropped through the trunking and into the red lighting, the watertight doors were banging shut. He fell from the steep angle the boat had taken up, the captain falling in a heap on top of him.

'Blow Q!' the first lieutenant commanded above the controlled chaos. As the foul air roared from the venting of the emergency diving tank, the first depth-charges exploded. The boat jumped. Glass shattered and, as the red lighting flickered out, the pale emergency lighting snapped on.

'I've got her, Number One,' the captain called above the din. 'Don't go below sixty feet or we're stuck.'

Brawdie struggled to his feet while the boat levelled out, the pointer of the gauge touching 59, 59, 58 . . . There was a faint, clicking sound as the second E-boat whirred overhead, her propellers beating the water. As Brawdie's gun's crew were struggling to their feet, the next batch of charges exploded.

'Too bloody close,' Hawke muttered. 'Take her down slowly, Number One. We'll bottom and sit this one out.'

The gunlayer glanced at the clock: nine-thirty already. The moon rose after midnight. If they dodged this heat, they'd be pushed to get in a charge before the morning: they'd have to reach the deep field first. The sand was scratching beneath the keel and as the captain stopped the motors, *Urgent* slid to a stop. The depth was forty-five feet: less than a cricket pitch of water above their periscope standards. Snagge, the HSD, was removing his earphones, always a bad sign, when the enemy began his next run-in.

'Silent routine,' the captain ordered. 'Pass the word, not a sneeze from anyone.'

And as they waited, their faces turned upwards towards the deckhead, Brawdie recalled his last memory of Lang's body caught in the guard rails, six feet above their heads. Fergie, the hard-bitten old three-badgeman and a Catholic, was openly crossing himself.

'God rest his soul,' the gunlayer muttered. Harry was a good range-setter.

CHAPTER TEN

Gravy

'Thanks, Gravy, for asking me and for a super evening.'

'I'm sorry you've all got to leave so early. You know you're always welcome here, don't you, Steve?'

'The first thing they told me when I arrived at Lazaretto.' The jolly face hidden behind its ginger beard seemed always about to break into mirth. 'I'd better get back to my boat: *das luftwaffe* may be paying another call tonight.'

Wingrave Tench watched the rollicking CO of *Unruffled* disappearing down the road. A new boy to the flotilla, he had already drawn blood by sinking four ships and gunning a train. 'A natural,' Shrimp had murmured to Gravy over their gins tonight.

'Good night, Hammer. I'm glad you brought your Number One.'

Hawke had not been his usual comic self, had not performed on his concertina. He'd lost a man, Shrimp had told Greta.

'Thanks, Gravy. I'd better get back.' He glanced over his shoulder. 'Carbis is just coming; Toni is walking back part of the way with him.'

They all seemed so young, Tench thought, as he watched Hammer hurrying towards the door. Their youth was what upset Greta most when they failed to return from patrol . . . but, though losses were still inevitable among these submariners, pray God last April and May would never be repeated.

'Sorry to be the last, sir,' John Carbis said as he bade his adieu with Toni de Marco. 'But your wife and Toni have been explaining why the whole island knows you by your nick-name.'

'He hasn't experienced your soup kitchens, sir,' Toni said. 'Thanks so much. I'm just sorry Dolly couldn't come.'

Gravy watched his Protection Officer and the tall, laconic Carbis striding down the drive. He wondered how Hammer was getting on with his new first lieutenant: such an eccentric and volatile a character as Hammer must take a bit of getting used to . . . the Central Region

Protection Officer slowly closed the door of Pembroke House on his departing guests. He returned to the drawing room where Greta was trying to persuade Shrimp to share pot luck with them.

Captain George Simpson, Captain *S10* – 'Shrimp' to everyone, officers and sailors alike – was standing as he always did: feet apart, his thick-set frame leaning slightly backwards, his head back, his chin out. He held the glass of gin in his left hand, the cigarette in his right but, with his forearm horizontal, in that typical posture of his, his elbow stuck out above his hip.

'He won't stay,' Greta said. 'He's going back to Lascaris.'

The blue eyes of his closest friend turned on Gravy's.

'Pay no attention,' Shrimp said. 'But there's a biggish thing on at the moment and it's not quite finished. All a bit of a pierhead jump.' The wise, humorous face lit up in that slow smile of his, the piercing eyes twinkling. 'We're getting into our stride again, you see.' He turned and gave Greta a peck on the cheek. 'Say goodnight to Sue if she's not already in the land of Nod.' He stubbed out his half-finished cigarette, walked to the door and found his cap.

'Good night, both of you. Thanks, as always.' For an instant, unusually for him, he was serious. 'You know how it is: I don't know what I'd do if I couldn't come to your Pembroke House.'

Greta took Gravy's arm. Together they watched that amazing man wobbling down the road on his bicycle.

'Watch how you go, Shrimp!' Greta called after him. A hand lifted in farewell and the leader of the Tenth Submarine Flotilla was hidden from sight.

'I'm sorry there weren't more of them tonight,' Greta said as they locked the door. 'But Shrimp couldn't let us know beforehand, obviously. He sent out all the boats he could, he said. We laid the party on too far ahead.'

'You know it's always been like this,' Gravy said. 'He lives from hour to hour, does Shrimp. He reads the enemy's mind: you can only do that if you live with it every second.'

'Pat said that guessing the enemy's every move was Shrimp's greatest quality.' She added softly: '*Una*'s returning soon with the others.' They'd become used to concealing their fears from each other. If Shrimp could live with the permanent anxiety, they could.

Pat Norman, CO of *Una*, had been out here longer than any . . . he'd commanded *Upholder* temporarily, been wounded badly, then taken over *Una*. How long did luck stay with a man? Greta sighed:

they'd seen Shrimp bear it all silently, alone, when so often his submariners failed to show up off Delimara Point. More than half had been killed in action, yet not one man had shirked patrol, despite the terrible losses. Sixteen of his submarines had never returned to Lazaretto since he'd formed the Base . . . *Talisman* lost only four weeks ago, on passage from Gib: mined in the Sicilian Narrows, they thought. How did Shrimp bear this burden, this appalling strain which he could share with none of his officers, not even his Staff Officer, Bob Tanner; nor Sam Macgregor, his sterling Engineer Commander.

Greta was sharing her husband's thoughts when there was a distant, rumbling bang.

'What's that?' she asked anxiously.

The bangings continued, but something different this time.

'I'm not missing a naval engagement for anything, Greta,' said Gravy, and bounding upstairs, he took up his favourite look-out position on the roof. The night was dark: no searchlights, no gun flashes.

'You silly old thing!' Greta cried from downstairs. 'It's only the door banging and you've woken Sue.'

'Sorry, darling.'

He carefully closed the balcony door behind him: he needed a few moments up here before turning in. The anxiety on Shrimp's face had worried him, for he always exuded confidence and optimism, the spark which inspired his men and the Maltese with whom he came in contact. Morale to him meant everything: he never spared himself to obtain the best for his crews, to help take their minds from their war. The pig farm, the rest camp, the officers' Oleander Villa on the edge of St Paul's Bay, the ridiculous wardroom antics, these were all part of his leadership, his thinking.

He'd been an outstanding submarine co himself, was one of Max Horton's* most trusted subordinates, so Shrimp knew what submarining was all about. Above all he regretted that, at the age of forty-one he was now precluded from being out on patrol with his friends. As his young secretary had told John Carbis, Shrimp's endearing trait was his dealing with people: he treated everyone, from the most junior seaman and from the most simple Maltese to the most senior admiral, as equal to himself. This natural humility was his strength. But, as several of the captains had told Gravy, there was a steely side to him. Woe betide anyone exploiting Shrimp's amiability or failing to treat

*Flag Officer Submarines, Admiral Sir Max Horton.

the enemy as ruthlessly as he expected. But anyone could ask Shrimp for help and his advice was never rationed.

Wingrave Tench was gazing into the starlit sky when he heard the distinctive purring of twin-engines: the Beaufighter night-fighter patrol was hidden somewhere up there in the darkness. Kesselring's onslaught last night had been brutal, one of the worst of the siege. Beginning at dusk, the attacks had continued until dawn: but the RAF, marvellously led now by Park, the Battle of Britain leader, had clawed the Fliegerkorps II from the night. Strange that tonight the enemy had not begun yet . . . this intense blitz had begun ten days ago and had been one of the worst onslaughts since it all started two years and four months ago. Perhaps Kesselring's pilots had had enough of trying to destroy this unsinkable aircraft carrier?

The RAF had shot down its thousandth plane last week, on 13 October: and 'Pedestal', though not relieving the food situation greatly, had hurled Park's pilots back into the air: *Ohio*'s petrol was saving Malta and each day which passed was strengthening Park's hand. Aircraft were beginning to trickle through regularly from North Africa, carried by 'Woolworth' carriers in convoys to Takoradi on the Gold Coast, then overland across the 2,250 miles of hostile terrain to Malta . . .

The Beauforts were droning overhead, but where *was* the German Air Force? Gravy felt unable to rationalize this peaceful night, so different to those he had shared so often with Shrimp. The tall man smiled in the darkness at a particular memory . . .

Shrimp had been at Pembroke House one night when the phone rang. An old lady was bothered because what seemed to her to be like a Baby Austin was hanging from a tree in her garden. While Gravy busied himself with evacuating the area, Shrimp rang through to the army, the police and everyone remotely concerned. The parachute mine was rendered safe, as were also two others: one near the walls of Mdina, the other between Floriana and Valletta.

These wasted enemy efforts were enjoyed by everyone, as were the nightly forays of the Italian Cant bombers which entertained the inhabitants of Sliema, St Julians and everyone on the route to Valletta. The Cants flew in after dusk, homing-in on the white house at St George's Bay, behind Pembroke House and St Julians. Turning for Valletta, the Italians, as soon as the searchlights picked them up, jettisoned their loads; sometimes a jet of sparks streamed from a plane as the bombs were loosed, setting the aircraft aflame. The Cant would turn for the sea, a fire glowing inside the fuselage. Three times this happened and how the Maltese cheered at the enemy's futile efforts!

On another bad day, when Lazaretto and Shrimp's submarines were getting a roasting from the Stukas, Gravy rang up to ask his state of health. 'Pay no attention, Gravy,' Shrimp had replied. 'Sadly, Sam MacGregor's bagpipes were last seen at a hundred feet and still gaining height: otherwise, all is reasonably well.'

Here, in the darkness and solitude of his roof, Tench was feeling an unusual fit of depression. Two immutable decisions from on high always got him down when he was exhausted: first, all his efforts at joining the army had been refused. Authority insisted on his continuing as a civilian so that he could carry on with his work. And second, he was irritated by the unfairness of the censorship decision regarding the Maltese.

They had been through so much, these brave and loyal Maltese. The tragedy was that he, as Chief Censor, as well as being the Director of the Communal Feeding Department, was not permitted to tell them the facts. The people *should* be told the truth – and Gravy was certain it would be better to do so: the enemy knew our plight well enough.

The sour paradox was that, in spite of 'Pedestal' and even at the ration of 800 calories a day, there remained only *ten days'* supply of food on the island. The population had existed on this starvation level for several months now and scurvy was taking its foul toll, particularly with the children and the elderly. In ten days Malta would have to capitulate, whatever protestations the population made.

He had been appointed to act as Assistant Lieutenant-Governor if the enemy succeeded in invading, and had been issued with an armband to denote his authority in such circumstances. He was also commissioned to organise a civilian resistance, a difficult job because of the necessity for secrecy. When recruiting agents, he could not divulge the identity of others. He had approached one Maltese and, as usual, opened the batting by stating:

'If the Germans take over the island, I want you to help by becoming an underground agent . . .'

'We're *not* going to be defeated, Mr Tench.'

'But we must be prepared. That's why . . .'

'Please don't talk to me about it any more,' the man replied angrily, bringing the conversation abruptly to a close.

As head of the central resistance he was to work clandestinely, but the secrecy had its embarrassing moments. He had acquired another house for use as the Underground's head-quarters and communication centre, an acquisition carried out in total secrecy, even his own family being unaware of his actions. A major had come to see him to complain that he could find nowhere to live. Gravy had been away from home and the officer had found only Greta to whom to air his grievance. It was unfair that Mr Tench should have two houses in his name, when army officers had nowhere to live . . .

Greta was astonished, but said nothing to the major . . . but she had given Gravy 'stick' with her suspicion that he had set up house for another woman. Ah, well . . . but no stauncher partner could he have found for a wife than his Greta. Life at Pembroke House, apart from the joy she experienced with her submariners, was hell for her . . . How *could* the local, starving Maltese understand that the home of the head of the Feeding Department could never hoard *one* extra calorie than the legal ration?

Once when he was away in Valletta, a mob of desperately hungry women had forced their way into his house and ransacked it in search of food. Their little daughter, Sue, had been terrified; and being the daughter of the Director of the Communal Feeding Department, her schoolmates persecuted her to the limits, making her life a misery. Being the only British child remaining on the island, it was time to get her home, but how *could* this be arranged?

Alistair Mars had volunteered to take her home with him, if the authorities would find the aircraft space. Mars had finished his time in *Unbroken* and was due for rest and leave. He was bound to lose out on leave with his wife whom he had not seen for a year, if red tape held him up because of Sue. But he'd promised to escort his charge safely home, come hell or high water.

The Siege had brought out the very best in the brave Maltese: their loyalty and friendship was reciprocated and Gravy's love for them was something which perhaps they would never understand. The Maltese opened their homes, shared all they had, with their British partners: from sailor to admiral, other rank to general, airman to air vice-marshal, all were truly welcome. For a people being so cruelly hurt because of the presence of the Services, this was a miraculous thing, a thing of the spirit, of the heart. Often Gravy wondered how the island had managed to hold together.

Of one marvel he was certain: had it not been for the Three Good Men as he termed them, Malta would have capitulated months ago:

what an amazing paradox this was – Plymouth Brother, Roman Catholic Archbishop and Jew. The Three Good Men had welded this individual, independent people into an implacable foe for the Axis.

Pre-war relations had been bad between the politicians and their Roman Catholic Church: a situation which made it impossible at the outbreak of war for the Governor and the Colonial Office to maintain happy relations with both factions at the same time. Each camp suspected that the other was being favoured. Then General Dobbie arrived, a Plymouth Brother, an appointment much criticized by both Church and politicians alike. Dobbie ignored the politics, declaring that he took his guidance only from God.

The general's attitude delighted Archbishop Caruana. A friendship and trust grew between them; Church and State worked together as one. The Maltese people, always obedient to their priests and religious establishment, accepted the harsh measures which the government were forced to impose in order to survive the Siege.

The Jew was Andrew Cohen. Over six feet tall, he was an unorthodox and courageous administrator; he took responsibility on his own shoulders when red tape bogged down the works. As assistant to the lieutenant-governor he made things work under impossible conditions. To save petrol he rode a motorcycle, to the terror of the Maltese and to the detriment of himself and the machine. Battered was the driver, bent was the machine before he was forced, through the agency of an open crater, to desist.

Inevitably, these three clear-headed, determined men made enemies but it was a measure of the quality of these leaders that they succeeded with the Maltese people.

Gravy was not surprised when Lord Gort, vc, arrived from out of the blue to relieve within two hours, the exhausted, saintly Dobbie. Within days, the tough, indefatigable Gort, survivor of the Dunkirk miracle, was knocking together the heads of the vips and visiting every corner of the island. Order and faith in victory was revived, not least among the military men . . .

Gravy sighed. At thirty-six years of age, he was beginning to know the pangs of disillusionment. Would history ever realize the debt that Malta, Britain and the world owed to these dedicated men?

For his own part, he never could explain how he had become plunged into it all. He was only a businessman after all, a director of Simonds Farsons Brewery. But he could not refuse when the Governor asked him to run the Censorship and become Director of the Communal Feeding Department, the CFD. Depending upon the state of the siege, the convoys and the bombing, the civil administration would decide how much food could be issued daily. It would be Gravy's job to see that the daily ration was meticulously shared and issued.

Realizing the impossibility of his task if he was to comply with Treasury Colonial Regulations, he accepted the appointment only on the condition that no Treasury official was sent to his office. So he was given the job, at which point he employed a chartered accountant to submit monthly accounts to the lieutenant-governor's office. It was Gravy's headache to make sure that each child, woman and man comprising Malta's quarter of a million inhabitants received an equal share of the available food.

He decided to consult the Marquis Barbaro St George who had started a fool-proof rationing system at St Paul's Bay: stores of food were rationed to the wholesalers, so that they could provide their shop-keepers with the equivalent amount of food represented by their customers' ration cards. The Marquis was put in charge of the Central Food Distribution Office in Valletta while Gravy recruited three thousand helpers from the solid Maltese civil service, from the teachers and other willing citizens of the island.

When a ship arrived, she was unloaded at the dockyard as swiftly as possible, however vicious the bombing. The stevedores were given augmented rations, otherwise they could never have achieved such splendid results. The army then rushed the lorries (the few vehicles allowed petrol) out to the depots of the CFD. Once, when the stevedores were working round the clock unloading a precious ship, Gravy was ordered to provide extra food for the exhausted workers. His horse, Skylark, became stew for them and the ship was unloaded before being bombed and sunk. This sad decision followed shortly after he was forced to destroy Greta's dog because there was no food for it.

Gravy's first apparently insoluble difficulty was how to apportion one hundred thousand tins of peas between two hundred and fifty thousand people. Victory Kitchens were set up all over the island: elementary soup kitchens where everything edible was chucked into a boiler, cooked and ladled out to the queues of hungry people. The Services improvised by inventing every conceivable type of cooking gadget: wood, paraffin, diesel oil, sawdust for the boilers: crude but it worked. There had been no food riots, no blood spilt because everyone suffered equitably.

Horses were used to transport the stores from the depot to the Victory Kitchens. Any animal which refused or was incapable of working between the shafts of the flatcarts was condemned for the notorious 'meat loaf': donkeys, old goats, and unidentifiable constituents . . . Tench smiled ruefully as he stood alone in the soothing breeze, in the darkness on his roof; he had not acquired his nick-name for nothing.

There had been the day when he had been summoned to Andrew Cohen's office to meet a delegation of people making a complaint about the bread. Gravy placed a sample of the dreadful stuff on Cohen's desk. Andrew was absent-minded: deep in thought while eating an orange, he would eat the peel without realizing it; on one occasion, all the bones of a fish. And, while ruminating on the official bread complaint, he had eaten the evidence as the delegation assembled.

Milk for the children and their mothers was a constant headache. When the war started, the goats which scavenged in the streets were milked from doorstep to doorstep, so only the highest bidders enjoyed the commodity. The droppings which the goats left behind them were a worry for the health authorities. It was Lewis Farrugia, the Managing Director of Simonds Farsons Brewery, who solved that problem: he set up depots all over the island. All goats were registered and had to be milked at the depots; the milk was then pasteurized at the brewery.

Being the Central Region's Protection Officer hardly added to Gravy's popularity: he had to provide a roof for everyone, an unpleasant job when, night after night and day after day, the Luftwaffe flattened homes into mounds of rubble and heaps of stone which, mercifully, could not burn. Knocking on the door of a palatial house to ask its owner to quit so that twelve refugees to a room could be accommodated, was not conducive to winning friends.

The worst of his headaches had been how to cope with sanitation, but an enterprising fellow from the Public Works Department had volunteered to install his Dry System in no time at all. The genius deserved promotion for his drive and initiative. But the Central Region's Protection Officer had just discovered that this famous Dry System consisted of a bucket and a hole in the ground. An association of ideas made Gravy chuckle out loud when he remembered Francis Gerard's experiences.

The Information Officer, Major Gerard, had been forced to attend a call of nature and was privileged to be using a splendid, modern water closet. An arrogant Glaswegian sergeant began battering on the door: 'Git outa there, ye durrty Malt! Make way for His Majesty's Forces!' Major Gerard opened the door. The behaviour of the sergeant was exceptional and naturally the Maltese resented such arrogant loutishness. Shrimp and Gravy made sure that no such arrogance was allowed to creep into the attitude of their own men. A deep affinity existed between Maltese and British – and especially with the navy.

A wholesale grocery importer named Paul Busutil was in the CFD and he enjoyed visiting Pembroke House. Any excuse to gossip with Greta was seized upon, but it was difficult for her not to be discourteous when she was up to her eyes in work. Eventually the man would receive the hint that it was time to leave: '*Meestair* Tench,' he would protest. 'Let me go. I must go back to my wife, poor fellow . . .'

It helped to treat their adversities as one long joke, but there were so many fine people among the middle ranks to be taken most seriously: the little chap, as an example, who had been sent out from Britain to organize shelters for the people. In no time he had them digging out shelters all over the island. He had been a tunneller all his life and knew exactly how to carve out the entrance at the right angle to deflect blast: a veritable tiger, with his energy and leadership, he received no credit for his pains. Whenever Gravy now dashed into a shelter, the unique smell of damp reminded him always of London's Underground: the ground lifting under you when the bombs struck; the *swish!* of air; and the smell of humanity in its rows of bunks . . .

The island's soft sandstone was saving its people from annihilation. Joseph Cassar, Gravy's driver and a clever mechanic, was typical: he hacked out an underground shelter for his own family while he spent his life driving Gravy across the island – a very brave man, he merited the MBE which had been bestowed on him. It was as miraculous for him to be alive as it was for Wingrave Tench to have been spared.

The latter's luckiest moment was when the Governor sent Gravy in the destroyer *Packenham* to Cairo to meet the Australian Red Cross representative: that generous nation wished to send money to ease the Maltese people's agony. They would return in an RAF aircraft which had been priority booked. When Gravy and his Australian companion turned up for their flight, they were furious to find that they had been baulked of their seats and they were forced to catch the next plane. The aircraft in which they should have travelled crashed, killing all its crew and passengers.

Andrew Cohen had braced himself to visit Greta to break the sad news of Gravy's death, but Gravy reached Pembroke House first. Greta pushed him into a wine cupboard. Andrew arrived, pale and distraught, not knowing how to break the news. Greta said she thought he needed a drink and invited him to pour himself one. Cohen opened the wine cupboard door. Even death was a joke these days . . .

One of the worst moments was sharing *Illustrious'* agony, after she had been so badly mauled by the Stukas. During one of those terrible days when they had tried to repair her in the dockyard amidst the bombing, Gravy had gone up to the Union Club. He would never forget that solitary figure, Denis Boyd, the captain of *Illustrious*, who had just returned from visiting his wounded men in Bighi Hospital. The expression on his haggard face would remain for ever in Gravy's memory. He'd seen it once more, and once only, on Shrimp's: the responsibilities which men like them have to bear must be appalling . . .

Like Boyd, Shrimp never showed the stress gnawing within him. Instead, he always brought brightness, was never sad nor tired whatever awful news he was hiding. Only once, as with Denis Boyd, had Gravy seen Shrimp beaten: when he came to Pembroke House one evening, on the day that *Upholder*'s sinking off Tripoli was confirmed. Though David Wanklyn had insisted on one more patrol, Shrimp would blame himself for ever for the loss of his friend and one-time first lieutenant. Wanks' death was, to Shrimp, the same agony as Boyd's for *Illustrious*.

There was something special about the submarine cos. Shrimp had asked Greta and himself to ease the strain which these men bore by opening Pembroke House to them. Gravy was not to refer to their experiences; but they unburdened themselves to Greta, and Gravy was sure it helped. They seemed so close even now, even those who would never call again.

The rumbustious, roly-poly Dick Cayley of *Utmost*, with his mouth organ, in Britain to take over *P311*; the shy, retiring Johnny Wraith of *Upright* now lecturing to the factories in Britain to boost morale, before commanding *Trooper*. (Of two large ships which he had recently sunk, he reported to Shrimp, 'They simply committed suicide, sir. Just ran into my torpedoes . . .') Boris Karnicki of *Sokol*, the endearing and magnificent Pole, back in Britain refitting: his ship's comrade, *Dzik*, had just been launched at Barrow.

And all those first cos who had borne the brunt of the first years: Darling in *Usk* lost without trace; Livesay mined in *Undaunted*; Galloway depth-charged in *Union*; Kershaw in *P31* back in England; Whiteway-Wilkinson in *P33* and Abdy in *P32*, both lost by mining off Tripoli; Hemingway, *P38*, mined off Tripoli; Edmunds, *P36*, bombed in dockyard; Marriott, *P39*, bombed in dockyard . . . Gravy wondered cynically whether these men and their companions would be remembered once this was all over: they had played their parts, some of them for only a brief moment, but they had done their duty before their stars were extinguished.

Of those first boats, thank God, some had survived to refit in England before coming out again under new captains to carry on the fight: Harrison in *P34* had recently gone home . . . and now, these successors to Wanks, Tommo and their comrades were carrying on the fight. That they were five to eight years younger than those whom they followed was evidence enough of the severity of the battle: the most recent addition, Roxburgh, who had just relieved Tom Barlow in *P44*, was twenty-three years old, while the average age of the cos had lowered to twenty-five.

What a resilient bunch this new generation was! The old man of them all, who had survived from the beginning, was Pat Norman in his beloved *Una*. There was the tall and angular Lynch Maydon in *P35*, immensely successful; Alistair Mars in *Unbroken*; Halliday in *P43*; John Stevens (Steve) in *P46*, rapidly making his mark. Working up at Gib and shortly to join the Tenth were Tubby Crawford, Wanklyn's Number One, in *P51*; Mike Faber, with *P48*; Mossy Turner, *P45*; Lakin in *Ursula*; Oxborrow in *P54*; and, of course, Basher Coombe who had taken over *Utmost* from Dick Cayley.

Greta knew them all, each co's foibles, his character: Pat Norman making her weep with anger by the enthusiasm with which he pruned her roses; Dick Cayley arriving with a white angora rabbit as a present for Sue – and which instead they ate for lunch. Teddy Woodward hurling a protesting Greta to safety from a screaming bomb . . . and the anonymous sailor who one day popped a wadge of chocolate into Sue's bicycle basket.

Greta had insisted on Sue sharing it with her schoolmates; but, in spite of putting an advertisement in the paper, 'Will the person who gave a little girl chocolate please come to Pembroke House in St Julian's?' there had been no response. *Parthian* had recently made her

store-running trip through from Gib, bringing canteen stores . . .
After discharging lubricating oil, diesel and torpedoes for the flotilla,
she had sailed for Beirut, taking amongst her mixed stores, in
response to a missing commando's last beqest, a dachshund puppy
for the Princess Aly Khan. The chocolate must have been submariner's perks. Dear God, we *were* pushed; we still are, though there's
hope now if the Eighth Army with Alexander and Montgomery
continues to whip Rommel . . .

Thank God, thought Gravy as he turned towards the roof door, for
the lighter moments. They'd go mad without them. It was *this* which
Shrimp understood and which cemented their friendship. Who else
would have re-acted as Shrimp did when the German invasion last
month was imminent?

Gravy had started life as a wireless operator in the Eastern
Telegraph cable company; since then, as a director of a brewery in
Malta, he had had close contact with every bar, restaurant and hotel
on the island, and these two qualifications had evidently appealed to
the Secret Service people. He had accepted their invitation to become
a leader of the Underground should the Germans overrun Malta.

The secrecy was such that even the Governor was ignorant of the
plans being laid and of course Gravy could not tell his family. But he
had asked for permission to discuss it with Captain Simpson. Shrimp
promised, when the Germans came, to look after Sue and Greta: he
would smuggle them out in a submarine if it was humanly possible to
do so. The lifting of this worry made life bearable for Gravy who was
then better able to prepare Malta for the worst.

Such was the friendship which Shrimp gave and which Gravy
reciprocated. Tonight Gravy was anxious for his friend. 'The cruel
joke is this,' Shrimp had told him confidentially this evening. 'Just
when things *might* be improving for Malta, they're becoming very
much worse for my men. The enemy has improved his anti-submarine
measures considerably. And as Alexander and Montgomery chase the
Afrika Korps westwards, Rommel's supply lines are shrinking. The
enemy can concentrate his anti-submarine escorts into target areas
which constrict daily. To get at the enemy, I shall be asking my
submariners for almost the impossible.'

The drawn face broke into that infectious grin: 'But pay no
attention, Gravy,' he added briskly, reaching for his cap. Without
another word, he had walked out into the night.

Wingrave Tench pushed open the door and tiptoed to bed.

CHAPTER ELEVEN

Piccadilly

On his way to his captain's cabin, the first lieutenant of *Urgent* paused at the seaward corner of the upper balcony. From the shelter of this first arch, he could watch the green sea lumping in, cold and inhospitable, all the way from the Aegean. The black buoys of the protective boom lunged to the swell and below him, even at the berth alongside the wardroom, *P50* was plunging to the scend. Lofty Small was there with his part of the watch, shifting the fenders and adjusting her after-spring. The other boats were moving too in their trots off the Lazaretto buildings, the pontoons leading to them bobbing about with lashings of spray: a filthy day on which to sail.

December was as unpleasant here, directly open to the north-east and its gales, as anywhere else – and almost as cold. He turned and walked along the upper balcony, past the name boards of the different cos – most of them returned now from their patrols following 'Torch', the operation featuring the North African landings: John Roxburgh, *P44*'s new captain; 'Steve' Stevens, *P46*; Alistair Mars, *P42*; Pat Norman, *Una* . . . and Hawke's *Urgent*. John Carbis glanced through the archway to the creek: Danberry and his cable party were huddled on the casing and waiting for the off: *Urgent* looked 'taut', he must admit, pugnacious in her new blue paint, her plating dripping from the spume in the pale sunlight. The dockyard had done a remarkably swift repair job.

Squaring off his black tie, he pulled down the khaki collar which persisted in nudging above the collar of his reefer, then knocked on the white door marked c.o. *URGENT*.

Hawke was at his table, his sailing orders spread before him. He glanced up coldly as Carbis tucked his cap beneath his arm.

'Ready for sea, sir. All hands on board.'

'Very good.' As Hawke resumed the perusal of his patrol orders he asked, 'How's Lang's relief progressing?'

'Ordinary Seaman Purdis, sir? He's enjoying being a Brawdie pirate more than one of the TI's torpedomen.'

'Still no relief for him?'

'Not until *Clyde*'s next trip with passengers.'

'Happy with your trim?'

'Reasonably, sir.'

'What's the trouble?' Hawke glanced up swiftly.

'The dockyard's patching up: I may not have compensated enough. Better light than heavy for the trim dive, you told me, sir,' and John Carbis smiled faintly.

'You're learning, Number One.' The return smile was as chilly as the blue eyes of this Ulsterman.

'No spuds this patrol, sir. Powdered only, I'm afraid.'

'Dehydrated cabbage?'

'Tons of it, sir.' Carbis smiled: 'The cox'n has won a rabbit.'

The ginger eyebrows raised in question.

'A bottle of yeast from the dockyard; we'll make our own bread.'

'Give me ample warning,' Hawke laughed shortly. 'Can't be worse than the stuff we load: it goes mouldy after three days.'

'That's what we thought, sir. Wescombe's over the moon about it. I didn't ask what he swapped for the yeast. Ticklers, I reckon.'

'Fair enough.' Hawke began to gather his papers. 'O'Brien's put my gear on board?'

'In your locker, sir.'

'Give me five minutes with Captain 'S'.' Hawke looked up and nodded. The pre-sailing interview was terminated. Hawke was a cold fish behind his tomfoolery, thought Carbis as he closed the door behind him. Relations between them had remained coldly correct after the Burat patrol. Carbis could not dispel the suspicion that Hawke wished he had a Jimmy who was not a 'pressed' man. This doubt made Carbis prickly and the resentment bottled within him must be getting through to his captain. To hell with Hawke: he, John Carbis, wasn't the first Jimmy to find Hawke's antics a pain sometimes . . . if only he would use the gun less, be less rash: many of the married men preferred a skipper who thought that the torpedoes were the submarine's main armament. You're being bitter, John Carbis muttered to himself. It's time you forgot 'gens' and made the best of this lot . . .

He trotted down the steps at the end of the balcony, glanced at the carved crests, picked out *Utmost*'s weather-cock: Basher Coombe had reported his position when on his way home from Marittimo, having fired all his torpedoes. And *Utmost* was overdue and presumed lost: Captain 'S' had told his cos never again to transmit unnecessarily, especially when passing through Piccadilly, as the run through the minefields south of Marittimo and along the south coast of Sicily was known. Basher's recent loss grieved everyone, and particularly his chum, John Roxburgh, in *P44*. Carbis walked on thoughtfully, along the lower arcade: *Urgent*, too, was bound for Marittimo, Hawke had said.

Lofty Small was signalling across from *P50*'s plunging fore-casing. Placing a foot on the low wall between one of the arches, Carbis leaned on his elbow to watch his friend finishing off the boat's fendering. *P50* had experienced three blank patrols since joining the flotilla, but nevertheless Carbis hoped that Lofty would be spared a Burat-type adventure.

After Lang's death (his body had disappeared by the time *Urgent* eventually surfaced), the boat lay doggo until the E-boats' counter-attack eased off to the north of the sandbanks. The moon was full when *Urgent* finally planed to the surface, having crept off into the deep field. Shortly after starting the charge, a coast-crawling convoy was sighted steering northward.

Hammer chased it for hours up-moon, the ships with their escorting F-lighters (armed with their vicious 88s) standing up like houses in the moonlight. Carbis was on watch for the first part of the slow over-hauling and was amazed at Hammer's calmness, his patience while *Urgent* slowly reduced the range. The gunlayer at last shouted that he was within range of the rear ship but, at the first round of the flashless cordite, the stern escort immediately opened fire. The F-lighters had been inveigling *Urgent* into their trap, having sighted her for some time. The 88 shells splashed uncomfortably close but, diving at once, *Urgent* retired without serious depth-charging.

The remainder of the patrol was blank and on the way home Hammer read the burial service for Lang. Carbis had been moved by the simplicity of these submariners and their stoical acceptance of the risks they accepted daily. His Channel war had been a tea-party in comparison; he might soon begin to feel part of their select club. If only Hawke wasn't such an untrusting, cold fish. There were times when John Carbis hated the chap's guts . . .

Lofty was the lucky one: there could be no more likeable captain than Matthew Fairfax, the quiet, languid two-striper whom Carbis was beginning to know also as a friend. Their first acquaintance had begun thirteen years ago, as schoolboys when Matt had been captain of the school. This bond had drawn them together now and they'd spent several evenings in the mess chatting over old times. He'd been involved in 'Torch' too, but at the other end of the North African landings, that being his first patrol and, like most of the others in the flotilla, a blank.

'Hold on, John,' Lofty shouted against the wind. The wooden plank to the shore bounced beneath his weight and then they were exchanging the banalities which passed between friends when leaving for patrol. But today was different: Lofty mentioned Anna, a subject they rarely discussed together now.

'I thought you'd better be the first to know, John,' Lofty said. 'We're going to marry as soon as we can.' He seemed embarrassed. 'Anna's agreed, but her parents aren't all that keen.'

'Good for you,' John Carbis said, her name as always jerking a chord inside him. He could picture her, that glorious pale-faced girl with the dark, mysterious eyes. She'd asked him up to Mdina to meet her family. Lofty had been in great form, but there had been tensions and John felt them. So the couple had made their decision: good luck to 'em . . .

'Of course, I had to tell Matt,' Lofty said. 'But not everyone's for it. "Upsets things in the boat," seems to be the general drift. And her parents have asked me to postpone our wedding, wait till this bloody war's a bit more settled.' He was looking straight at John, seeking his verdict.

'If Anna's happy, I'd get on with it, if I were in your shoes, Lofty. Good luck, chum.'

Small grinned. 'Thanks.' He turned as a shadow moved across the flagstones.

'Just off, John?' Matt Fairfax asked. 'Have a good trip. I'm off at the weekend on a cloak and dagger lark.' He smiled that slow smile of his, the lazy eyes wandering over his submarine. 'She's riding better now, Number One; better set an anchor watch until this lot eases down.' He turned to Carbis: 'We'll be back before you, so good hunting off Marittimo.' He laughed shortly: 'It's always a hot spot, but not the best billet for the gun, I'm told. No more stars below your crossed-guns for your Jolly Roger!'

Carbis smiled too. 'The nuns have stitched on our Burat star, sir. But we've had blank patrols, too, since you were with us in the Gulf of

Sirte.'

'It's a rotten November, after all our high hopes,' and Matthew Fairfax grinned ruefully. 'See you when you get back.'

Carbis strode on, past the wardroom courtyard to the end of the arched frontage; past the workshops, through the archway and into the sunlight bathing the pathway bordering the creek. He jumped down to the oil-drum pontoons, balanced himself by the hand-ropes of the plunging catwalk and paused to glance once again at *Urgent*'s draught marks, fore and aft: a short-cut which *P44*'s Jimmy had taught him. If she was level by her marks, she *must* be right for trim – a dodge which saved hours of meticulous calculations. Ross was calling the cable party to attention. Carbis scrambled up the brow, returned their salute and nipped up the rungs of the conning tower.

'Thanks, Doug. Secured for sea below? It'll be rough outside.'

'All secured, sir,' the cox'n reported at Carbis' elbow. Wescombe stood by the bridge wheel which was connected up for 'harbour stations'. 'The LTO's running a temperature, sir. I'll turn him in after leaving harbour.'

'Has he seen the doc?' Carbis asked. Mott was vital for the working of the boat. He had begun suffering from headaches since his mauling during the ammunition-ship patrol.

'No, sir,' Wescombe murmured. 'He'd rather see you and not risk missing the patrol.' The older man smiled: 'Nothing which a number nine pill won't put right, sir.'

'I appreciate his faith in *Urgent*'s "doctor",' Carbis muttered. 'But I'm no expert on smacks on the skull.' The first lieutenant shared his medical responsibilities with the imperturbable cox'n.

'Captain's coming, sir,' Wescombe said, glancing towards the shore.

Carbis stood on the bridge seat. 'Properly at ease,' he called down to the cable party. Sub-lieutenant Danberry alerted his five men and the second cox'n, while the wind whipped about their oilskins.

Captain 'S' was walking slowly down the archway with Hawke deep in conversation beside him. They disappeared behind the workshop buildings, then emerged into the sunlight where, at the shore-end of the catwalk, Shrimp watched Hawke striding across the bobbing pontoons. When he reached the brow, Carbis called the hands to attention. Returning his first-lieutenant's salute, the captain clambered up to the bridge rail and jumped down on to the bridge.

An instant to check that all was well on the casings, a final salute to the lonely figure at the end of the pontoons and Hawke turned to the job in hand:

'Obey telegraphs. Group up. Let go stern rope.' Not until the after-warp was clear of the water did he turn his attention to the fore-casing: 'Let go for'd.'

The head-rope splashed into the water and then the hands were running it aft to stow beneath the fore-casing with the wires and fenders.

'Slow astern starboard.'

'Slow astern starboard, sir,' the cox'n repeated.

At *Urgent*'s stern, the surface churned briefly as the starboard propeller bit the water. The bow paid off towards Torpedo Creek, the stern swung inshore.

'Slow ahead together. Take her out, cox'n. Steer for St Paul's cathedral.'

The sleek blue submarine forged slowly ahead into the swell lumping into Marsamuscetto Harbour.

'Secure for sea.'

Hawke went to the port side, stood to attention as he saluted Captain 'S'. The lone figure waved, then began walking slowly back towards the arches to keep pace with the departing *Urgent*. How often had he done this, Carbis wondered . . . and how often had the departing boat never returned? A cluster of friends abreast the wardroom waved and that was it. The signalman unshipped the white ensign and in no time the boom was lunging ahead, the seas breaking white over its glistening black buoys.

Carbis turned for his final check aft. The ropes had been stowed, and astern Lazaretto was already assuming toylike proportions: *P44* lay in the trots with *P43*, *51*, *46*, and *48*, all back from their patrols following 'Torch'. The cable party was scrambling, wet and dripping, over the bridge, Danberry bringing up the rear.

'Secured for sea, sir.'

Carbis glanced at the few Maltese waving from the St Elmo battlements, then dropped down through the tower to shift into his patrol rig of sweater and serge trousers. *Urgent* was on her way at last.

'We should be home for Christmas.'

Urgent was approaching Sicily, thirty miles along the coast east of Cape Granitola; her captain was ending his talk, his men gathered around him in the control room and in the doorways. 'I repeat, silent routine is to remain in force until we reach the far end of the minefield. We'll be trail-blazing through Piccadilly and so we can help the navigating officer by being careful with our depth-keeping and trim. Ask permission before moving about in the boat . . .' His glance settled on the burly leading stoker. 'Especially you, Davies.' The man grinned as his messmates pulled his leg. When Ewan Davies walked from the fore-ends to his station in the engine room, his shift of weight, unless compensated along the internal trimming line, could cause a break-surface in bad weather.

'Stop the Freon,' Hawke ordered. 'We don't need it in this cold weather.' The refrigerating machine was too noisy. He turned to his first lieutenant: 'Diving stations, please. You can go to Watch Diving once I've got an accurate position.'

At 0755, the end of twilight, *Urgent* came up to twenty-seven feet, a good start to this Friday, 13 December. Carbis sensed the tension as Danberry took over Watch Diving. 'Use the periscope as little as you can,' Hammer urged. 'Ten-second looks, at the most. I'm only four miles off-shore.'

Carbis was waiting for each compartment to report that it was shut off from depth-charging, each a watertight unit on its own, each its own minuscule world.

'Engine room shut off, sir,' the telephone operator reported.

'Boat shut off from depth-charging, sir. Silent routine in force, Freon stopped.'

'Very good, Number One. Come and have a look at the chart.'

Hawke, crouching over the chart table between Ross and Carbis, went carefully through the patrol orders: 'Blaze the trail' first, then round the island of Marittimo to Cape St Vito to catch the convoys sailing from Palermo: a straight-forward patrol and always active, for the enemy had to round St Vito to reach Tunis and North Africa, his route guarded by the mine barrage stretching across the Narrows.

'We're here . . . ' Hammer drew a circle around the pin-prick he had made on the chart. 'I've got a fix, using the Macauda tower, to the left of the mouth of the Verdura river, in transit with Caltabellotta peak: it's the snow-covered mountain at three thousand feet.' He indicated the tower again. 'Don't muddle it with the other to the right: Macauda is the broken-down one, on the cliff-top. For the other two bearings I've taken Cape Bianco, the flat-topped headland to the right of the Macauda tower; and to the west, the reddish cape, Cape St Marco: it's got a white round tower on it, with white cottages.' He paused, speaking to himself as he picked out the track which *Urgent* had to follow. 'I'm half a mile to the south of the line, Pilot: fix every ten minutes and get me on track. Then the officer of the watch can take over.'

'A pity that Etna's in the clouds today,' Ross said.

'The foreshore would blank off the volcano, we're so close, Pilot.' Hammer spoke quietly. 'This is my first trail blazing. For the rest of the flotilla's sake we've got to get this right.' Carbis felt Hammer's eyes on him: 'Happy with your trim, Number One? The gale's eased, thank goodness.'

'A trifle heavy for'd yet, sir.'

'Keep her like that. A break-surface will spoil our whole day: we're within spitting distance from the shore. They'll be expecting trail-blazers, after poor old *Talisman*.'

They remained silent. The *T*-boat, sailing from Gib six weeks ago to reinforce the Tenth, had never arrived at Malta. There were reports of enemy mining activities in the Sicilian Narrows, so she probably fell victim to this most lethal of all weapons: the invisible mines sown across the Narrows, 12,000 of them laid at the beginning of the war and most of them undeclared. Swinging from their mooring wires, at varying depths, the deep-laid mines had accounted for over half our submarine losses so far.

Hammer laughed grimly. 'If I thought about mines, I'd go barmy,' he said. 'Ignore them. The MDU (Mine Detection Unit) is useless: the enemy hydrophones can pick up its pinging miles off. I'm sure Basher was depth-charged before he started through Piccadilly.'

Carbis had not heard Hammer talk like this before. *Utmost* was the last *U* to be sunk. *Traveller* was up in the Gulf of Taranto at the moment, where the minefields were as notorious as those of Piccadilly. She was on a recce for a chariot attack against the *Littorio* battleships in Taranto harbour.

'Well, that's it, then,' Hammer finished brusquely. 'I'll be in the wardroom.' He looked up at Carbis: 'How about a cuppa?' He glanced at the watertight doors which were shut and clipped. 'Hell, then, we'd better open up the doors. We can't survive without our char.'

The interminable day wore on, the circles of the fixes creeping along the track line through the mine barrage. During Carbis' second watch of the day, he sighted Cape Granitola growing larger through the lens of the search periscope. His back ached from the continuous crouching, from the regular five-second looks: checking, taking bearings, watching the trim. So far the boat had not been forced to speed up and thereby lose precious amps; he was feeling satisfied and, what was more, Hammer was not his aggressive self. The tension came from creeping through this mine-field.

Only a few aircraft were patrolling along the coast: Cants mostly and a few JU 52s. The only incident had been a floating mine which had bobbed down the port side during Ross' watch in the afternoon. All was peaceful. Carbis had taken his last fix before he'd be turning over to Danberry at 1600. Tea and a zizz; the evening game of 'liars' before supper; then surfacing south-west of Marittimo.

'Up periscope.'

He was still amazed, even after his sixth patrol as Jimmy, by the detail which showed up of the enemy shore. There it was, the long-awaited Cape: the brand new lighthouse, white and prominent, a hundred feet high, was perched on a flat, low building resembling a gun emplacement. To its left, he could see a broken-down tower, the old light presumably, rearing from the low-lying, rocky coast where the seas broke lazily over the off-lying rocks. 'Bearing THAT . . .'

'Red eight-three, sir,' chanted the periscope reader, the stoker PO, as he jotted down the relative bearing.

The white tower at Menfi on its rocky point and the red rocks of Cape St Marco completed the fix. *Urgent* was a cable inshore of her intended track when Ross took over his watch.

'I've over-corrected for the south-easterly set,' the navigating officer told Carbis. 'I'll get her back on track again.' He added, 'Danberry's having all the luck at "liars"; three full-houses in a row.'

John Carbis sank wearily on to the settee. Alongside him sat Danberry, the leather cups in his hands as he prepared to shake the two remaining dice; the other three, all Jacks, waited in the centre of the table. Two safety matches were already displayed there.

'*My* two lives,' Hammer explained, looking up from his book. 'Pilot and the sub have ganged up against me. Mutiny!' He watched attentively as Danberry carefully shook one dice. From the other side of the bulkhead drifted subdued laughter from the chiefs' mess where the chiefs and POs were holding their uckers league. Danberry threw one dice open across the table: a King. With a grin on his leering face he slid the other pot across to Hammer: 'Full house,' he announced, 'Jacks on Kings '

And so the game went on, the murmur of voices the only sound in the boat as she neared the end of her long day. They were tired but it was winter and the heat was tolerable. O'Brien appeared with the aluminium teapot and its stewed tea. A grubby napkin hung over his left fore-arm for he affected the graces of the Ritz's head waiter as he slickly laid the cups and saucers. The dollop of thick condensed milk hardly made the brew more appetizing. He always added brown sugar before anyone could stop him, a habit which infuriated Hammer.

'You're the worst flunky I've ever had the misfortune to suffer, O'Brien,' Hammer said, his blue eyes flickering with amusement. 'You'd better do a steward's course with the pussers when we get home. How'd you like that?'

'*Me*, sir?' The broad Glaswegian accent gladdened Carbis' ears. 'When this lot's over, you'll find me in The Central, Glasgie: I'll see that you get a good steak, sir, with . . .' and he mumbled something which no-one around the table could fathom.

'With what, O'Brien?'

Carbis enjoyed this traditional evening's entertainment: the Scot usually dished out more than he received.

'With what sauce, you miserable flunky?' Hammer was sticking his head forward truculently.

'Arsenic sauce, sir – reserved for Sassenachs and Irish Micks.'

'O'Brien, one day I'll get my own back. It's Christmas soon and I'll cook for you. Just wait . . .' and Hammer nodded knowingly.

'Boiled eggs, sir?'

Carbis and Danberry snorted: when 'Cookie' Brawdie had been closed up one evening, O'Brien had prepared supper. Not certain how to cook boiled eggs *en masse*, he had referred to the cookery manual. He got his sums wrong and for thirty-three four-minute eggs he managed to boil them for four hours each . . .

'You miserable flunky! What's for supper?'

'Your favourite, sir. Train smash: bangers and bacon in Australian tomatoes – lovely drop of stuff, sir.'

'Let's have it before we surface, then. I can't face looking at your culinary efforts through my dark glasses.'

'Aye, aye, sir.' The gaps of his broken teeth showed through his grin and O'Brien quit the wardroom to prepare supper with the gunlayer.

By consent the dice were abandoned. The quiet interval before supper and surfacing had arrived, the one moment during the long day when thoughts turned to home, writing letters and reading. Hammer picked up his book, Danberry extracted his writing pad; Carbis climbed up into his bunk which ran along the ship's side at the foot of the table.

He needed sleep, as they all did. He watched the cockroaches scampering along the pipes above his head, heard the snores from the adjoining compartment, registered the orders given by the officer-of-the-watch, Ross, in the control room. This was the moment when he allowed his innermost thoughts to turn over in his mind, the private dreaming of the future when this war was over, finished once and for all. Her image always came back to him now, her exquisite, pale face with those dark mysterious eyes, her soft, red lips. Lofty *was* a lucky devil to be marrying her and had never realized how nearly he'd lost her to his friend. John knew for certain that Anna had, for a brief moment, loved him too. That day, not long ago in Bighi, she'd practically admitted the fact . . . but it was too late now. She'd asked him never to refer again to those precious memories.

Sleep, elusive sleep . . . he felt drowsy, tired by the long hours trying to prepare the boat in time for patrol after the dockyard visit. It was restful to be on patrol again and things were no worse between Hawke and his first lieutenant. He himself was intrigued by this closed society of submariners: it was like a family. The crew were accepting him now, as they did also their 'press-ganged' messmates; he was beginning to feel more sure of himself. His eyes began to close as drowsiness crept over him and he twitched the hairy edge of the blanket up to his chin. As he turned on his side towards the boat's side, he heard it, a distant, faint scratching. For'd somewhere . . .

'*What's that?*'

Hammer was sitting upright and placing his book face-down on the table. Carbis turned, resting on his elbows. And as the metallic scraping grew in intensity he rolled noiselessly from his bunk. Sitting opposite his captain, he slipped on his shoes.

There was no need to identify the sinister noise. Hammer had half risen from his settee, one hand gripping the fiddle table. Danberry sat rigid, pen poised above the sheet of blue writing paper. The scene was like an Athenian frieze, the actors frozen in time.

'Shut all watertight doors,' the captain shouted, to be heard the length of the boat. The doors swung silently, the clips snapping home, the black levers turned from the far side by invisible hands. Carbis followed his captain swiftly into the control room.

'Stop together,' Hawke ordered quietly.

The scraping had become a rasping screech; a twanging sound was reverberating throughout the hull. Carbis watched the log, as the speed came off her: 2½ . . . 2 . . . 2 . . . 1½ knots.

'We're dragging the bloody thing down on top of us,' Hammer said.

The scraping was scything abreast the control room, see-sawing back and forth like a tyro violinist: was the mine-wire snagged around the standards? If the boat went ahead, she'd pull the mine down on her fore-ends. If she went astern, the chances were that the half ton of explosive would snag even worse. The jumping wire *should* be effective, even if the bow cutter had failed.

Urgent was poised on the edge of eternity with the wire see-sawing against her like a violin string. Carbis' nails dug into his palms; the stoker PO's lips were moving, as he fingered the rosary beneath his shirt. The boat was stopped and rapidly losing trim. Her bows were sliding away and, after this long day, was bodily heavy. Hammer was motionless between the periscopes, hands on hips, head canted as he tried to judge the whereabouts of the wire. The twanging sound was all about them, rasping metallically against some protrusion. Carbis closed his eyes, prayed, feeling Death breathing down his neck. *Urgent* was gaining depth rapidly. He *must* go ahead if he was not to lose control: forty-five . . . forty-eight . . . fifty-five feet . . . *TWANG*! He jumped, his nerves bar taut. The ghastly din ceased.

Carbis turned to meet Hammer's eye.

'All requests for reversion to general service will not be entertained until we get back to Malta,' Hammer said. 'Half ahead together. You can pump, Number One.'

The young telegraphsman, Ordinary Seaman Tarr, broke into brittle laughter. Ross raised his eyebrows. 'Phew!' breathed Nick Fell, the black-bearded giant on the after-planes. 'Permission to change my trousers, sir?' Laughter rippled through the control room.

'Slow ahead together,' Hawke ordered. 'Report when you've caught your trim, First Lieutenant.'

Ten minutes later, the hands went to supper. *Urgent*, excitements permitting, would be surfacing at the end of the trail in an hour's time. She was on track and almost through the mine barrier: the rest of the mines, it was assumed, were sporadic lays off the Egadi Islands where everyone had to take his chance. The PO Tel was waiting to transmit his short transmission back to Malta and John Carbis wondered what quip Hammer would use. It was difficult to beat *Utmost's* during the early days: 'Next please,' Dick Cayley had signalled.

Urgent should be rounding Marittimo at midnight. By dawn she'd be on her sure-fire billet off Cape St Vito – the enemy was now forced to use this main road to Tunis. Carbis turned the watch back to Ross, then returned to the wardroom for O'Brien's 'train smash'. He heard laughter from the fore-ends, felt the atmosphere returning to normal. As Wescombe had said, they could put up with anything except mines. You couldn't do anything about them, so there was little point in worrying. Logical, Carbis thought, as he slid to the wardroom settee. These men were difficult to understand at first; but once you were one of them it would be difficult to find a finer breed . . .

He had not realized how many pressed men there were among the ship's companies. He might be one of the few officers, but many sailors were being forced into 'the boats', for with these losses how were the submarines to be otherwise manned? Except for a few like Brown who was so different to O'Brien, the conscripted matelots were treating their fate with the customary good humour of the lower deck. There was little discrimination between the volunteer and the 'pressed man' among them, so why, for heaven's sake, should *he* be feeling so sore about his own status?

He clambered into his bunk and, arms beneath his head, began a critical analysis of his own attitude: if the troops could set such an example, perhaps he'd do better by indulging less in his own critical, self-pitying attitude. Hammer *could* be right with his opinion of his first lieutenant . . . and as Carbis drifted into sleep, he decided for the first time that he'd show his captain that he was not a bloody-minded, half-hearted conscript. Never before had he hoped that *Urgent* would encounter a whopping, rich target soon: it was difficult to choose a better spot than St Vito, though the enemy's anti-submarine measures were red-hot in these parts.

CHAPTER TWELVE

Marittimo

The dawn sky was slashed with a silver streak in the greyness of this winter twilight. It was 22 December 1942 and, as Hammer had promised, *Urgent* would be home in Lazaretto for Christmas. As Carbis waited for breakfast he sensed an expectancy throughout the boat when she dived at 0700. Even O'Brien and Cookie had excelled themselves.

Eggs were on the menu, the ones they'd saved until now, not fresh enough for boiled eggs, but tolerable for 'train smash'. *Urgent* was homeward bound through Piccadilly this afternoon. Though the gash buckets were over-flowing, the rubbish would not be ditched until she was well clear at the other end. Hammer had decided to follow the same track home through the minefields, on the assumption that lightning never struck twice in the same place. He was poring over the chart table, checking his last fix of Marittimo with Ross.

It's strange, John thought, how some place names possess a sinister ring: Marittimo comes top of the list. This most westward of the Egadi Islands, outpost to Sicily, was only twenty miles from Trapani, where the enemy's First Eleven was based: the crack anti-submarine destroyer flotilla, the fast, four-gunned, two-funnelled *Navigatoris*. No-one knew what detection gear they used, but in addition to asdics they evidently carried highly sensitive hydrophones: they could sniff out a submarine, even when bottomed in a remote bay off the Sicilian coast. Presumably, they worked in conjunction with the shore-based listening gear. Marittimo – even the sound of the beastly name turned his stomach.

The island reared from the deep like a stranded whale, its Mount Falcon at the north-western end, over two thousand feet high being the whale's hump: it stood sentinel, malevolent and sinister, beckoning submarines like the Syrens. Encircled by mines, Marittimo provided concealment, night and day, for listening E-boats and patrol craft. They knew that if we were to get at their convoys from Naples, Messina, or Palermo, we had to round Marittimo. The westerly tip of the island was Mugnone Point which gave shelter to Bianca Cove where the E-boats harboured; the southern coast stretched eastwards to the cliffs of Bassana Point, the southern extremity of Marittimo. The dark, brooding mass of rock had seemed distinctly too close when Carbis had come off watch during the early hours. The captain, as always when Marittimo was being negotiated, remained on the bridge. He liked to keep outside the fifty-fathom line, clear of the deep minefield encircling the island.

'Your breakfast now, sir?' O'Brien asked, poking his head through the doorway. His voice was subdued, as was everyone's until they were clear of Marittimo.

'When the captain's ready.'

Urgent slid slowly past Libeccio Point: the new lighthouse, close south of the rocky finger sticking westwards, was a prominent landmark.

'What's for breakfast?' The captain, his face behind the ginger growth, was grey with tiredness. 'Bring it in, O'Brien. I'm hungry.'

'Eggs, sir.'

'At half-a-crown each? Good-o.' Hammer slumped on to his settee.

They were settling down to their breakfast when Carbis heard Danberry's summons:

'Captain in the control room.'

The eggs lay untouched in their tomato 'smash' as Hawke moved swiftly to the search periscope.

'*Diving stations!*'

While Carbis took charge between the depth-gauges, men dropped what they were doing and began streaming silently to their stations. Danberry, as Torpedo officer, was already at the Torpedo Calculator (the 'fruit machine') and setting the captain's estimations. Ross leaned over his chart table to run the plot. The cox'n was settling on the stool in front of his after-planes, while Fell, the second cox'n, came tumbling into the control room to take over the fore-planes.

'*Start the attack!*'

Carbis' adrenalin still pumped when he heard that command, the executive order to put into practice the killing they had been trained to do. Their lives, and the fate of the target above them on the surface, were being decided at this instant. A pencil of light was streaming into the captain's eyeballs from the lenses: the interpretation which his brain made of those signals was critical for the existence, perhaps, of thousands of our soldiers . . .

'Bearing *THAT* . . . starboard fifteen. Eighty feet. Group up, half head together.'

The handles clacked shut as Hammer stood back and the periscope hissed down into the well. He turned to Danberry.

'Target: modern trooper, ten thousand tons. Speed twenty. Escort: five *Navigatoris*. Three weaving ahead, one on each quarter.' He stared at the dials of the fruit machine while Danberry tuned in the settings.

'*Stand-by all tubes* . . . What's my course for a sixty track?'

The mauve lights glowed '*stand-by*' in the torpedo order instrument above Carbis' head. They'd be busy in the tube space and Carbis had to be bold with his flooding when the torpedoes fired: a break-surface with five *Navigatoris* up-top would spoil everyone's day . . .

'Course, sir,' Danberry piped up: 'Three-four-o. Your DA (Director Angle): Green twelve . . .'

The drill was faultless and, as Carbis was levelling her off at eighty feet, *Urgent* settled on her course of 340°.

'Periscope depth. Bring her up fast, Number One. Stop together.'

Hawke moved to the attack periscope. Carbis could hear Hammer's finger and thumb flicking for the periscope as the submarine swooped up to twenty-eight feet.

'Put me on my DA.' He was crouching on all fours, grabbing at the handles of the slim attack periscope as it emerged from the well. 'Don't dip me . . .' Dale, the stoker PO, swung the stick round, held it finally on the DA.

At sixty feet, the roar of a destroyer thundering overhead had swamped the boat, then faded swiftly across the quarter. Hammer was inside the escorting screen. Light streamed again through the eye pieces. Hawke whistled, his fingers clenching the handles:

'*Fire one!*' Handles slammed shut. Orders crackled from him as the snap attack reached its climax:

'Fire by time interval.' He shot a glance at his first lieutenant.

'One hundred and twenty feet. Flood Q. Group up, full ahead together. Starboard twenty. Keep her stern down, for God's sake . . .'

Carbis felt the bows dropping, checked the cox'n's dive on the after-planes. Q was holding her, taking her down, thanks be . . .

'Shut off from depth-charging,' Hammer commanded above

Danberry's orders to fire the other three torpedoes. Carbis blew Q, vented it inboard, its foul air roaring into the boat.

At sixty-five feet there was a clang against the hull then, seconds later, another. The cheers rang through the boat when Snagge reported from his asdic set:

'Two torpedo hits, sir. Diesel HE from merchant ship has stopped.'

'Group down. Stop starboard. Starboard ten. Stay at one hundred and twenty feet. Steer one-two-o.' Hammer ordered: 'I'll slip away to the south-east. Course for Piccadilly, Pilot?'

'Breaking-up noises, sir,' the HSD announced in his monotone.

They could all imagine the horror. The large trooper was already disintegrating as she plunged to her grave in this deep water. At a thousand feet bulkheads buckled, compartments exploded, boiler rooms disintegrated. What happened to the human beings, enemy or not, was best not contemplated.

Carbis concentrated on his trim, pumping like mad, so that, when the counter-attacks started, he'd not have to use the noisy pump: it was too deep to use the quieter centrifugal. He'd shut the Kingstons and the boat was sealed; the main vents were open, so that no air bubbles could be trapped to betray their position . . . drill, drill, drill. He was beginning to understand: drill replaced the necessity for memory, minimized human error.

'Boat shut off from depth-charging, sir.' Each compartment was now a world on its own, communication being by phone to the ends of the submarine. She was silent as she could be, moving ahead at 'slow together' and grouped down with the batteries in series to consume as few amps as possible.

'HE, Green one-two,' Asdics reported. Then: 'Turbine, sir.'

And so the counter-attack developed, *Urgent* sidling away to the south-east at three knots. Men relaxed at their diving stations, talking softly to each other. Tails were up: a prize target sunk; the heat negligible, with only a few distant charges dropped where *Urgent*'s torpedo tracks originated. On firing she had cleared her tracks at full ahead, 'grouped up', while the clatter from her running torpedoes drowned all else. Piccadilly was within reach: home for Christmas!

Then Carbis heard it, and Snagge confirmed the sound they all loathed . . . *tick-tick* . . . *tick-tick* . . . *tick* . . .

'Destroyer in contact. Red eight-five.'

Hammer was leaning against the chart table. 'That's another, is it, HSD?'

'Yes, sir. The first is right astern.'

The captain grunted and moved to his favourite position. Hands in pockets, he was sizing up the picture forming in his mind. 'I saw five destroyers.' He called to his helmsman: 'Starboard ten.'

He wasn't using much wheel; Carbis was thankful because he did not want his tolerable trim upset. Large wheel movements dragged down the boat's stern. He would then have to pump, because speeding up was out of the question; but pumping meant noise.

'What's the pressure showing?'

The barometer was to the right of the torpedo order instrument: 'Three inches,' Carbis said.

Hammer rubbed his chin, a habit of his when under stress. The atmospheric pressure was too high, if a long hunt was to develop. The high-pressure air which discharged the torpedoes from their tubes was vented back into the boat automatically to prevent air bubbles bursting on the surface; the air from venting Q inboard also had to be added to the innumerable air leaks. But when they surfaced tonight to charge, the pressure would be released when the hatch was opened.

'Transmitting interval decreasing: range, five hundred yards. Second destroyer, sir: Green one-two-o. HE increasing . . .'

Carbis could hear her now, starting her run-in . . .

'Starboard twenty,' Hammer ordered. 'Don't speed up, even if we go deep. Pass the word, "Silent routine".'

Carbis tried to hold her on the planes, but with this amount of rudder she dropped to one hundred and thirty-two feet as the *Navigatori* rumbled overhead. They listened for the faint, unmistakable clicking of the depth-charge detonators springing home, the sign of an accurate pattern. But there was nothing, only fading HE and then three clangs harmlessly astern.

'Midships . . . Meet her: steady.'

The helmsman steadied on 290°. Hammer's last-minute alteration had thrown the attacker off her stride; but *Urgent*, though stern-on to her foe, was inevitably beam-on – therefore presenting a maximum target – to another destroyer working in consort. Fresh *tick-ticking* was pervading the boat.

'Third destroyer in contact: Green two-o, sir.'

Hammer rubbed his ginger chin while the HSD silently completed his all-round listening sweep. Carbis had brought *Urgent* back to one hundred and twenty feet, and he too was watching Snagge as his sensitive fingers rotated the ebonite knob of his set:

'Five destroyers, sir. Spread in a circle around us. Breaking-up noises have stopped.'

Carbis met his captain's eyes. 'The Trapani First Eleven,' Hammer said softly. 'The professionals.'

There was no need to explain the opposition against which *Urgent* was having to adopt her evasive tactics. Men spoke softly, padded about in gym shoes or bare feet. A spanner dropped now was a sentence of death . . . you didn't trifle with the Trapani boys. Less than a month ago, Basher Coombe had piped up on his wireless transmitter for a few seconds. *Utmost* was promptly sunk by a Trapani torpedo boat . . .

The five hunters above *Urgent* suddenly began saturating the area with depth-charges. Their counter-attacks were haphazard, but they continued for two hours. Twisting and turning, Hammer kept *Urgent* end-on; by exploiting the churned-up water which was upsetting the enemy's asdics, *Urgent* succeeded in sidling away from the holocaust. But by two o'clock, after seven hours of counter-attacks and seventy-two depth-charges, the enemy was evidently reverting to his copy-book, methodical tactics. The captain relaxed the 'depth-charge state' to 'one clip' on the doors; the cook's corned-dog, hard-tack biscuit sandwiches were handed through the boat. On 'slow one', *Urgent* was slinking south-west to the edge of the destroyers' five-mile circle and was slipping through the net.

'Destroyer in contact: Red six-o, sir.'

Carbis' innards knotted inside him: so nearly escaped. But time and time again they were picked up on the edge of the circle and now the hunt was starting again. Hour after hour it had persisted: Hammer, sitting on his camp stool, back against the for'd periscope, calmly focusing the surface picture in his mind. Carbis had been on his feet since the initial attack, trying to hold *Urgent* at her depth of one hundred and twenty feet: she was getting heavier and soon he would be compelled either to run the pump or speed up, each action potentially suicidal. The planes were carrying permanent rise now.

'Port ten,' Hammer ordered. 'I'll vary the menu and run straight for him this time. Bearing on asdics?'

'Red four-o, sir.'

And as *Urgent* settled bows-on to her hunter, poised for a head-on clash, Snagge removed his earphones and called out:

'HE increasing, sir: destroyer running in to attack.'

CHAPTER THIRTEEN

The First Eleven

Vincent Bolder, the TI, lay stretched on the corticene in the fore-ends, his hands beneath his shoulders, listening to the propeller beats of the approaching destroyer. The murmur of voices around him ceased as the racket from the racing propellers became a wild crescendo. His reverie of Marie and their last leave together faded as he dragged himself back to the present. He sat up this time, inclining his head to judge the angle at which the *Navigatori* would cross overhead. He watched the others, most of them new hands to the game, particularly O'Brien and Brown, the TI's mate. Brown, a Cockney, was dark with sullen, brown eyes: a cheeky devil, he was always demanding explanations for every bleeding thing. A 'Hostilities Only' rating, he was, like O'Brien, a conscript into submarines. But unlike Pat O'Brien, he nursed a permanent chip on his shoulder. Today he was getting on everyone's wick.

O'Brien flicked a cockroach from his forehead; he leaned forward from the toolbox on which he was sitting beneath the starboard torpedo racks. His lips were pursed while he too glanced upwards at the deckhead, listening to the pounding reverberations. He looked pained at having his sleep disturbed; seemed bored by this submarining game which, at times, became effing dangerous. Bolder smiled to himself: blokes like this young Glaswegian were good value, unlike that Brown . . .

Above the whistling of the fore-planes, as they juddered in response to the planesman's wheel in the control room, the noise of the threshing propellers could not be ignored: pounding, pounding away above him. This time it was to be close because he heard the charges smacking the water. He waited while they sank through the depths, then heard distinctly the 'click', 'click' when the detonators sprung home: seconds now . . . He clenched his fingers together, prayed to his God . . .

The boat jumped twice. The hull sprang inwards, bounced out again. But the heat was not so close as last time – no cork spattering down from the deckhead; the light bulbs still intact. The racket subsided swiftly, while the enemy made off across their starboard quarter.

Brown was on his feet. His round face working grotesquely, he shouted at Ewan Davies whose rotund figure was wedged into the hatchway of his pump room:

'All right for you, Stokes!' he grimaced. 'You asked to join this effing lot. I effing didn't.' The more Davies grinned goodnaturedly at the able seaman, the more his amused indifference seemed to infuriate Brown. 'Ninety-six charges so far,' the seaman blurted. 'And what do we get for all this bollocking?' He swivelled his eyes first on O'Brien, then on Bolder. In a pathetic gesture, he opened wide his arms, speechless, in despair at his messmates' incomprehension.

'We've sunk a trooper, Frankie,' Davies said soothingly. There was an embarrassed silence while they waited for Brown's outburst. The TI climbed to his feet when Brown blurted: 'And what effing good will that do? A few thousand Huns sent to the bottom won't stop Rommel. The Old Man should have let it go . . . we were on our way home, weren't we?'

Fergus, the grizzled, squat three-badgeman, met Bolder's eye and dragged himself to his feet.

'Hawke's crazy,' Brown mouthed wildly. 'You bloody know it, all of you.' He spread wide his arms again, appealing to them: 'You ain't got the guts.'

'Shut your mouth, Brown.' And as the TI squared up to the deranged man, Fergie let him have it. The seaman slumped to the deck; shaking his head, he curled up into the corner by the gash bucket. And that was the moment when they heard the whispering of propeller noises beginning again. The time was half-past six: eleven and a half hours since diving this morning.

At 2315, an hour before moonset, the hunt was drawing away to the north-east; it became sporadic, then ceased altogether. Carbis could not credit the fact until Snagge wearily announced that his all-round sweep was negative. Hammer waited another thirty minutes then allowed the doors to be opened. The grinning, pale faces were like creatures from another world.

'Remind everyone, First Lieutenant, that we're still at silent routine. They could still be listening for us up-top.'

For over thirty minutes, there had been no depth-charges to add to the score of one hundred and thirty-six; no asdic pulses, no propeller HE: silence up-top. A wan smile creased Hammer's grey face as he sat on his canvas stool.

'If all's clear in half-an-hour, I'll surface, Number One. We can still get in five hours' charge on our way to Piccadilly.' He rose slowly to his feet: 'What's the pressure now?'

'Four and a half inches, sir.'

'Time for fresh air.'

The stuffiness was thick, like a blanket about them; the air was foul and the pressure was too high. They'd been dived now for nineteen hours, the longest experienced by Carbis so far.

'Stand-by to surface,' the captain announced. 'I'm getting dressed, Number One. Let me know if anything comes up on the asdics.'

Carbis had to contain the exuberance spilling through the boat as the tension eased: the lookouts were buttoning themselves into their rustling Ursula suits; men bustled through the boat to shift into red lighting; the familiar surfacing drill was a shot in the arm for everyone. God! It would be good to hear the generators clattering again, drawing down the cold, clean air. At 0030, half an hour into 23 December 1942, Carbis took *Urgent* up to periscope depth. The lookouts were in the tower, the signalman waiting at the upper lid. Hammer was having a rapid all-round look through the periscope. No future, hanging about here: too dangerous with nil visibility . . .

'Plane her up, Number One. Start the blowers now. *Surface!*'

Hawke climbed up the ladder, the lookouts standing back on either side of him in the darkness. He felt the signalman's feet on the rungs, clasped his ankles. With this high pressure, the man at the top could be whooshed over the side and drowned . . .

'Fifteen feet!' the first lieutenant called from below.

'Open up,' Hawke ordered.

Kipps was grappling with the short handle; then the long, and . . . *whoosh!* – Hawke's eardrums blew out as the gale of air rushed upwards. The stars were swooping wildly in the night sky above him; water was sloshing over his head. 'Stop both,' he shouted downwards.

Then he was crouching to grab a hand-hold on the slippery, dripping bridge. He jerked up, wrenched the glasses from around his neck for a swift search around the dark horizon.

The stars he would always remember; those glittering stars, bright and sparkling in the great bowl of the universe. As he was raising the binoculars to his eyes, he glanced over the side.

He would never know who was the most surprised. Twenty yards abeam to port wallowed the dark outline of an E-boat: stopped and listening. A sailor stood mesmerized, glued to the upper deck in bemused astonishment; a cigarette hung from his mouth, its end glowing red in the darkness. His arm jerked and pointed. There was a howl of alarm. On the E-boat's bridge, shadows moved like flies.

'*Dive, dive, dive!*'

Kipps was already through the lid when the captain pressed the diving push. But as Hawke hurled himself towards the dark hole, he snatched a glance around the horizon. On the starboard bow, a thousand yards off, was the smudge of a destroyer's silhouette – stopped and listening. Two others were to the right of her, but further off.

Hawke swore, jumped on to the signalman's head and pulled the upper lid shut after him.

The renewed counter-attacks were immediate and vicious. Carbis took *Urgent* down, blowing Q on the way, to her customary, evasive depth. Hammer tumbled down in record time, allowing the stoker PO to peel his Ursula jacket from him while he waited for the first lieutenant to settle at one hundred and twenty feet. Doors banging shut, the boat resumed 'slow one' and silent routine.

'I walked right into it,' he murmured to Carbis. 'Played straight into their hands, the cunning buggers.'

He had no time to elucidate. The first destroyer was thundering over them in minutes, but astonishingly, only three attacks developed during that first hour. The counter-attacks were losing their precision; there seemed a frenzy about them: more speed than accuracy.

'They'll be running out of charges,' Carbis said, trying to console his captain. To remedy his mistake, Hawke seemed grimly determined to be one leap ahead of their hunters. On the fifth counterattack, at 0245, as the *Navigatori* was rumbling directly over them, Hammer grouped up and went full *astern* at the critical moment.

Carbis was wrestling with his trim when the pattern exploded ahead of *Urgent*'s bows. Cork was shaken from the deckhead but only a few light bulbs shattered in the fore-ends.

'Group down, slow ahead port . . .'

And so it went on, the fury and accuracy gradually diminishing. By 0300 the attacks were becoming desultory, but always, always, when reaching the edge of the circle, another destroyer (*Urgent* unable to avoid being beam-on to one of them) would pick her up again.

'The sods must have restocked at Trapani,' Hammer said, 'or they'd have run out of charges by now.'

'The other three are probably doing the same,' Carbis said. 'Perhaps they'll send their two chums home for more soon.'

Hammer twisted and turned, calmly and patiently judging the precise instant when to put the wheel over, when to increase speed. His fortitude was infectious, Carbis putting all he had into trying to hold his trim; the cox'n wrestling with his after-planes; Fell imperturbable but swearing softly as he swung off on his fore-planes. It was miraculous that there had been no mechanical failure so far; not pleasant to contemplate in these depths . . .

By 0340, when the attacks started to ease off again, a general tiredness began to seep over them. The captain kept the boat at silent routine and Danberry took over the watch, his orders being to keep end-on to the hunters. There was one unspoken question in everyone's mind: how were the batteries to be charged with only three hours of darkness left – and the enemy still waiting up-top? Carbis had already dispatched the LTO, Mott, to recheck the battery readings. How to survive another day without a charge?

Leaving Ross trying to work out their position, Carbis spread the battery graphs before him on the wardroom table; methodically and silently he began working out how much life there was left in the main batteries. On the other side of the table sat Hammer trying to contain his patience. When Carbis looked up finally, he saw trust for the first time in Hammer's blue eyes.

'What's the score?'

'The LTO's double-checking the densities, sir. If his first readings *are* correct, at "slow ahead" on *one* propeller the batteries have eighteen hours of life in them.' He stretched back against the settee and watched the man who was to decide the fate of everyone on board.

'Only eighteen hours at slow one?'

Carbis nodded: 'Not a minute more.'

Hammer's eyes were on the clock: 'Till nine tonight?'

'2130, sir . . . without *any* other electrical consumption. No pumps, galley, lighting.'

They faced each other, meeting the other's gaze. There could be only one decision.

'We've under three hours' darkness left to surface for a charge,' Hawke said. 'The opposition's waiting for us, "hunting to exhaustion" as the pundits put it so eloquently. There's little future in surfacing now.'

Carbis nodded. Blown out of the water when they baled out; the survivors taken prisoner for the rest of the war; the captain scuttling the boat as he scrambled up the conning tower: as if to stress the realities, the *tick-ticking* of a destroyer gaining contact again whispered all around them. Danberry was already altering course, Ross supervising behind his shoulder.

'What about air?' Hammer asked, speaking his thoughts aloud. 'We've been dived for nearly twenty-four hours and the air's already thick.'

'We've done twenty-four hours once before, sir.'

'Nineteen,' Hammer corrected. 'Never thirty-six. We can't surface again until after twilight, you know that.'

'1900, sir.' Carbis glanced at the clock. 'In fourteen hours' time.'

'*If* we've thrown off our hunters.' Hammer passed his hand across his forehead. Rubbing his chin he looked up tiredly:

'This is my first small boat, so I've no experience to go by. We *should* cope with carbon dioxide poisoning if we start using the Protosorb crystals at once.' He halted as his weary brain remembered. 'My God, John!' He had never used Carbis' Christian name before.

'We left the Protosorb and the trays in dockyard, sir. Took up too much room and useless, we agreed.'

Hammer sat motionless, the muscles in his face working as he realized the consequences which their over-hasty decision was causing. Men were already suffering headaches from the onset of CO_2 poisoning.

'You've checked the oxygen cylinders?'

Carbis nodded: 'One in each compartment, sir.'

'You're my second-in-command, John. It would be best if we reached the same decision. Take your time.'

Carbis replied at once: there was no choice.

'Stick it out, sir. We don't know what the effects of lack of oxygen and too much CO_2 will be. We may make evening twilight quite easily.' He paused while they listened to the distant hunter crossing astern. Then he went on: 'But we know for sure what to expect if we surface now.'

Hammer nodded. 'If only we could bottom to save amps. I daren't make for the shallows.' He rose slowly to his feet. 'Thanks, John.' He slipped from between the table and his settee. 'I'm going round the boat to tell the hands myself. We'll remain at diving stations but keep the doors open to let the air move a bit. Keep an eye on things in the control room.'

Carbis watched the stocky figure levering himself through the doorway, on his way to the fore-ends. The ship's company had been at diving stations for twenty-four hours and would be so for another *fourteen* . . .

Hawke's rounds took over half-an-hour: he explained to them all, fore-endsmen, the Chiefs and PO's, the control room watch, the engine and motor room team, the choice facing them – an untried marathon about which they could only guess; or baling out against overwhelming odds on the surface.

Lack of air was the principal danger: therefore no talking, no eating; minimum movement; sleep as much as possible. To conserve the precious oxygen, the boat would immediately assume watch diving; watches would change at four-hour intervals instead of two, to minimize movement. Their lives depended on strict obedience to his orders. He returned to his camp stool between the periscopes. If the hunters were determined cats, Hammer's *Urgent* was to be an elusive mouse . . . Ross took over the watch. Carbis and Danberry turned into their bunks.

Just the effort of turning-in made Carbis' chest heave, as he breathed in deeply to fill his lungs: what's it going to be like, he wondered, in twelve hours' time? An ache behind his forehead was nagging persistently, the first symtoms of excess CO_2 he supposed. Lying on his back, hands beneath his head while the faint beat of propellers faded across the stern, he tried to imagine what it was like up-top for the hunters. He must be one of the few on board who had been on the other side of the fence, dropping depth-charges on suspected contacts. Certainly a more agreeable pastime . . .

'First Lieutenant, sir?'

He opened his eyes to see Reginald Plumb, the Chief ERA, standing at the end of the table. With the cox'n, he was the senior rating in the boat, a wise counsellor and 'father' to his engineering department. But those humorous eyes had lost their twinkle.

'The captain is starting the oxygen now, but I've no gauges in my stores for the cylinders. Have you got 'em, sir?'

Carbis propped himself on his elbows, tried to think. Giffard, when handing over, had mentioned that the six gauges for the oxygen cylinders had been overlooked when sailing in the last-minute rush from England. The chances of their ever being required was nil; to order them from England, to take up precious space and weight in *Clyde*, had seemed irresponsible. Carbis felt the nagging ache when he shook his head.

'Sorry, Chief. We'll just have to crack the valves on each cylinder. We'll have to guess: five-second bursts?'

'I shan't know how much oxygen is left after each issue.'

John began crawling from his bunk. 'We'll have to chance the ration, Chief.'

'We'll see what effect it has.' He smiled wanly. 'I'll take it on, sir. You've been on your feet for twenty-four hours.'

Plumb, a tall, lanky man with a blue-jowled face, had already climbed through the doorway and was shuffling in his slippers to the fore-ends. Carbis resumed his bunk and slumped back on the blankets. He was surprised by his breathlessness, by the need to inhale deeply for the life-giving air. He had never noted before how his lungs worked, how his diaphragm moved like bellows, heaving regularly up and down. But now breathing was an effort, a deliberate, conscious struggle each time he inhaled. How much longer would this have to go on? His wrist-watch told him it was 0733 – only half-an-hour since they passed the twenty-four-hour mark. *Surely* more time had passed? He peered again at the clock: 0734 . . .

Morning twilight would be merging soon into a winter's Mediterranean sunrise. He could picture the glow from the crimson-slashed sky reflecting on the wet superstructures of the destroyers; their crews up all night, too; tired, hungry and fed-up; longing for food, dirty from the night's work. He could smell the acrid stench from the brass voice-pipe of his chasseur, the stale odour of tobacco smoke and warm cocoa wafting upwards from the wireless and asdic offices. Perhaps Italian captains of Latin temperament hadn't the patience to 'hunt to exhaustion', as did our boys in the Western Approaches? The battle in the Atlantic, where the war would finally be lost or won, was ferocious at the moment: the U-boats were marauding in the South Atlantic too . . .

'Excuse me, sir?'

Plumb was waiting, the wheel spanner in his hand.

'Of course, Chief.'

The oxygen cylinder was slung on the deckhead above the pistol locker; four feet long and six inches in diameter, it looked pathetically inadequate. Standing on his toes on the captain's settee, Plumb stuck his wheelspanner into the spokes of the valve; twisted, listened to the hiss while reading his wrist-watch; spun the valve, shut it briskly. He dropped back to the deck and, panting, disappeared into the control room.

Danberry and Carbis had turned towards the hissing oxygen. The relief was exquisite, the refreshing oxygen reaching to the depths of Carbis' lungs. He felt satisfied, without labouring for breath. For nine whole minutes by his watch, the relief lasted. But, remorselessly, the laboured breathing began to assail him again: 0746 – only *twelve* minutes since he had last glanced at the time? He *must* discipline himself or the hours would never pass. He was dragging deeply for air, panting laboriously, his forehead beginning to pound across his temples. The headache was bearable – but when would the Chief be back again to crack the oxygen?

He turned to the ship's side, seeking sleep but the position cramped his lungs so that he could not inhale: gasping, he slumped again onto his back. Danberry's face was cracked in a forced smile.

'Number One,' he was murmuring. 'Number One . . .?'

'Save your breath, Sub.'

'We haven't a chance, have we?' His look was accusing; the intelligent, brown eyes were shot with fear. 'Answer me, Number One,' he persisted angrily.

'Shut up. Get to sleep. We'll get out of this.' He watched the heaving body, the blond head turning away.

For the first time, Carbis began to ponder what a slow death through suffocation would be like. Painless, drifting into a sleep from which you never awoke? Or agonizing, horrible, with all the frightfulness of an American film? Oblivion crept over him and he dropped into a fitful sleep.

Carbis took over his watch from Ross at 1500. The minute hand creeping around the dial seemed not to move. Hammer was dozing on his stool and leaning against the shining cylinder of the for'd periscope. Apart from the stentorian breathing of everyone around him and the murmur of the officer of the watch, there was no sound –

the boat creeping silently north-westwards in another attempt at escape. But the silence now had a menace about it: deceptive and dangerous, the CO_2 poisoning and lack of oxygen were beginning to take their toll.

Only ten minutes ago, the boat was bodily heavy: Carbis was forced to order the pump space operator to 'pump on M'; Davies had carried out his drill, reporting 'pumping on M'. Instead, he was flooding. At this depth, in seconds water was overflowing the tank beneath his feet and beginning to flood into the pump space. Carbis felt, through the soles of his feet, the sudden angle, sensed the gain in weight. He immediately checked the leading stoker's report and the valve was shut in time. CO_2 poisoning and lack of oxygen were having a pernicious effect. A man would add two and two and be certain it totalled five. Having opened a valve, he would believe sincerely that he had shut it. Afternoon was drawing into evening and taking on a nightmarish quality.

Men lay panting in hammocks, stretched on the deck, waiting for the 'Chief with the Spanner', greedy for those minutes of relief following his opening of the oxygen cylinder. This hiss of the escaping oxygen jerked awake those who had found restless sleep; they lay, gasping like beached fish, sucking in the air. Floundering in their sweltering hammocks or twitching in corners on the oily corticene, they would be woken by an outburst of gibberish from a sleeper, threshing in the throes of a nightmare. Time became unreal, detached, interminable. The hands of the clock stood still.

John Carbis staggered on his rounds through the boat every hour: everyone was reacting differently. Some lay curled up, resigned to their fate like dying animals, in remote corners; others showed a brash cheerfulness as they gasped and retched spasmodically for the precious air. Everyone had excruciating headaches; some were vomiting into any container they could find. The stench and the atmosphere were becoming foul. When he reached the motor room, Able Seaman Nunn, the LTO's mate, was looking up at him from all fours; he was bending over the rigid body of Michael Mott.

'Somefink funny's 'appened to 'im, sir. Sudden like: just went stiff.'

The LTO was lying in the blistering heat, on the plating between the switchboards.

'What's happened, Mott?' Carbis knelt alongside the stricken leading seaman. Mott could not speak, was totally paralysed. Only his eyes moved: wide open and with huge, black irises. Terror stared from them, as they swivelled to follow Carbis' movements.

'How long's he been like this, Nunn?'

'Just 'appened, sir.'

Leaving Nunn on the switchboards and collecting two hands from the control room, Carbis carried the paralysed man for'd. They turned him into a bunk in the petty officers' mess. 'Mott,' Carbis gasped. 'It's heat exhaustion. We'll soon have you right.'

Prising the purple lips apart, the cox'n was trickling a cup of lime juice between Mott's lips. The Outside ERA, Sandy McVicker, stayed with the LTO, bathing his forehead. Carbis and Wescombe returned to the chiefs' mess to look up the medical manual.

When John Carbis returned to the wardroom, he slumped to the vacant settee, Ross being on watch and Danberry turned into the upper bunk. Carbis leaned on the table and cradled his splitting head on his arms. His forehead throbbed less in this position and when he'd recovered his strength he'd climb up to his own bunk somehow. After lugging Mott for'd he was pooped. His chest was bursting, his ears sang and vision was becoming fuzzy. When, for God's sake, would the chief be along to issue the oxygen? Was that a far-away, faint voice calling from the upper bunk?

'Are you listening, Number One?'

Danberry again. His grey face peered over the lip of his bunk. 'They're still in contact?'

'Yes . . . in contact.'

'Still two hours before twilight?'

'Right,' Carbis snapped. 'Shut up.'

Danberry was leaning over, trying to catch Carbis' eye: 'I'm bringing up blood now,' he whispered.

'You're not the only one. Stop nattering.' John hauled himself upright, glared at the terrified eyes less than six inches from his own.

'I can't breathe,' Danberry gasped. 'How *can* we last another two hours?'

Carbis itched to grab the man's throat between his hands. 'For God's sake,' he whispered, 'pull yourself together, Sub. There's many worse off than you.'

The pallid face worked grotesquely, as Danberry fought for mastery of himself. From the corner of his mouth, a gob of crimson froth dribbled. Carbis reached up, trying to prop him into a sitting position.

'*What's up, Number One?*'

The captain was standing, gasping, behind him. His blue eyes were pitiless. The sub's spluttering subsided, as Carbis lowered him against the grille of the gyro panel.

'He's taking it badly, sir,' Carbis murmured. But why was Hammer standing here in the wardroom?

'They've lost contact, Number One.'

'*Not in contact?*' Carbis refused to believe it. He slumped at the table, while Hammer fell on to his settee.

'They *could* still be listening. Remember the E-boat?' Hammer asked.

'It's five-thirty, sir . . .'

'Another hour and a half.'

There was a scuffling out in the passage. The cox'n was holding on to the grille of the gyro panel. 'The chief's passed out, sir. I've turned him in.'

'The first lieutenant will issue the oxygen.' Hammer nodded at Carbis across the table.

The imperturbable Wescombe smiled: 'Doesn't do much good now, sir, does it? Tickles your fancy, nothing else . . .'

'Pass the word, Cox'n: the destroyers seem to have lost us. I'll be surfacing in ninety minutes. Tell 'em to hold on . . . not long now.'

'Thanks, sir.' And as Wescombe shuffled from the wardroom, Hammer grinned across at John Carbis:

'Off you go, John. Issue the oxygen to the wardroom last: it's no bloody good anyway.'

CHAPTER FOURTEEN

Taste of Eternity

Carbis allowed the wheel spanner to slip through his fingers on to the wardroom settee. His legs buckling beneath him, he slumped to Ross's bunk and lay back, fighting for breath. The familiar surroundings blurred, then drifted into focus. Hammer was murmuring from the other side of the table:

'Surfacing in an hour, John. Rest a bit: the oxygen does no good now.'

Carbis shook his head and stretched out on Ross's bunk. Above him Danberry was moaning. Hawke lay down again, his breathing laboured as he fought for air. *An hour?* Sixty more minutes of *this?* thought Carbis. They'd have to 'stand-by' in half-an-hour, then . . . he'd need all of thirty minutes checking *Urgent* was safe to surface, in the state in which they all were. And as he made superhuman efforts to expand his diaphragm, struggling in vain to draw in the air to the bottom of his lungs, he accepted for the first time that they could *not* make it: a question of arithmetic.

Mott remained paralysed. The chief was semi-conscious. On John's recent rounds, someone had pinned a notice on young Tarr's hammock: 'Sixpence a look!' The wretched ordinary seaman's balls were swollen to the size of melons. Unwin, the Tel, had been sick so violently and for so long that he had lost consciousness; he had been rescued from asphyxiation only at the last second. And, just above Carbis, lay the pathetic Danberry, demoralized and useless . . . *and there was still an hour to endure.*

The Burat patrol: was it really three patrols ago? It seemed to have occurred in another life. How clean and swift death from an exploding depth-charge seemed compared to this! It wasn't as if *Urgent* could sit on the bottom and they could quietly snuff out. The submarine had to be worked, demanding the utmost attention; tantalizing them all with hope, while beneath her keel a thousand feet of hungry sea awaited them. Down there her steel hull would crumple like an eggshell. And each hour which passed was accentuating the hazard of men's slipping minds . . .

He was ready to die. He had (as he imagined they all had) always refused to think about the inevitable. He believed in God, as he was pretty certain they all did when it came to it. And He would take them home when the moment came. They'd tried, tried, hadn't they, in their own violent way, to hasten the end of this ghastly Nazi tyranny? Better to be professional killers, as they all were, than do nothing except to hold up pious hands. News of unbelievable horrors concerning the Jews was percolating through from Europe: even women and children, it was rumoured, were being thrown alive into ovens. If this *was* true, how could *anyone* stand aside? If this *was* fact, he'd rather be doing his duty by exterminating the perpetrators of these horrors than be branded a pacifist . . . and he felt proud that little *Urgent* had played her minuscule part in the final deliverance which he knew his God intended – provided free men remained true. She'd sent a troopship to the bottom thirty-six hours ago, hadn't she? Another thousand fewer Germans to kill our soldiers – and when the Eighth Army most needed help . . .

When the Tenth had sailed on Operation Torch (to nobble the Italian fleet if it sailed to intercept our invasion convoys) Malta had only *thirteen* days' food left. A disguised merchant ship had made a desperate dash to relieve the island but failed to get through. The precarious situation was saved temporarily by the store-carrying submarines *Parthian*, *Clyde*, *Traveller* and *Thrasher*; and the fast minelayer, *Welshman*, made another of her 40-knot dashes with supplies. A near-thing but thanks to them, Malta was able to play her part in Operation Torch . . .

He could not resist turning towards the wardroom clock. He'd try limiting his breathing, try counting the excruciating efforts at drawing breath. He was sweating and waves of nausea were sweeping over him. He must think of anything, anything but this struggle for air . . .

On 8 November the boats on patrol received news of the successful Algerian landings, but Operation Torch had been a disappointment for the Tenth. *P43*, *P46* and *Utmost* all missed marauding U-boats; but though *P35* missed a *Littorio*-class battleship on passage from Taranto through Messina to Naples, *P46* torpedoed the cruiser *Attilio Regelo*. After a stalk lasting five hours under glassy conditions, *P44* fired at the damaged ship, but missed at extreme range. The rest of the flotilla were denied a sniff of the Italian fleet which did not attempt, apart from a cruiser force's foray to Cap Bon and back, to interfere with the 'Torch' landings. When Shrimp reported to the Admiralty the escape of the *Littorio*-class battleship, he remarked that it was unfortunate that he had not received his orders to redispose his submarines a day later, 'but that on consideration these battleships have never done anyone any harm' . . .

Another twenty minutes. Carbis longed to crawl from his bunk, break free from this steel coffin. The stabbing pain in his head was unbearable and concentration was impossible . . .

The Germans had occupied the whole of France on 11 November, gone into Corsica and Sardinia with its Luftwaffe on the 14th. For the submarines these next four weeks were proving the most unsuccessful of their war – and tragic, too. *Utmost* was lost on 24 November; and during the same week, *P54*'s captain and her two lookouts were washed overboard and drowned on surfacing in a gale. And now *Traveller* was overdue from her Taranto reconnaissance. A rotten month . . . the boats were over-concentrated, each captain having to spend too much time in careful navigation to avoid collision with his neighbour; the enemy's anti-submarine tactics were intensive and efficient; and the weather, appalling . . .

Once more he turned guiltily towards the clock: seven-and-a-half minutes to go. Now he *knew* they still had a chance . . . seven more ghastly minutes, gasping for breath. His hands clasped about his chest, he shut his eyes, willing the minutes to pass . . .

The Siege of Malta was lifted. The Spitfires were there in numbers and the Stonehenge convoy had brought them their high octane: no longer could the mass-murderers roam at will and unchallenged in the skies above the island, no longer terrorize the stubborn, brave Maltese. The Spits, under Park, were clawing them from the skies. Our store-carrying submarines, having saved Malta for 'Torch', were no longer needed. It had been a close-run thing.

Was the tide turning at last? On 27 November, the final tragedy to the French fleet occurred when, ignoring Darlan's plea from Algiers, the Vichy mob scuttled their fine ships at Toulon. In Russia, the Germans were tasting their own medicine at Stalingrad; and on the other side of the world, the treacherous little yellow men were being held and trounced at Guadacanal by the Yanks. Was there a ray of hope after these two years and five months since the Siege of Malta had begun; three years since the Hun had swept into Warsaw to obliterate the marvellous, gallant Poles?

It was too much to hope: our National Days of Prayer seemed to be unanswered, our hopes dashed . . . but if *Urgent* ever reached Malta; if they got out of this, he, John Carbis, would never complain about anything again. He'd share Anna's and Lofty's happiness with their rushed marriage – and sail the dinghy which he'd bought in partnership with Shrimp's secretary . . . *Boojum*, her name – but how inconsequential it all seemed now! How beyond reach, how impossibly ephemeral the dream of sailing a white-sailed cockleshell on blue, blue seas! The reality was today's filth, foul air, spilling gash-buckets and overflowing heads. Was that Ross' voice from somewhere?

'Captain, sir . . .' then again, more urgently between his gaspings: 'Captain, sir: six-thirty . . .'

The body stirred from the other side of the table: 'Stand-by to surface,' Hawke said jerkily. 'Shift to night lighting and go to diving stations.' Hauling himself to his feet, the captain waited for Carbis to precede him to the control room. Gently shaking the upper bunk, Hammer's quiet words came spasmodically: 'Come on, Sub.' He shook the bunk more forcefully: 'I need you.' Waiting to meet the young officer's terrified eyes, he then staggered into the control room.

'Take your time, Number One,' he panted as he grabbed the hoist wire of the search-periscope. 'No balls-up now.'

Carbis was swaying before the gauges and trying to bring his double vision into focus. Behind him men were hauling themselves to their stations, some on all fours; on arrival, they needed minutes before they were able to take over from the watchkeepers. Stoker Gooch, on his way aft, was supporting Danberry to the Fruit Machine. 'That's all right, sir,' the man murmured when he left the sub clinging to the torpedo calculator. And while the control-room team gradually assembled, Carbis was checking and double-checking the orders he gave; Hawke was watching behind him, as methodically they prepared *Urgent* for surfacing. At 1845, Hammer ordered an all-round listening sweep. This last, essential precaution added the final tension: if there remained anything up-top now . . .

'Lookouts ready for the tower, sir. Permission to open the lower lid?' Carbis asked.

Paddy Kipps, the jovial signalman, stood ready, itching to enter the skirt, the two lookouts, Brown and Swinley, dressed and sweating behind him. All three were fidgety and swaying on their feet.

'Open the lower lid,' Carbis said. 'Lookouts in the tower. Keep silent.'

At 1856 exactly, the first lieutenant faced his captain: 'Ready to surface. Main vents checked shut, sir.'

'All-round sweep completed,' Snagge called softly from his asdic corner. In the silence, a sneezing cockroach would have sounded like thunder: 'No HE. No asdic transmissions.'

Carbis felt no elation. This was it, then. Straight up for air. Even if the Italian battlefleet was waiting for them, *Urgent* was surfacing.

'Periscope depth,' Hammer gasped. And at sixty feet, as *Urgent* adopted her bow-up angle, he raised the for'd periscope. A swift look in high power, just in case . . .

Forty . . . thirty-five . . . thirty-one . . .

'Twenty-eight feet, sir,' Carbis panted as he watched his captain, the light streaming into his eyes, sliding round on his heels . . . If he checked now with his search . . . if there was something there . . . God, why couldn't Hawke put them out of their misery? When he stood back, gasping, the corners of his mouth were twitching.

'Eighty feet,' he choked. 'Eighty feet.' John Carbis could not believe the command.

'Eighty feet, sir,' he repeated. 'Less dive on the after-planes, Cox'n.' But he wasn't thinking of the trim: there must be something there, waiting. They'd been tricked again. *He*'d had enough, whatever was waiting . . . For God's sake . . . AIR! Gun action would be Hawke's next order. He turned towards his captain. Why had he left up the periscope, why was he smirking?

Sixty feet – sinking nicely to eighty, the planesmen choking from their efforts . . . then, behind him, he heard a scuffling. A muffled, garbled shout. When he turned, Brown was already on the top rung of the control-room ladder. He was tearing frenziedly at the clips of the lower lid.

'Restrain him,' the captain gasped. He stood back, nodding at Bill Dale and the stalwart Outside ERA, Sandy McVicker. The crazed seaman was mouthing stupidly, his eyeballs huge and rolling grotesquely in their sockets as he flung Swinley from him. He had already freed the first clip and was wrenching at the second when Dale encircled his flailing boots. Jock had him by the collar and, with Swinley encircling his chest, the three managed to tear the man's grip from the lower hatch.

'Take charge of him, Cox'n,' Hawke murmured. 'Put him under

close arrest and turn him into his hammock. Sedate him and place two men over him.' He nodded at the first lieutenant. 'Put the torpedo officer on the after-planes.'

Danberry quit his Fruit Machine and Wescombe slipped from his stool. The struggling Brown was being bundled through the watertight door.

'And, Cox'n . . .'

'Sir . . .?'

'D'you understand? Any force necessary is to be used to restrain him if he refuses to quieten down: he's endangering the submarine.'

'Aye, aye, sir. I'll get Fergus to stand by him.'

'Stay with him yourself.'

'Aye, aye, sir.'

Hawke wiped a sweating hand across his forehead.

'We'll stay at eighty feet for half-an-hour. It's still daylight up-top.'

A resentment smouldered through the control room . . . another thirty minutes of this . . . too bloody cruel. Carbis could not trust himself to turn and face Hawke.

'Nothing in sight, Number One. Nothing. Not even an aircraft.'

Then slowly, through the dazed and poisoned brains, the import of their captain's remarks percolated slowly through the boat. One by one, each forced a grin, quietly slid down to the corticene. Men clasped hands, grinned, dug each other in the ribs. Ross bent guiltily over his chart table, trying to concentrate in working out again a revised time of twilight. They'd been dived now for over thirty-six hours – and ten minutes.

'Dark at 1928, sir . . .' The navigating officer gave a wan smile: 'Certain of it, sir.'

'Continue all-round HE watch.' Hammer glanced at the clock above the helmsman's head. 'Surfacing in . . . *twenty minutes' time.*'

Carbis felt his legs trembling, something he could not control. Like everyone in the control room his stare was fixed on the black hands of the clock. If they ever reached the half-hour, this would be the longest twenty minutes of their lives.

Petty Officer (Telegraphist) Stanley Gawn was six feet, two inches tall. Like the others, he was squatting, his back propped in the doorway of his minuscule wireless office. This bloody business was making his mind reel; if the Old Man wanted to pass a signal to Malta, Gawn hoped he'd give his PO Tel enough warning. He had to warm up his set and, if they wanted him to catch the missed routines, he still needed time – particularly as Swain had nobbled Olly Unwin, his telegraphist, to replace Brown in the tower as lookout. Rotten business that; no-one enjoyed it much, least of all the Old Man, Gawn reckoned . . .

Olly was developing into a useful Tel. Jimmy had urged him to work for his Higher Trade exam; Paddy Kipps had helped him with morse on the aldis lamp and the lad was being encouraged to try also for his higher substantive rate. Gawn must arrange for Unwin to attend Signal School at St Angelo and, if there was time during this next rest period, he'd accompany Olly. St Angelo's Chief Tel was an old mucker of Gawn's and they could share a tot together. Success meant a shared gin, too, from the wardroom's wine locker: the skipper and Jimmy never begrudged their precious ration because advancement meant extra pay to be added to the successful candidate's submarine allowance of half-a-crown a day; somehow, the whole process restored normality and an objective to all their lives . . .

Olly was now accepted also as a lookout: he'd been training in the darkened room at Lazaretto which had been built recently to simulate night conditions on the bridge. Even with carrot pills and knowing how to keep a watch, the lookouts' eyesight could never be too good: the boat's existence depended on their competence and concentration. At night, whoever sighted the other first, survived . . . but, if the entire Wop fleet was up-top now, *Urgent* would be surfacing, Gawn was sure.

Poor old Jimmy, there: rocking on his pins . . . another eleven minutes. And he wondered pessimistically whether he need bother about learning his lines for the next Sods' Opera due in the canteen during the rest period. They'd press-ganged him for the part of Eskimo Nell but, even if *Urgent* survived this, they'd never get back for Christmas. Swain had told him they were still west of Piccadilly. There was still ten minutes to go but the Old Man was tapping Jimmy on the shoulder.

'Stand by to surface,' the skipper croaked.

And as Gawn watched, remote, like an observer from another world, Jimmy was trying to act normally while he methodically went through his surfacing drill. '*Check. Check* again. Main vents? Main vents?' The bloke's words were slurred and he was swaying on his feet while he pumped from for'd to aft along the trimming line. The minutes ticked away, agonizingly slowly. Then at 1928, Chris Snagge, his voice as monotone as ever, was gasping from the other side of the panel which separated the asdics from Gawn's w/t office:

'All-round sweep completed, sir.' A long pause. Again, everyone had stopped breathing . . .

'No HE.'

'Ready to surface, sir,' from the swaying Jimmy. 'Main vents shut.'

The skipper pulled himself to his feet.

'Surface. Straight up, Number One.'

From his corner, the PO Tel watched them; they were like marionettes in a puppet show: the lookouts waiting for the skipper to fumble his way through the canvas skirt; their mumbling while the skipper followed the signalman up the tower. The gasping lookouts slowly disappearing, the red lighting turning them into gnomes from the netherworld; a garbled shout from above when they released the first clip; Jimmy swaying in front of the depth gauges.

'Thirty feet . . . twenty-five . . .' he gasped, bending his knees now, poor devil, barmy, trying to keep the boat down.

'Eighteen.'

Any second now. The PO Tel staggered to his feet. Any second now . . . air, please God . . . AIR.

A sudden draught of air. His eardrums popped. Any minute now, those generators, the chief's diesels, would be sucking down fresh air into the bowels of the boat . . .

They were like mummers from the past. The first lieutenant, hand on the ladder, staring through the lower hatch and up into the tower. Every man's eyes straining towards the dark cavity . . . every man waiting, praying . . . what *was* up there, for God's sake? No-one moved; a total, tangible silence save the *swish! swish!* from somewhere while *Urgent* rolled slowly in the swell . . . *Had they sighted the enemy again, up there on the bridge?* The helmsman was gazing stupidly at the bucket which he held below the bell-mouth of the voice-pipe: why wasn't the usual water gushing down, when the skipper opened the valve on the bridge? And by Gawn's right shoulder stood the Chief ERA, while they held him upright in the engine-room doorway. Their eyes met and neither spoke.

'Captain, sir?' Jimmy was shouting up the tower, his white face distorted. '*Captain, sir – Are you – all right?*'

The inactivity had persisted for too long: but still the silence, this agonizing wait. And just as Gawn felt he could stand it no longer,

Jimmy turned to him:

'Nip up top, PO Tel. See what's going . . . on.'

Then the PO Tel, unusually for him, was crawling into the trunking, clammy canvas scraping the back of his neck. Through the lower lid; the flat plate beneath his feet, his arms flailing upwards, hand-over-hand, feeling for the slippery ladder rungs in the blackness. Then, his lungs bursting, he was levering himself into that indigo aperture through which the glittering stars were swooping in the heavens. *Up* . . . and through. And as he knelt there, trying to haul himself upright in the semi-darkness of the bridge, he collapsed, tripped by a jumble of bodies lying prostrate across the deck of the bridge. His head began swimming as he breathed in the sweet air to the very depths of his lungs, this delicious air. Oh God! *Thank Christ* . . . The air, the clean, cold air sucked down, down, down to the very core of him. And during those seconds the swimming stopped in his head; his mind began functioning again. He shoved his chin across the lip of the upper lid, as the first body beneath him began to stir:

'Control room!' he yelled. 'Control room: they've all passed out!'

He heard Jimmy acknowledging his report, felt the captain's frame extricating itself, saw him staggering to the bridge side and lifting his binoculars. Becoming rational again, Gawn clambered down the ladders, then fell out of the skirt into the control room; he was caught by the circle of gasping men. He heard the seawater flushing into the helmsman's bucket.

'*START THE GENERATORS* . . .!'

Gawn shoved his way through the waiting circle and stood back to watch. There they were, a dozen men, mouths open like bloody fish, hands on each others' shoulders, waiting, waiting. Jimmy, by the gauges, motionless. Sandy McVicker, his hands poised over the main vent levers on the diving panel, just in case . . .

A jolt; a faint vibration and then . . . *phrrrummp*! The first diesel churned over a couple of revs, then burst into life . . . The gasping circle by the trunk leaned forward, heads held back . . . the first gush of fresh air streamed down the hatch, through the control room and into the hungry diesels. The second engine rumbled, drawing the airstream into its avid cylinders. Jimmy started the ventilation and from for'd Gawn heard the cheers. They had been dived for thirty-six hours, twenty-seven minutes – and now they had another chance to live. AIR . . . sweet air . . . that wonderful life-giving force . . .

Men jigged up and down, beating each other on the back; and the exquisite feeling, the indescribable relief of his lungs once more having air to breathe was an experience which the PO Tel would never, never forget.

The blowers were started, the batteries put on charge, the zig-zag begun. Leaving Ross on the bridge, the captain came below. He was laughing as he emerged through the trunking, blood streaming down his forehead. Jimmy was stepping towards him: 'I'll stitch it up for you, sir.'

The skipper recoiled, as if bitten by a snake.

'Don't touch me, you miserable doctor,' he grinned.

'You'll be scarred for life, sir,' Carbis said, in his best bedside manner.

'I'd rather live,' said the Old Man and slowly retreated to the wardroom.

The whole boat shared in the spontaneous merriment. And when, fifteen minutes later, as they were settling into their zig-zag for Piccadilly, Ross had to dive because of a Wellington's low-level attack, no-one gave a fig.

CHAPTER FIFTEEN

Rest Period

Stan Gawn, the PO Tel, cleared *Urgent*'s ETA when she was within sniffing distance of Gozo, but the sweeper did not appear until the submarine, having surfaced off the islet of Filfla, reached Delimara Point. So it was late into the forenoon of Boxing Day, 26 December 1942, when *Urgent* finally reached St Elmo on that bright and crisp morning, two cables astern of *Speedy*, her favourite minesweeper.

Somehow, through the mysterious circuitry of the bush wireless which the Maltese seemed to operate, the people knew that *Urgent* was overdue: otherwise, Carbis was thinking to himself on the bridge, why have all those hundreds of people, men, women and children, gathered on the battlements stretching beneath the fort of St Elmo?

John had to dodge to the other side of the large black flag, the Jolly Roger, flapping from *Urgent*'s after periscope. Its new hour-glass emblem and the white bar from the sunken trooper had already been stitched on temporarily by Kipps: he'd be taking it up to the nuns during the rest period to have it sewn on properly. The grim skull and cross-bones looked good there, streaming in the breeze.

Urgent was surging towards the boom and he could hear the cheers from the people thronging the walls, the children jumping up and down; the women, in their black dresses and coloured shawls, weeping, some of them, with joy. And John Carbis felt a surge of pride that he belonged to this stubborn little ship and her thirty-three officers and men.

She'd survived all that the enemy could hurl at her; she'd made a dent in Rommel's supply chain, killed hundreds of soldiers. No pleasure the last, but that's what she had to do . . . And as he waved back, he felt a lump rising in his throat: it was touching to see such loyalty in these simple, brave people, bombed to bits so that the Services could hit back at the loathsome foe. Their joy, as they waved and cheered there, was not only the pent-up emotion of vengeance:

they sensed that they too, by their fortitude and sacrifice, were taking part in what *Urgent* and her sister submarines were achieving, day in, day out, patrol after patrol.

'*Harbour stations . . .*'

At last! The captain's summons which they had not expected to hear again: it was only forty-eight hours ago, wasn't it, that interminable trial? Carbis stood to one side while the cable party clambered up the tower to prepare the wires and fenders on the casings. *Harbour stations . . .* these two words were music to submariners. And at last Carbis felt he belonged, that he was accepted by this staunch, elite brotherhood, with its unique humour and rough camaraderie. And as he watched Hawke, crouched over the wind baffle, his chin on his hands, that distant look in his cold, blue eyes, Carbis now appreciated what that tough, eccentric man had had to endure. For him, this moment must be some compensation for the recent unpleasantness.

Urgent was through the bobbing black buoys which protected Marsamuscetto Harbour from external marauders. Sliema Creek was opening up to starboard and he could pick out Toni de Marco's house. Kipps was wetting the bosun's call between his lips, waiting for this one moment of ceremonial. There was Lazaretto! The old base: they bore a love–hate for this haven of theirs . . . no food, no booze, no women; no comfort, but it was home, *home* to them, its battered walls enfolding the warmth of comradeship which they all shared. The wardroom; the troops' mess and the canteen they loved; and the tiny chapel hewn out of the sandstone. Sunday tomorrow, wasn't it? He would not be the only one from *Urgent* attending the simple service of Holy Communion which the chaplain never missed. Men found peace and strength there for a brief moment.

There was a surprising number of boats strung round the base, like blue gems in a necklace. He was surprised to see the long, distinctive shapes of three *T* boats, large cylinders on their casings, whales in comparison to the minnows represented by the *U*s dotted among them. There was no blanketing smoke from the canisters, so presumably the RAF was in the ascendancy at the moment. And as his gaze swept fondly across the sandstone buildings, he picked out the broad figure of Captain 'S', 'Staffie' at his side, standing by the dhaisas' rocky landing-place at the bottom of the steps which held the carved crests. Carbis nodded at Kipps who stuffed the call between his lips.

Hawke was climbing on to the starboard seat.

'Attention on the casing,' Carbis called down from the bridge. '*Pipe!*' Standing to attention himself and saluting while Kipps piped 'The Still', *Urgent* slid silently on main motors, the swish of the water curling along her pressure-hull being the only sound. Shrimp raised his hand in salute, captain to captain; then, with a welcoming wave, he turned to walk slowly along the bottom balcony towards *Urgent*'s buoy. Kipps piped the 'Carry on' and five minutes later the submarine, turning tightly, rove her headrope through the buoy off the engineering workshops.

Captain 'S' was standing on the pontoon below her bridge; he was smiling as he looked upwards to chat with Hawke. A minute later *Urgent*'s CO was over the side and both men were walking along the pontoons to the shore.

It was 1145 before Carbis could dismiss the hands. Unwashed, unshaven, their bedding mouldy, grey-faced and tired they made their way happily ashore to showers and food. What more could they ask? The mail, if there was any . . . And then John Carbis himself was wobbling down the gangway. His sponge bag under one arm, his 'steaming bag' beneath the other, he glanced at the dinghies bobbing between the pontoons. Where was *Boojum*, the dinghy of which he was part-owner?

He was unable to prevent a half-smile of delight from creasing his freshly-shaven face. He felt a surge of gratitude to be sucking in fresh air again, for being alive. Wet, wasn't he? But dear God, how marvellous it all was: he'd collect his mail first. As he rounded into the courtyard leading to the wardroom, he looked into the shack on the right which housed George Hardinge, the captain's secretary. He pushed open the door.

'Hello, George! Where's our *Boojum*?'

The sub-lieutenant's back stiffened in his chair. The long, lugubrious face turned, looked up in disbelief.

'Good God, John!' he said slowly. 'You're supposed to be dead.' He laughed that slow guffaw of his. 'I've dispatched your overdue signal.' He rose from his chair, poked his friend gingerly in the stomach. 'It really *is* you John,' he said. 'Welcome back: *Boojum*'s sunk.'

'How'd it happen, George?'

'Gregale. It blew like hell, but we're raising her as soon as Pop Giddings can spare the hands. I'm afraid we won't get her up for your rest period this time.' He smiled again. 'See you at lunch. I'll buy you a gin.'

Normality: it was so good. John moved on towards the open door of the wardroom. The sun was shining coldly in the courtyard where on Sundays and for 'clear lower deck' they all gathered. There was slime on the paving stones and the doorway to the chapel in the far wall looked cold and bleak, so different to summer when the bourgainvillea showered the courtyard in purple bloom.

It seemed dark in the cavernous wardroom, the large hall with its corrugated-iron roof replacing the original which was blown off in the bombing. At the seaward end stood the bar and its depleted stocks; in the middle was the tortoise stove, its tin chimney leading to the roof and down which, during a gregale, the smoke blew back. At the rock-end was the dining section, with its two long tables. Carbis walked to the letter rack between the stove and the tables.

Three letters were stuffed into the 'C's and his spirits rose when he recognized his mother's handwriting. The second was from Pam and the other was postmarked 'Rabat and Mdina'. He stood back to scrutinize the rack, the quickest and least painful means of discovering who was missing. It seemed as if *Traveller* was overdue then? He moved to the noticeboard on the right of the letter rack to read the Newsheet.

There it was: *Traveller* overdue and presumed lost. And *P222* had not returned to Gib from patrol, presumably lost off Naples which had been her billet. Three boats in a month, a *U*, an *S* and a *T* – 150 submariners – and *Urgent* had nearly joined the list. Now for the 'chat': Tubby Linton had arrived with his *Turbulent*. He was the most experienced of them all, with a reputation for ruthlessness and for seldom firing more than two fish in a salvo. Jacky Whitton had taken over *P54* at sea when Oxborrow and his lookouts had been washed overboard and drowned.

The areas between the Eighth Submarine Flotilla and the Tenth had been reorganized, each keeping to their own side of the line drawn from Cape Bon–Marittimo–west coast of Italy. *Seraph*, following her landing of General Giraud for Operation Torch in North Africa, had on her next patrol rammed a U-boat at sixty feet and, due to the damage, was going home. But the cheering news was that the Eighth Army, having trounced the Afrika Korps, was maintaining its advance westwards across Tripolitania: Rommel's Panzers were halted through running out of petrol. To meet Rommel's frenzied cry for supplies, the enemy was de-fuelling his big ships, apparently, to keep his anti-submarine escorts operational for defending the convoys.

Our boats' sacrifices weren't in vain, then? *Rorqual* had made a successful mine-lay off the Cani Rocks at the entrance to Bizerta, which had already claimed one victim. And four days ago, the Arctic convoys having started again after PQ17, the convoy JW51B to Murmansk had been successfully defended against *Hipper*'s and *Lutzow*'s attacks. Our destroyers had taken on Hitler's pocket battleship and heavy cruiser – and won. *Perhaps* 1943 was heralding the turning of the tide? Carbis subsided into one of the few chairs and opened his mail.

Mum was fine, but worrying as always now that Dad was in hospital. Nothing serious, she said – but that made John's anxiety the worse. She never told the bad news, but this letter was better than no news. Servicemen were suffering from stomach ulcers: because of worrying for their families at home operational efficiency was being affected. The blitzes on Plymouth and the home ports were difficult to bear without news. Thanks to Shrimp, a twin-engined Mosquito fighter had been stripped of its guns and once a week it flew to Malta with mail for the flotilla. Flying high, with extra tanks, it made the direct flight in one hop. The ulcers had disappeared overnight.

The letter with the Maltese postmark was from the Segunas. Lieutenant John Carbis was invited to attend the marriage of their daughter, Anna, to Lieutenant Nigel Small, Royal Navy, in Mdina Cathedral on 2 March 1943. RSVP to Mrs Charles Seguna, The Old House, Bastion Square, Mdina. But would *Urgent* be in harbour then? John had already declined to be Lofty's best man, because *Urgent* was running alternately with *P50* at the moment. Perhaps things would change?

Twisting the third letter over in his hand, he deliberated whether to open it: he could identify that rounded handwriting anywhere. He ripped it open, glanced at the two paragraphs. Washed up for good, but no hard feelings. And she wished him luck, wherever he was. Yours, Pam. Nothing more. He shredded it and strolling towards the open doorway, dropped it into the waste-basket. Another chapter behind him and probably all for the best. He knew that it was probably pride that made him feel rejected – but it damn well hurt . . . He'd get hold of Luigi and see if he could rustle up a bath for him, if he hadn't already gone to dinner. It took time to warm those cans of water.

'Well John, what d'you think of Lofty marrying?'

Matt Fairfax, captain of *P50*, was ensconced in the battered arm-chair to the right of the door. His arms hung limply over its ancient leather arms. His bent knees half-concealed his sensitive, pleasant face while he chatted late into the night with his friend. John Carbis regarded him with understanding and, above all, with respect: he'd known Matt since their schooldays when they'd both been working to enter the navy. Matt, four years older, seemed vastly senior at the time, but now, with Fairfax 'in command' and John a 'Jim', the gap had vanished. Their friendship was unusual, for first lieutenants did not hob-nob with COs. And so, when they did have a chance they chose a moment such as this, when most of the others had turned in. And out here in Malta, sharing the fiery crucible of war, men concealed little from each other: it helped to talk things over with friends. Tonight, Friday, 4 January 1943, Matt was looking strained and tired, Carbis thought.

'It's his decision,' Carbis replied to the question, sipping down the last of the 'red biddy' which a French submarine had brought from Algiers. 'It's perhaps neither the time nor the place, but he's very happy with Anna.'

'Super girl, I thought. Mother's nice, too. Always look at mum: your wife will be like her twenty years later.' He added, 'But there's something not right, John.'

Matt was thinking aloud. He'd left his newly-married wife at home; he lived for nothing else but to finish this foul war so that he could get home and be a family man.

'He's a lucky chap,' John said. 'There're not many Annas about.'

'I hope Lofty realizes it,' Matt said. He was hiding his thoughts. 'He's so hopelessly overboard with her.'

'What's worrying you?' John asked.

'I wonder whether Anna feels the same, but I'll be glad when my first lieutenant's spliced. His mind's on another job at the moment,' and they both smiled. 'It's tricky for me now, John.' The CO of *P50* was hesitating. Then he began to talk softly, his deep-set, brown eyes fixed on his friend. 'I suppose it's my fault: I'm beginning to lose confidence in myself.' He stared hard at John: 'I've done four patrols since joining the Tenth. They've all been blank.'

'It's not your fault, Matt,' John said. 'You know what they say:

right place, right time. Some have more luck than others.'

'That's why I've asked for the Tunis bottleneck: I can't fail to find a target there.' He looked up. '*Urgent* is joining me a day later, Hammer tells me.'

'Is she?' John did not have to conceal his misgivings. Tunis Bay was a hot spot at the moment and the memories of *Urgent*'s last patrol were still vivid. 'We're sailing the day after tomorrow. We loaded torpedoes this forenoon.'

'I'm off tomorrow morning,' Matt said. 'But I'm tired, John. Feel whacked.'

'I guessed so,' John said. 'Are you fussing about your blank patrols?'

'I've fired twenty-four fish,' Matt replied. 'No hits. And what with the torpedo shortage . . .' He paused, then went on: 'I *have* to keep cheerful: the troops are damned loyal, but I'm letting them down. It's not much fun serving a captain who collects all the heat without sinking anything. Lofty's loyal as loyal, but I'm worried about morale, nevertheless.' His head jerked up. 'Wouldn't you be?'

John could see the pain behind those trusting eyes. He chose his words carefully. 'Wanks was the same, wasn't he? Shrimp almost had to relieve even *him*, but he became the most successful of you all. Wanks must have gone through what you're suffering now.' John smiled across at this modest man who was hiding nothing. 'Don't you see, Matt, you're passing through the most difficult phase of your command? It's easy when you're hitting: must be hell for you when you're missing.'

'I'm beginning to ask myself whether I *do* have a periscope eye.' He spoke softly: 'I'm considering asking Shrimp to relieve me, if this next patrol is another failure.'

John realized that the co was making a statement, not asking for comfort. To soft-soap Matt would be insulting.

Carbis said: 'I think you should go to Captain 'S', but *not* for your reasons.' Fairfax slumped deeper into the chair, raised his eyesbrows.

'You're bloody tired,' John went on. 'Admit it.'

The blond head nodded. 'I am.' He paused, then murmured half to himself: 'I don't know how to go on sometimes. The strain . . .' He passed a hand across his brow, but did not continue, his mouth clamping into a firm line.

'Why don't you go to Shrimp, just to talk it over?' John insisted.

'I'm sailing tomorrow, remember? It's almost midnight now.'

Carbis shook his head. '*He*'ll understand,' he said quietly. '*He* knows what it's like. There's too much at stake, you know that . . . the boat and your ship's company. *Of course* Shrimp won't mind, even if he's turned in, which I doubt.' John leaned forward, touched his friend's forearm, willing Matt to heed him.

The captain shook his head slowly. 'I can't,' he said. Lowering his voice, he added, 'A sort of pride, I suppose.'

'He'll understand that, too. Nothing to be ashamed of, for God's sake, Matt. You cos have to take a lot.'

Fairfax was climbing to his feet. 'I'm off to bed,' he said. He smiled a strange, sardonic grin, unusual for him. 'Right as rain after a good night's sleep.' He dug Carbis in the ribs. 'Thanks for listening, chum. Keep it to yourself, won't you?' He disappeared into the darkness of the courtyard, calling over his shoulder:

'See you on the billet, John.' The sound of his footsteps faded into the night, '. . . or at the wedding.'

CHAPTER SIXTEEN

The Tunis Run

Once again the first lieutenant of HM Submarine *Urgent* lifted the binoculars to his tired eyes. Once more he checked that the two lookouts, one on each side of him on the lonely bridge were on their toes. This billet at the entrance to the bottle-neck of Tunis Bay, slap on the enemy's convoy route from Palermo to Tunis and Bizerta, must be the most unfriendly place in the world at the moment. He began his all-round sweep once more, starting from the dangerous, northern sector whence the targets might appear. He searched the horizon to the eastwards while *Urgent* coughed back and forth on her diesels, zig-zagging inside her five-mile circle of operations to complete her charge before dawn, ready for another tense day. The right-hand rim of his circle of vision darkened: the dim outline of Zembra Island. The name sounded sinister now, almost equating with Marittimo.

Zembra . . . dark and brooding, with its three 1,300-feet-high peaks and under this half-moon resembling St Paul's cathedral. Zembra was only three miles off when *Urgent* doubled back to her westerly leg. Five miles on a mean-line of 280° would bring her back to the edge of *P50*'s billet; then, reverse course again, return; and so on all night long. The grim joke was that each boat purported to ditch her gash on the edge of the other's billet, but it was too early yet for the nightly ritual . . .

Zembra, its rugged cliffs at the north end showing in the moonlight, stood sentinel, ten miles to the west of Cape Bon, and was the gate-house into the Gulf. He could just pick out the low-lying islet of Lanbretta, like a cheese slice, between Cape Bon and Zembra. He searched carefully southwards, identified the Cape of Zafran at the eastern entrance to the Bay of Tunis itself. He could not see Tunis and its low-lying canal, but Cape Carthage was just visible at the opening to the bay. Even now, nineteen hundred years later, the very name still stirred the imagination. Those centuries ago, the Carthaginian galleys had plied here, challenging the power of Rome. There was an analogy somewhere.

Then up to the north-west, to the invisible Plane Island and the Cani Rocks where *Rorqual* had laid her mines; onwards to the north to where the Skerki Bank forced the convoys into this bottle-neck . . . and another all-round sweep was finished. The helmsman was calling up the voice-pipe: 'Permission to ditch gash, sir?'

Carbis took another look without binoculars: 'Ditch gash.'

O'Brien's face appeared in the upper hatchway. Six buckets of garbage were handed up and clanged across the bridge rail. The holed tins rattled against the pressure-hull, the gash splattered into the sea and in less than a minute, with the conning-tower jammed momentarily, the dangerous but essential chore was finished. In another twenty minutes Ross would be relieving him and he could catch his best sleep in the twenty-four hours. His night watch was from 0100 to 0300 and he was accustomed to it now. It was the spell when the captain slept his soundest at the back of the bridge in his chair, where he now was. Uncanny how Hammer stood it: these past weeks had been the most hectic in *Urgent*'s short life.

Urgent arrived on her billet during the early hours of Tuesday, 8 January of this new year, 1943, Matt Fairfax in *P50* preceding her by thirty hours. The area of each boat's operations was prescribed within a five-mile circle, the circles being on a line between Zembra and Plane Island, to the west. Both boats were permitted to attack all *laden* ships bound for Tunis, but *P50* was better placed for the Bizerta-bound traffic, an advantage about which Hammer, John knew, was pleased for Fairfax's sake.

They'd spent the first three days prowling up and down their line at periscope depth waiting for the convoys and the enemy's air cover was intense. The approach of a convoy was heralded by a bevy of surface and air escorts. Yesterday morning, *P50* hit something well to the north, because in *Urgent* they heard the distinctive double clang of two torpedo hits, followed twenty minutes later by a couple of hours of depth-charging. During the afternoon *Urgent* fired a full salvo of torpedoes at a floating dock under tow. The range was extreme, because of the danger of firing across Matt's patch; the fish ran under, Hammer was certain, because there were no distinctive clangs. During the first watch this night, they had sighted *P50* on the horizon, zig-zagging to the westward while she charged. Like *Urgent*, she was trimmed right down, only her conning tower being visible –

but the silhouette had certainly been *P50*'s, so she was safe.

Thank God, thought Carbis, the Germans haven't yet installed radar on Zembra. If they had, the two submarines could not charge at night on the surface. At Spartivento, the Italians had erected an enormous revolving aerial which covered the whole area: the trick was to surface directly under the cliff for a charge, a dodge which fooled the enemy. But if they installed a radar on Zembra . . . *kaput!* for the submarines. *Urgent* had been put down by low-flying JU 52s seven times tonight already. Most were troop- and store-carrying, but you never knew when one of them could turn out to be an anti-submarine patrol.

During the day, this Palermo–Tunis run was like a main road: down the middle between the minefields ran the convoys, protected on each side by a string of escorts; above them flew the circling anti-submarine air patrols, the Cants, JU 52s and the JU 88s. The Germans were making superhuman efforts to save their Afrika Korps. Von Arnem was now commanding, apparently; Rommel, exhausted and sick with worry at his lack of petrol and supplies, was back in Germany.

Yesterday was glassy calm. Working the periscope was tricky, needing furtive, swift looks. Hundreds of six-engined troop-carrying Heinkels were lumbering overhead at two hundred feet. They were difficult to identify but they looked like flying Box-Cars. Some were packed with troops, others carrying tanks and petrol. A stream of these Heinkels, flying low all day above the periscope, did not calm the nerves. In a few hours it would all begin again. Carbis sighed, feeling weary himself, when the call came up the voice-pipe:

'Permission for Lieutenant Ross on the bridge, sir?'

Good old Duggie! He was never late and the new sub, Geoffrey Tonks, was a punctual relief also.

Breakfast was the best moment of the day for John Carbis. After the tension of the night (*Urgent* was put down nine times in all), it was good to feel the normality of routine starting again; using the mirror on the heads door at the foot of the wardroom table, he brushed his hair while men went about their business around him: substituting white bulbs for red; Mott, the LTO, apologizing as he crouched on his knees at Carbis' feet to take the battery readings. His unshaven, tired face staring back from the mirror was grey about the jowls and chin; his brown eyes were sunken and, dammit, there were definite flecks of white at his temples. If he grew a beard, he'd have a leaner, more piratical and laconic image than ever. He turned and, stretching his aching limbs, flumped down on the wardroom settee. Hammer, waiting for him, pushed across the jug of condensed milk. Ross was flicking through the signal log; O'Brien, hovering in the background with the teapot.

'Baked beans?' Ross asked, without glancing up.

'On fried bread, sir. Lovely drop of stuff.'

'You must have cooked it, then?' Hammer murmured.

'Sort of, sir. Cookie had the "morning".'

Stirring the condensed milk into the black tea, John felt a drowsiness creeping over him. He barely noticed when the new third hand, Sub-lieutenant Geoffrey Tonks, shyly poked his head round the corner. (It was sad about Danberry, but he'd be happier back in 'gens'.) When Carbis looked up, he knew from the expression on Tonks' face what was coming. Aggravating, because the day had begun peacefully: they'd dived at dawn and went straight down to find the layer at seventy feet. *Urgent* was remaining at one hundred and twenty feet until breakfast was finished, when, up-top, there would be sufficient light to see through the periscope.

'The HSD has picked up HE on 350°, sir,' Tonks said quietly. 'Across a wide arc, sir.'

Hammer shoved his teacup into the centre of the table and John followed him into the control room.

'A fast convoy, sir,' Snagge reported from his asdic corner. 'The HE's increasing rapidly.' He was crouching even lower over his ebonite knobs.

Hammer glanced at his watch: doubtful whether there was enough light up-top. He met John's glance.

'Periscope depth. Diving stations.'

He was taking her straight up, risking collision from deep. But now, instead of being silently critical, Carbis felt a total confidence in his sturdy captain standing, rubbing his chin, between the periscopes. In the fore-ends, unfinished cups of tea were being pushed aside to steam on mess tables or in oily corticene corners. Men were tumbling to their stations, silently cursing as Carbis swooped *Urgent* upwards.

'Twenty-eight feet, sir.'

'Up periscope.'

This was the instant when John's innards turned over, felt literally like water; so what must it be like for his captain, swivelling the search periscope round, waiting for the smear of water across the lens to evaporate before he could see clearly? Hammer was jamming his face forcefully into the rubber shock-guard and light excluder: to the west, nothing: to the south, the greyish-green haze of the Bay of Tunis; then swiftly east to Zembra which took in his whole field of vision. By daylight the island was a mixture of dirty brown and lifeless green, a white circlet of surf curling lazily around Lantorcho Rock, close north of the island. And far in the distance, mauve in the haze, Cape Bon; with its low, outlying point, it resembled a smaller Gibraltar . . . Cape Bon, the nearest African point of land to Sicily, only ninety miles distant. As the sun rose, the Mediterranean would become a sparkling blue, rendering the glassy calm surface deceptively serene . . . Hammer's back was stiffening.

'Bearing THAT: Cant fifty-two. The sky's stiff with aircraft.'

'Green one-six-five,' the lugubrious McVicker, the Outside ERA, sang out. Hammer flicked to low power and swung to the north. *Steadied* . . .

'Cripes!' He was grinning behind the eye-pieces. '*Start the attack*! Stand by all tubes. Down periscope.'

The executive command to attack now made John's stomach sink, unlike a few months previously. He *must* concentrate on his trim, must *not* dip his captain whatever else happened. 'More rise on the after-planes, Cox'n,' he ordered. He could picture the image etching into Hammer's brain: the screening destroyers creeping nearer, the white cross-trees of their masts swiftly mounting above the horizon, their bridges beginning to show; then the for'd guns and their foc'sles with creaming bow-waves at their stems and, with luck, a wisp of white horses if there was an off-shore breeze, the perfect sea for a periscope attack. The wide front of the convoy would be spreading across the horizon; the destroyers weaving, altering course imperceptibly, turning under continuous rudder, their angles-on-the-bow impossible to predict . . . and always moving closer.

'Target THAT: five-thousand-ton freighter, army tanks on deck. I'm ten degrees on her port bow.' Clapping shut the handles, Hammer stood back, while Tonks applied the settings on the Fruit Machine. Carbis was holding *Urgent* well: she was a trifle light for'd and he would have to flood boldly when the torpedoes left their tubes. A break-surface in front of this lot . . .

'Judging by her bow-wave, give her eighteen knots, Sub,' Hammer said. 'I'll try to get a range on my next look.' His face was grim.

'There're so many bloody aircraft about, might as well ignore 'em.' The captain was waiting, hands in pockets, for his next look. 'They're running us down fast, Number One. I'll need all the time I can get.' He turned to the helmsman: 'Port fifteen. Don't dip me, Number One. Don't speed up. Course for a hundred and twenty track?' He flicked his fingers. The thicker, search periscope hissed upwards. He jammed his face into the eye-pieces.

'That's better . . . *there*: a weaver, right ahead. Green and white cross-bars. Dazzle camouflage; can't tell her angle on the bow. Ah! Her angled bridge structure gives it away.' He was talking to himself: 'Going like hell. Another weaver, on the target's other bow. One, two . . . four, five aircraft overhead. Range . . . THAT. Down periscope.'

'Twelve degrees,' the Outside ERA read off.

'Course for a hundred and twenty track, sir, is 230°,' the sub announced crisply. 'Your DA, Red twelve.' The four mauve 'ready' indicator lights were flicking on above his head. 'All tubes ready.'

The attack was developing fast. Hammer went deep under the first destroyer, her propellers beating rhythmically as she passed overhead. Carbis brought her up swiftly, settled her at twenty-seven feet, only seconds before the DA came on.

'Put me on my DA. Stand by . . .'

Standing behind the crouching captain, with both hands the Outside ERA held the periscope firmly on the DA. 'Stand by,' Hammer repeated. 'She's a bit close . . .'

A sudden, crisp *clang!*, then another, rapped against *Urgent*'s hull.

'God!' Hawke whispered to himself. '*Break off the attack*.' He slammed shut the handles. 'GO DEEP! Flood Q. Group up. Full ahead together. Starboard twenty. Shut off from depth-charging. Keep her tail down, Number One . . . *Up periscope!*' and he took his final look before *Urgent* gathered way.

And as organized chaos reigned in the control room, Hammer shot out his comments in the short intervals when he could be heard. As he was about to fire, two huge water spouts had shot up beneath the target's bridge. Matt Fairfax, in *P50* on the other side, had found his mark. The ship had broken in two suddenly, the gigantic explosion bringing down an aircraft in flames across her derricks. The after-part of the ship was plunging stern-first into the depths; the life boats, which were hanging from her derricks even before the torpedoes were fired, were being dragged down with her.

'Water noises astern,' Snagge reported. 'Target breaking up.'

'Steady on 040°,' Hammer ordered. 'Group down. Stop port.'

Carbis stood astride, feeling the angle coming off her as Wescombe eased back on his after-planes. The bubble in the inclinometers slid for'd, settled in their fluorescent tubes at two degrees bows-up.

'One hundred and twenty feet, sir.'

'Silent routine.'

Urgent was creeping silently from the scene when Snagge glanced across from his corner: 'Submarine HE, Red one-one-o, sir. Target's breaking-up noises are fading, sir. Green, one-seven-o.'

Hawke was looking worried. He stood, rubbing the stubble on his chin, feet astride and stooping forward in that typical stance of his when concentrating. 'Investigate the submarine HE,' he ordered.

Snagge crouched even lower across his set and readjusted his earphones.

There followed the most heart-rending half-hour, while Snagge chanted his methodical reports of the three destroyers hunting *P50*. Carbis longed to rip the headset from the HSD's skull. *Contact.* Speeding-up. The run-in by one destroyer, while another conned the attacker over the firmly held contact. Then the *clang! clang!* – and the rumbling explosions, the crescendo mounting with each minute that passed. It was horrible, listening to the murder from down here at one hundred and twenty feet, creeping away undetected while the enemy concentrated on Matt, Lofty and their company. Then mercifully it stopped, the distant whispering of propeller beats dying away. If only, Carbis thought, we had no imaginations, we could bear it. To listen to their friends being blown to bits in three hundred feet of water was beyond bearing. By a few seconds only, *P50* had sealed her own fate when it could have been *Urgent* . . .

'Breaking-up noises, Red one-two-five.' Snagge's words were monotone. He was slowly removing his headset. When he turned to face his captain, his mouth opened but his voice broke. Tears were rolling down his grimy face. *P50*'s HSD was his best friend; they'd been boys in *Ganges* together. Snagge could listen no more to *P50* disintegrating under those enormous pressures: her bulkheads buckling; the compartments imploding, her hull squeezed and crushed as if in a giant's hand; the overwhelming, final deluge . . .

'God keep them.' Hammer's eyes were closed as he whispered the prayer all those around him in the control room shared. The time was already 1140. At noon, the escorts having steamed at speed towards

La Goulette, *Urgent* relaxed from silent routine, opened up from depth-charging and resumed her periscope patrol. After the subdued dinner hour, men went silently to their hammocks, each with his own thoughts.

At 1405, the tall, aesthetic Gawn, the PO Tel, appeared silently in the wardroom. He coughed discreetly. The sleeping form on the for'd settee stirred, opened his eyes and sat up.

'What is it, PO Tel?' the captain mumbled.

'Immediate, sir. One-time pad.'

John felt a hand shaking him and he tumbled from his bunk. Ten minutes later, Ross and he had de-ciphered the signal:

IMMEDIATE:

From Captain S10 to Urgent *(repeated to all submarines on patrol) Italian radio claim sinking P50 by destroyer attack.* Urgent *to withdraw forthwith to new patrol area limits of Marittimo and Cape St Vito.*

(The 'own-movements' followed, detailing the whereabouts of *S10*'s and *S8*'s submarines.)

Time of Origin: 011213

Hammer pushed the pink signal slip to the centre of the table. 'Can't say I'm sorry. It's a bit hot around here. Nothing but Heinkel Box-Cars at two hundred feet all day.' He waited for Carbis to precede him to the control room for his afternoon watch. 'Come and take a squint at the chart, Number One.' They moved to the chart table.

'We might as well go straight up the middle of the swept channel, John. It's as safe as wandering through the minefields on either side.' He traced the red-hatched minefield limits on either side of the 'main road' which Ross had etched on to the well-worn chart: The Tunis Run.

Down this corridor, the enemy were pouring their supplies in their desperate effort to save their Afrika Korps which, up to a few weeks ago, was ruling the roost: ships laden with stores, vehicles and ammunition; troopships, oilers. Overhead, the hundreds of lumbering Box-Cars, six-engined monsters. Back and forth through this corridor, protected on each side by minefields, streamed the convoys: southerly, loaded to the gunwales; northwards, in ballast. Forming a protective, physical screen, the Italian A/S escorts, destroyers and torpedo boats, maintained their continuous vigil, weaving and zigging, ready to pounce on every submarine contact. High overhead the Luftwaffe fighters patrolled, in control of the skies. Hammer was pricking off the distance: at ninety miles a day, *Urgent* should be round Marittimo by this time tomorrow.

'We've still got four torpedoes left, if we meet anything.' He smiled ruefully, glancing at his first lieutenant. 'Even though it's a mixed salvo.' Carbis realized what difficulties this posed for his captain. There was a desperate shortage of the modern Whitehead Mark VIIIs; and the Mark IVs, the First World War torpedoes, were being issued to make up the deficiency. Not only did the older weapon have a shorter range, but it could float at the end of its run like the old Mark VIs; embarrassing for the next boat taking over in the same billet. It was incredible that we had no silent torpedoes, such as the Germans' homing electric fish. Ours followed a straight line: the submarine had to be pointing along the calculated course down which the torpedoes ran, their tracks bubbling air to the surface. How much easier it would be, and how many fewer losses we would suffer, with trackless torpedoes in this mirror-like Med . . . Carbis crossed to the gauges and took over the watch from Tonks.

Urgent was steering north-east, down the centre of the enemy's swept channel. Carbis was crouching much of his time, to show as little periscope as possible. It was 1516 when, right astern, he sighted the first white cross-tree on a bearing of 222°. He lowered the stick, counted thirty, raised it again. Flicked to high power, found the bearing. The lens cleared and there, on the same bearing two tiny crosses showed, the first now larger – and the top of a funnel showing. His stomach dropped: 'Captain in the control room!' He handed over the periscope to the captain and took up his position by the ladder, while the hands scrambled to their diving stations.

'Five destroyers,' Hammer summarized, 'those bastards who were escorting *P50*'s merchant ship. That's them all right. Three *Navigatoris*.' He paused, taking a longer look. 'One has a single funnel and arrowhead camouflage, Sub. Could be an *Aviere* . . . Turn her up in *Jane's*.' He swung to port: 'And an old torpedo boat: two funnels; the break in her fo'c'sle is right for'd; and her bridge is like a box perched high.' The periscope swished down and he moved to the slender, after-attack periscope. 'I'll take the nearest, the *Aviere*.' He flicked his fingers. Crouching on all fours, he bounced up to the facepiece as it emerged from the well.

'What's her max speed, Sub? They're going like hell back to

Palermo.' He took another look and the stick slid downwards.

Ross was helping the sub flick through the pages of *Jane's Fighting Ships*. 'That's her,' Ross said. '*Audace*, sir. Thirty-one knots.'

And so the attack developed, Hammer firing four torpedoes at the *Aviere* before she began her next zig. The range was nine hundred yards and, as *Urgent* went deep, two hammer blows struck her pressure-hull.

'Group down, slow ahead port,' the captain ordered, beginning once again his evasive tactics. 'Shut off from depth-charging.' He glanced at Carbis.

'We've stirred up the hornets' nest, Number One. The First Eleven won't be amused.'

While *Urgent* began slipping away to the south-east towards the minefield, they heard the satisfactory but sobering noises of a ship disintegrating as she plunged to the depths. It was over a thousand feet deep here, and destroyer bulkheads were no tougher than a submarine's . . .

Tick-tick-tick . . . tick-tick-tick . . .

Before Snagge could make his report, Hammer said: 'Pass by telephone, fore and aft, "Silent routine". We're up against the pros again . . . and they'll be as wild as hell.'

'Thank God I've caught a trim,' Carbis whispered to himself, while the ache, like an iron-bar across his stomach, began throbbing again. 'I daren't run a pump: not this time.'

CHAPTER SEVENTEEN

'Straddle'

It was ten minutes to four by the fore-end's clock. Acting Petty Officer Vincent Bolder grabbed the phone himself when it buzzed on the bulkhead.

'Yes, sir. TI here. Dead quiet? Aye, aye, sir.' He carefully replaced the instrument into its holder.

'Here we go again,' he said to no-one in particular. 'Settle down, lads. Another long do, I reckon.'

'What I wouldn't give for a fag.' The moaner was, of course, Ordinary Seaman Brown, Bolder's mate. He lay on his back on the oily corticene, his arms beneath his dark greasy head. It seemed likely that the unpleasantness of the last patrol could start all over again. Fergie met Bolder's eyes: they'd tried to keep quiet about Brown's behaviour, and they were having no nonsense this time. The Old Man had taken a risk by giving him the chance to redeem his self-respect. But who'd have thought they'd be in for another dose of this lot?

'Keep your voices down,' Bolder murmured. 'Keep bloody quiet and don't move about. I want to get home to my family.'

He grinned sourly, but everyone else knew what he was at. They were watching Brown but, good-natured as ever, said nothing.

Tick-tick . . . tick-tick-tick

'Bugger them . . .!' Fergie, the three badgeman, was cursing half-aloud. 'They'll be mad as hell up top, losing one of their own.'

The asdic pulses were bouncing against *Urgent*'s steel hull and reverberating all about them. Then they heard the sound for which they were all listening: the beat of propellers, growing louder; steadily louder, louder . . . *now*, the beat increasing . . . *beat, beat, beat*. The whispering, a strange hissing and then the thunder as the bastard roared overhead.

'Stand by,' murmured the TI. 'Hold on.' Clutching the edge of the empty torpedo rack, he subsided to the deck. Less likely to damage your spine or your legs, if you were sitting on your arse; and, like the others, he glared upwards at the curved deckhead.

The gash buckets, hanging from the hammocks' hooks, jerked, swung, rattled against each other, like Egyptian belly-dancers, when the charges exploded. The first pattern was not close, but now for the second . . . and as the TI counted the seconds away, their world erupted in a cataclysmic roar. In the ensuing silence, while the boat trembled from the shock, cork began spattering down from the deckhead. This, the granulated cork to alleviate the condensation which was continually dripping during the winter, was a yard-stick by which to measure the proximity of depth-charges. A rain of cork: close enough. Granules and a few shattered light-bulbs, very close. A shower, all bulbs shattered and sudden darkness: too bloody close and time to request for reversion to General Service . . .

Brawdie was propping himself on one elbow and staring at Brown. 'How come, Frankie,' the gunlayer asked innocently, 'you didn't volunteer for this?'

The TI turned his face away. 'They're all right, this *Urgent*'s crew,' he mused, concealing his grin. 'Just like *P50*'s, I s'pose.' But it was this business of sitting, quite powerless, waiting for death which he found difficult. At least the Old Man had something to do . . .

Tick-tick . . . tick . . .

In the control room, as in the whole boat, all unnecessary lights were extinguished to save the precious amps and to keep down the temperature. What dim light there was came from the luminous gauges, the solitary light bulb above the helmsman's compass and the glowing dials of the Fruit Machine.

The pointers on the gauges showed eighty feet, a nice comfortable depth. They'd found the 'layer' at sixty-five feet on diving first thing this morning and there was a thousand feet under them. But the protective density blanket was proving disappointingly ineffective: the pinging of the enemy's first attack was passing straight through the layer which must have sunk much lower or vanished . . . but Carbis could hear it again, this infernal *ticking* sound when a destroyer gained contact. The pulses were like the faint noise between thumb and forefinger when you flicked them.

'Second destroyer in contact,' Snagge reported, 'bearing Green six-o.'

Hammer was already installed between the periscopes: 'Starboard ten. Steer one-two-o.' He was turning *Urgent* end-on to the transmitting destroyer on her starboard bow. And as she turned, the pulses passed ahead, diminished . . . vanished.

'Lost contact, sir,' the HSD said.

'Can you pick up the third one?'

'Haven't yet, sir.'

'Course one-two-o, sir,' the helmsman reported. *Urgent* was steering directly for the first hunter.

And so this game of cat-and-mouse went on. There can be only one loser, thought Carbis, and no-one is jocularly referring to 'The Heat' as once we did: those days are years behind us . . . but Snagge was cutting in:

'Red one-two-o. Destroyer's HE increasing.'

'They're good,' Hammer murmured. 'That must be Number Three.' If he turned towards the fresh threat, he would be presenting *Urgent*'s beam to the destroyer ahead.

'Bearing steady, sir. HE loud and increasing.'

The whisper of her propellers was turning into a rhythmic beat.

'Starboard fifteen.' Hammer was swinging her stern towards the attacker.

'Starboard fifteen, sir.' The helmsman's response was eager, but he moved his wheel slowly. Haste meant noise.

Snagge slid the earphones from his head:

'Transmission interval decreasing, sir.' The audible asdic pulses were swamping their ears in a staccato stream.

'Five hundred yards?' Hammer queried.

'A bit less now, sir.'

'Hold on, everyone . . .'

In seconds, the depth-charge pattern would be tumbling down through the depths to find *Urgent*. The destroyer's throwers would be firing at any minute; the depth-charges strapped to their stalks would leap in parabolas from each side of the quarterdeck. Simultaneously, the seaman on the racks would be yanking at his lever, and the first charge would roll over the destroyer's stern. Carbis had so often fired the patterns himself when hunting a contact in the Channel: he could recall vividly the calculated circular pattern, the charges set to varying depths, which was designed to destroy any submarine within that circle.

First, the hump on the surface of the sea when the first charge exploded; then more heaving hummocks of sea until, suddenly, the first spout of black, brown and yellow water leapt skywards. It was a sobering sight even from the upper deck of a surface ship.

Carbis took a final glance around the control room, checking, checking, always checking . . . then he heard the sound he was waiting for: the faint *slap-slap* of the thrower's charges as they hit the sea.

His knuckles were white where he waited, holding on to the ladder rungs. The Stoker PO put down the leather belt he was fashioning. He stood up, and braced his hands on the door clips. The Outside ERA was like a figure in a Grecian frieze: his lanky frame was bowed, motionless, where he bent towards the blowing panel, his crooked wheel-spanner poised in his hand. He, too, was peering upwards, waiting . . .

The young telegraphsman and phone operator, Ordinary Seaman Tarr, was sitting, his legs stretched and his back against the bulkhead; his eyes were like marbles as he stared upwards, waiting, waiting, his mouth hanging open. Wescombe, arms folded, sat motionless on his stool and staring at the gauge fifteen inches from his nose; Nick Fell, the second cox'n on the fore-planes, was chewing a matchstick; he was flicking it with his tongue from one corner of his mouth to the other in that infuriating habit of his, while tapping the rim of his wheel with his fingertips. His eyes, rolling in their sockets above his bushy, black beard, were following a cavorting pair of cockroaches above the lights. And Hammer, flexing his knees, stood feet astride between the periscopes, contempt for the enemy scored into his hard face.

Swish! swish! . . . swish! swish! . . . the beating of the propellers was audible, even above the thundering over the fore-ends. The rumble overhead passed its crescendo, began diminishing rapidly across the submarine's starboard quarter.

Then Carbis heard the *click-click*, several times. Very faint, but distinctive; the charges were close when you heard the detonators springing home. Any second now . . . Carbis was praying to his Maker, when the first charges (he could not count how many) blew their oceanic world apart, shattering the interminable tension.

The boat jerked, trembling along her length. The deck bucked upwards. The curved sides sprang inwards, recoiled outwards with a concertina effect which sucked the breath from his lungs as the explosions continued to burst around them, rocking her from stem to stern. Cork was showering upon his head, pattering on the deck. The tinkling of shattered glass; the instant darkness when all the light bulbs smashed. The faint glow of phosphorescence from the luminous paint on the depth gauges was giving the only light . . . and as Carbis fumbled for the codline lanyard holding the torch which had been jerked from his hand, he heard the first emergency lamp snicking on.

At the moment when they thought the attack was over, another pattern exploded about them, as close as the first. The sides sprang in-and-out again, but the emergency lighting failed to come on. Apart from the luminous dials and the small bulb glowing above the helmsman's compass, the control room was in darkness.

Carbis found himself on his knees and next to Hammer who was crawling on all fours. Impelled by the sudden bow-down angle, they were sliding for'd downhill across the deck. Bodies were piling up against the for'd bulkhead, when Hammer's voice cut through the pandemonium of gear breaking adrift.

'Torches!'

When Carbis flicked on his lamp, he saw his fingers were streaming blood where he'd clung to the lip of the attack-periscope well. The cox'n was hauling himself back towards his after-planes, his stool having been ripped adrift. His hands were clawing at the hydroplane wheel.

'After-planes jammed, sir, at *hard-a-dive*!'

Hammer grabbed Carbis' torch. 'I've got her, Number One.' He was wedged on the deck against the lip of the for'd periscope well. The torch beam swept to the planes: the bubble was at fifteen degrees bow-down: the depth, two hundred and ten feet.

'Tell the after-ends: "After-planes in hand",' Hawke snapped. Tarr hauled himself to the phone and tore it from its holder.

'Can't hold her, sir,' Carbis called out. 'Two-hundred and twenty-five feet.'

He knew, as they all did, there was nothing they could do now. Her safe diving-depth was two-fifty. He'd already shut off the main gauges to use the smaller, deep gauge. In seconds, it too would be against the stops.

'Telemotor pressure's off the board,' shouted McVicker who was trying to uncoil himself from the heap of bodies by the chart table. If the telemotor pressure line was fractured no machinery could work: *kaput* . . .

'Get it on, for God's sake,' Hammer said. 'Check the pump.'

Someone had switched on an emergency lamp. In the eerie gleam, the scene was one of utter confusion. Clawing bodies, trying to extricate themselves, struggling to regain their stations. McVicker, upon whom their only chance depended, was fighting uphill to the diving panel and the telemotor pump switch. Carbis was still clinging to the lip of the after-well and staring helplessly at the gauges. The angle was increasing with each second, the pointer moving inexorably around the dial: 240 . . . 250 . . . 280 . . . 300 feet . . . it was up against the stops. *Urgent* was plunging to her death.

Tarr's frightened voice yelled:

'After-planes in hand, sir. Water coming in through the stern glands.'

'Very good.' The voice was Hawke's, steady, controlled.

McVicker called out: 'Telemotor pump switch has been knocked off, sir!' He had reached the panel and was heaving himself upright. With a sweep of his arm, he lunged at the switch.

In that instant, seconds before catastrophe overwhelmed them, with everyone straining to catch the noise of the electric motor, came the barely audible, sweet sound of a motor whining into life; then gaining revs, it shrilled its message.

'I daren't blow main ballast,' Hammer called to Carbis, 'if you can gain control without. The bastards will only sight our bubbles when we vent.'

Carbis was mesmerized by the deep gauge: hard against the stop at 300 feet and the boat still going down. One faulty rivet now and she was gone. He thanked God for the Barrow builders, but . . .

'Planes are free,' the cox'n yelled in front of him. Wescombe was on one knee and turning his wheel anti-clockwise; the fore-planes were moving too. Then, imperceptibly, Carbis felt the angle coming off her.

'Group up,' Hammer called. 'Full-astern together.'

And as Tarr passed the command, his words were drowned by the shriek from the fore-ends phone. Tonks tore it from its holder. The sub's face was ashen when he turned towards his captain.

'Water coming in through the pump space, sir.' The pump space adjoined number one main battery compartment.

'All right, Number One,' Hammer said. '*Hold on.*'

And in that second, *Urgent*'s hull began trembling from the main motor's stern power. It was a race now: chlorine gas was a killer, the surest killer of them all should the bulkhead fail.

'May I pump, sir? I still can't hold her,' Carbis called out.

In spite of the gradual lessening of the bow-down angle, *Urgent* was leadenly heavy, so deep was she below her trimmed depth. The noise of the pumps would betray her presence, but there was nothing for it except for blowing main ballast: suicidal, with her hunters waiting hungrily on the surface.

Unnoticed at first, the lethal angle had eased, while *Urgent* pulled astern, away from those yawning depths. Men were struggling to their feet around him and John could see their grins as the light bulbs were replaced. Someone was sweeping up the broken glass and, while he wrestled with the trim, a semblance of order was being restored from the chaos. The pointer of the depth-gauge was slowly moving back: 290, 270, 255 . . .

'Shift to shallow gauges,' Carbis ordered and, as the planesmen leaned forwards to open the cocks, the pointers on the shallow dials twitched into life . . . 245 feet. The phones were howling again: the leaks were easing, fore and aft.

'Take over, First Lieutenant. Don't speed up.' Hammer pursed his lips. 'They won that round. The first pattern was over. I reckon that one was short, don't you?'

Carbis smiled: 'If they are gunnery types, the next should be a straddle.'

Hammer was not amused. 'They're so close, Number One,' he said. 'Even a gunnery officer couldn't miss.' The lights were repaired; the fuses replaced; and *Urgent* was settling on eighty feet. Hammer was leaning over the chart table with Ross when . . . God! *NO* . . . 'Destroyer in contact, sir. Green eight-o.'

There was no doubting Snagge's infuriating, monotone reports . . . *tick-tick* . . .

'Bugger them,' Hawke blurted. He took up his stance between the periscopes. 'Pass the word, fore and aft: *absolute* silence.'

Carbis glared at the gauges; at the clock which had stopped at 1533. He dared not face his captain, for naked fear was tugging deep inside: an 'over' and a 'short'; and now a 'straddle'? *Urgent* was cornered: one destroyer astern, poised to attack; and the other two, one on each bow, stopped, listening, pinging and directing. In whatever direction *Urgent* turned, one of her hunters was holding her in contact.

'Destroyer attacking, sir. Green eight-o.'

And so, once more, the agony began, but this time for the kill: in *Urgent*, everyone knew what they were in for. Numbed, men stared fixedly before them while obeying orders like automatons.

'Stop starboard. Starboard fifteen, half-ahead port.' Hammer gripped the periscope wire. His chin jutted; there was an aggressive-ness to the cast of his massive, rusty-haired head. He was cursing to himself as the pulses began once again to invade their world.

Snagge removed his phones.

'Five hundred yards?' Hawke asked. The HSD nodded. They knew it by heart. But hope was evaporating when the cacophony began to overwhelm them again. The destroyer was thundering above in a whirlpool of noise, her propellers beating, the swishing growing ever louder. Her stem must be cleaving the sea immediately above *Urgent* at this second; and then she'd be wheeling to clear the target for her next consort to take over.

John Carbis cared no more. He was resigned to die now. They all were, as they stared upwards, motionless. The destroyer's stern would be deep in the water, her wake boiling while she charged at 30 knots across *Urgent*. Now, *now* she'd be loosing her throwers, freeing the traps, the depth-charges flying through the air, tumbling from her stern.

The reverberating cacophony was terrifying. During those appall-ing moments, in their constricted world of the control room and in each isolated compartment – during those interminable seconds, John Carbis was feeling more closely bound to these men clustered around him than to any other human before in his life. Inhibitions caused by differences in age, rating or rank evaporated, were irrelevant: a gift beyond price, this comradeship could be forged only in the furnace of battle, conceived only through the sharing of fear. Alone, each man would be destroyed by terror; together, as comrades (a *fine* word this, in the fighting man's sense, John mused) we can face imminent extinction with dignity; this comradeship is binding each of us to the other in a common will: to hold on, not to fail each other . . . the thoughts flashed through his mind, as he watched his silent comrades. Dale, the Stoker PO, was fingering his rosary; Wescombe's lips were moving, his eyes closed. Well, we've tried, Carbis thought as he strained his ears to catch the *slap! slap!* of the depth-charges hitting the surface.

The racket above them . . . what was happening to it? It was drifting away to the port bow, the whispering beats of the propellers now identifiable again from the maelstrom. But the charges, the shattering explosions? Carbis slowly turned his head. Hammer was staring at him.

'I'll be . . .' he blurted, a grin splitting wide his face. 'Some poor sod's made a balls of his depth-charge drill,' he announced. 'Now's our chance.'

He turned to the telegraphsman: 'Slow ahead together.' Then, to the helmsman: 'Steer one-four-o.'

And as *Urgent* slipped away, Snagge reported a disorganized thrashing about on the surface. The destroyers were circling at high speed and the asdic pulses had lost contact. A bevy of depth-charge patterns exploded; none were close and each pattern further away. And with every minute which slipped past, *Urgent* gained distance. By 1630 she had escaped.

'Issue an extra rum ration with supper,' Hammer ordered his first lieutenant. 'Open up from depth-charging.' He turned to Ross: 'Course for Filfla, Pilot? Time to go home.'

CHAPTER EIGHTEEN

Farewell, Shrimp . . .

'Thank you, sair,' said Able Seaman Luigi Grima shyly, as he accepted the rusting tin of John's monthly ration of pusser's tobacco. 'There's no need, sair. Carmella was happy to take the letter.' He zipped up Carbis' canvas bag and, a smile on his cheery face, he left the cabin to serve the wardroom breakfast. John pulled on his sweater, picked up the bag from the bed and stepped out into the brittle sunlight of the fine, late January day of 1943. Passing the hallowed Byron name scratched into the sandstone outside his cabin, he strode along the upper balcony. A quick breakfast and he'd be off in *Boojum* before the weather changed.

The sunlight was streaming through the arches as he walked past the CO's cabins. He averted his eyes from the blank name-board which had once denoted Matt's cabin, walked past the quarters which, until nine days ago, had been Shrimp's. The great man was on his way to Beirut, having completed his long stint and built up the Tenth into the flotilla it now was. His relief, Captain George Phillips (*Ursula*'s captain off Norway three years ago), was settling in. A different character, a rock-like man of few words, he was already very much respected.

Carbis halted at the end of the balcony to watch *P43* sliding past, outward bound for patrol in the Gulf of Quabes. Anthony Daniell was her new captain and her pilot, John King, was a friend of Carbis'. A new team, they were proud of their gleaming, freshly-painted submarine which now boasted the name of *Unison*. John smiled to himself at the rumours of how every boat in the flotilla had been given a name.

Winston Churchill was affronted by the fact that our submarines, who were permanently in the front line, should only have been carrying numbers. He prodded the Admiralty to action, and now each boat bore a name.

The boats were finding it difficult to adjust, because even their numbered identities had developed personalities. There they were, their rust-splotched, blue outlines lying to their buoys: *P46*, Steve, was now *Unruffled*; *P44*, John Roxburgh, *United*; *P51*, Tubby Crawford, *Unseen*; *P37*, 'Otto' Stanley, *Unbending*; *P.42*, Alistair Mars, *Unbroken*; *P45*, Mossy Turner, *Unrivalled* – just returned from Hammamet, having enjoyed plenty of 'rough shooting' and sinking a couple of minesweepers; *P35*, Lynch Maydon, was now *Umbra*, but had already sailed for home and refit. Good old *Una* was in from Cape St Vito, with her new CO, J. D. Martin, Pat Norman having gone home for a thoroughly-earned rest. *Urgent* must have been the last boat without a number.

Urgent had entered harbour on 19 January of the new year, 1943, which had started so wretchedly for the submarines. She flew her Jolly Roger with its red bar for the sunken destroyer, but there had been no rejoicing. Matt and his company were gone, like so many others since our submarines had begun operating in the Mediterranean.

Shrimp must have stood here a while, before he left. What must have been his thoughts as he gazed for the last time at the boats he loved so much? To date, twenty-four British boats lost; plus the Free French *Narval* and the Greek *Triton*. Shrimp must have felt desperately sad at the latest losses – five in five weeks: *Utmost*, *Traveller*, *P222*, *P48* and *P311*. The two Ts, *Traveller* and the splendid Dick Cayley in *P311* had been lost during operations connected with the 'Chariot' attacks on shipping in Italian harbours. But the pain which Shrimp must have suffered was surely eased by the pride he felt in his men?

His Tenth had sent more than half-a-million tons of Rommel's shipping to the bottom; sunk five cruisers, eight destroyers and eight U-boats; seriously damaged a quarter-of-a-million tons of supply shipping, two battleships and four cruisers. The tanks of the Afrika Korps had ground to a halt in the sand. In his farewell letter to his men, which was pinned up on all the noticeboards in the Base, Shrimp had written: 'On arrival on the Mediterranean Station in December 1940, the Commander-in-Chief said to me, "Your object is to cut the enemy's sea communications between Europe and Tripoli." It was therefore particularly thrilling to me, when Tripoli fell to the Eighth Army before I left Malta.'

It was an emotional moment for everyone, submariner and Maltese staff alike, when that stocky figure with the greying hair and twinkling blue eyes left the Base for the last time. Captain Phillips and his officers were gathered at the rocky landing place. Shrimp, facing them from the dhaisa slowly plying its way across the narrow strip of water, was standing and returning their salute; all about him the cheers from the sailors and Base staff were echoing round the battlements of Marsamuscetto Harbour. He was taking passage to Alexandria in *Welshman*, the minelayer which had saved Malta with her 40-knot dashes from Gib.

All luck to the great man! He had loathed dispatching his friends into that hellish alley, demanding the impossible of them in the Tunis Run. But he had the satisfaction of knowing that, because of his men, the Germans were having the utmost difficulty in forcing their Italian allies to venture to sea . . . We'll miss him, John thought as he descended the steps: he's the one man in this blighted war I'd follow anywhere.

Through an arch he could see *Boojum* bobbing on her mooring. He'd better be off if he was to catch the wind and make St Paul's Bay on time. The caretakers in the officers' rest villa were expecting him for lunch. But first he'd pop in to see George if he was already in his office. He shoved open the Secretary's door.

'You're early, John,' his friend greeted him. '*Boojum*'s ready, though she's making a bit of water. I'm afraid she's strained a bit after lifting her.' George rose and they walked into the courtyard. 'Have a good rest in Oleander Villa. You've a couple of days, haven't you?'

'Sailing on the sixth,' John said. 'Hammer's coming back today but, thanks to Mr Warne, we've loaded torpedoes. We've fuelled and are all set for our next patrol. Thanks for getting the dinghy ready.'

'Forget it. Salaams to the caretaker. See you before you go on patrol.'

'I may get over to see the troops at Ghain Tuffieha,' John said. 'It's too cold for bathing from the rest camp, but the break will be doing them good.'

Breakfast was already underway in the wardroom. John saw that the weekly news-sheet was newly pinned on the notice board. The Mediterranean submarines had their tails up again. The Eighth Flotilla from Algiers had been busy: *Splendid*, *Seraph*, *Safari* and *Saracen* had all added to their score. But what of the Tenth, its successes, its losses?

Lakin in *Ursula*, having sunk a 4,000-ton German-manned ship, was rammed by a merchant ship during a moonlight surface attack north of Marittimo. Her standards and periscope were damaged but she got back to Algiers. 'Otto' Stanley in *Unbending*, after a cloak-and-dagger escapade off Tunisia, was involved in the 'Chariot' operation, as were Steve in *Unruffled* and Anthony Daniell in *Unison*; John Roxburgh in *United* had been busy off Marittimo, sinking the destroyer, *Bombardiere*. But lastly were the losses: *P50*; and the brief announcement that *P48*, Mike Faber, was also overdue. The Admiralty's announcements through the BBC were more loquacious. 'The Admiralty regrets to announce that HM Submarine . . . has not returned from patrol and must be presumed lost. Next of kin have been informed.' Those familiar, stark words said it all, covered neatly the slow or meteoric death of 34 officers and men – 60 in a *T*; 44 in an *S*.

John Carbis glanced at the letter rack: nothing for him, but there were gaps in the pigeon holes. He was becoming accustomed to ignoring in silence the empty chairs and places at table: this was how submariners dealt with Death. He sat down, unwilling to talk, and hurried through breakfast: pumpkin bread, bacon and pusser's marmalade. If he ever returned home, he'd never touch a pumpkin, baked beans or 'corned-dog' again for the remainder of his life. Pumpkin pie, pumpkin jam, pumpkin bread, pumpkin soup, pumpkin . . . ugh! Corned-beef slices, corned-beef 'cottage-pie'; corned-beef sandwiches, corned-beef mince . . . He pushed back his chair, grabbed his bag which he'd dumped at the doorway and hurried out into the sunlight.

As he strode along the mottled lower balcony, he could see *Boojum* waiting, bobbing at her mooring. There was a perfect breeze and he'd be away in ten minutes. He could be in St Paul's Bay in time for his clandestine rendezvous. His spirits lifted as he hauled the Canadian spruce dinghy towards him. It was a miserable commision he was undertaking, and one known only to himself: sad it might be and difficult, but he'd promised Lofty this. To see Anna again was compensation for all the wretchedness: his heart still quickened when he thought of her.

CHAPTER NINETEEN

Where Two Seas Meet

The breeze was steady from the south-west and, with George waving from the steps, *Boojum* skimmed out of Marsamuscetto Harbour. The peace-time destroyer anchorage of Sliema was empty except for *Speedy*, the minesweeper they knew so well. The dinghy listed to her gunwale when he hardened up outside the boom; then she was bowling along on her port tack, Dragut astern of her and Sliema Point coming up fast. She sailed better than he hoped, but she was making water through the garboard strakes. He would have to luff up every ten minutes to bale, so it was as well that Anna was crewing for him this afternoon: a good enough pretext, he thought, for inviting her.

The jumble of Sliema's battered houses was sliding past, and then he picked out Pembroke House above St Julian's. Tonio de Marco's home couldn't be far from Wingrave Tench's – there it was, with its angular red roof, not far from the shore. He ought to visit them again, but there'd been no time during this rest period. In his private moments, he had been absorbed as to how to accomplish this painful duty before sailing in four days' time for the next patrol. He'd promised Lofty, so that was that, even if *P50*'s loss was still officially secret. Anyway, inviting Anna for a sail was natural enough, though she'd not wanted her parents to know . . . But, hell, how *was* he to break the news? Direct . . . ? Or by inference, letting her guess the brutal facts?

Perhaps she was hardened by all the slaughter and would take it bravely? She was that sort. She'd probably lost members of her family: wasn't her father a psychological war casualty, locking himself up in his cellar for these three years? The casualty figures must also have left their mark: nearly 1,600 killed so far; 1,800 dreadfully wounded and maimed for life. She'd nursed *Illustrious'* wounded, too; had seen what war could do to those whom God had fashioned in His own image . . .

His wrist-watch showed 1030 and he hardened in the sheets until the sea was hissing along the washstrake. Dragonara Point slipped astern and then the orderly barracks of St George were peering down at him through their windows; the gun batteries still pointed their barrels skywards, ever on the alert, though daylight raids were becoming a rarity. How long it seemed since that awful night of the shelter disaster . . .

Thank the Lord it was a fine day, the sun sparkling across the troughs of the waves. The low-lying shoreline was opening up ahead of *Boojum* and curling away to Kaura Point, the eastern entrance to St Paul's Bay. Three-quarters of an hour later, the wind steady under Malta's leeshore, *Boojum* sailed into the bay; John, sailing close-hauled, began tacking towards the town. He hoped he would be as lucky for the return trip: dicey at this time of the year.

To starboard, St Paul's two islets guarded the western entrance. The smaller, at the seaward end, was joined to the larger by a low-lying strip of beach which, in these calm conditions, was sheltered from the wind. When it blew from the north or east, he could understand why the Apostle had termed the area between the mainland and the islets, 'the place where two seas meet'. It would be wild with broken water. A conspicuous, white statue of St Paul, facing out to sea and with his arms outstretched, stood up high on the larger island.

John tacked across to the north side of the bay, then went about. He could fetch the town in one reach. Oleander Villa was visible, tucked behind that fig tree which he remembered, though it was bare now of leaf. He checked the sheets and *Boojum* soared towards the little village of Bujebba. He'd make his number with the caretaker, dump his bag and ask them not to fuss about food. They'd like that.

She sighted the white splash of sail the moment the dinghy rounded Kaura Point. She had caught the early Sliema bus and though the driver had crossed himself before throwing in the gear, the rickety bus had dumped her safely here below the church in the town of St Paul's Bay. She was an hour earlier than she had expected; though she enjoyed these bus rides to visit her parents in Mdina, this morning's journey had dragged: the raucous chatter of her fellow Maltese, the squawking fowls and the continuous complaints of the three nanny-goats were not as amusing as they normally were.

Waiting for him here out of the wind, in this patch of winter sunlight, was delicious after the grim realities of the hospital ward. She leaned back against the gaily painted day-boat, with its black-and-white eye of Osiris, protection against the Evil One, glaring down at her from the jutting prow. The boat glistened in its fresh, green and yellow paint. The tang of tar; the smell of nets drying in the sun; the scents of the sea and of shrivelling seaweed were nostalgic delights of her childhood which she never ceased to savour. She sighed happily, nudging her shoulders against the warm planks of the boat.

She was glad of the extra red sweater she'd thrown on at the last moment, for it was always colder in a boat . . . ah, there was John's dinghy now, its sails fluttering, on the far side of the bay, off Gala Mistro, the cove below Selmun Palace. She could see him at the tiller, perched on the side as his tiny *Boojum* sped towards her and growing larger at every minute. She laughed aloud, utterly carefree, now that she had come to a decision after all the tortured thought whilst Lofty was on patrol.

She'd made her decision despite her parents' shocked disapproval. John had turned up at the right moment and she'd jumped at his invitation. Not only was he the only friend in whom she could confide, but he was the right person: he would understand – even approve, perhaps? She felt that quickening, guilty ache again below her heart, as the memories flooded back: those glorious moments they'd shared, high up above the upper bridge of the battleship, gazing down upon the ships of Grand Harbour. So long ago . . . three and a half years.

She reached for her canvas hold-all: she'd thrown a few rations together, in case John preferred a picnic. She'd even scrounged some chocolate, but she'd rather forget the cost: she knew she was being rooked in the market clustered around this beautiful church. Here, tradition proclaimed, St Paul had himself first worshipped the same Lord to whom the Maltese people were praying during these terrible, three long years . . . She rose to her feet to watch the dinghy disappearing behind the low headland which concealed the little village of Bujebba.

The memories were encompassing her again, those pure, delicious moments of childhood when with her brothers she'd swum from those rocks: another world, another existence, joyously carefree before the horrors of the Siege had driven her father mad. He'd been a hermit in his cellar since the bombing started. Mother, her darling Mum, was an old lady years before her time. And she felt again, as so often while she nursed those shattered, frightened men in Bighi's wards, a bitter hatred for the enemy, German and Italian alike. Lofty had told her that at twenty she should never feel hate, if her God was the same as his. She couldn't understand his logic with the job he had to do.

There! *Boojum* was curling round the headland. She ran down to the end of the stone jetty, loosened the crimson scarf about her head, letting her hair stream in the breeze. The dinghy was altering towards her and, minutes later, John was wrestling with the steering and lowering the big sail. Then under jib only, *Boojum* was waltzing into the restricted camber where bobbed the boats below her feet. She ran down the slope, the jib flapping noisily as she caught the painter he threw to her. Then the tall, lanky man was splashing through the water towards her.

She seems too frail to be handling *Boojum* as competently as this, John Carbis thought to himself while he tended the sheets. But she's a determined slip of a girl, he reflected as he stole another glance at the woman grappling with the tiller.

Anna was perched on the gunwale in her navy-blue trousers, her legs stretched to their limits, her toes forcing against the keel-box. A red scarf framed her pale face; and while she peered astern at the waves breaking along the shore, his eyes ran over the girl he'd once held in his arms. A finely chiselled face, with a small, straight nose; the wide-set eyes were darker than he remembered and sparkled with excitement. She was biting her lower lip while a half-smile curled at the corners of her wide, sensuous mouth. A glorious creature she was, slim but in perfect proportions, as fine as the porcelain figurines which stood on his parents' mantelpiece. Despite her tiny figure, her breasts jutted provocatively against the wool of her red sweater. She must be as tough as tempered steel to have survived all she's been through, he thought, as she turned and crouched down to get on with the baling.

'I'm so happy,' she sang out while the dinghy bucketed into the confused waters off the shoal. 'I've *always* longed to do this, John.'

Her eyes held his for an instant, lively, laughing with the fun of it all. 'It's unbelievable that St Paul was once here.' She jerked her head towards the statue: 'Nineteen hundred years,' she shouted, 'and he's still watching over us.'

They were already hardening up to round the outer islet; then, taking *Boojum* through the wind, they were on a broad reach and swooping towards the red and yellow cliff beneath the gigantic statue.

They exchanged places and, luffing up opposite the small isthmus frothing between the islets, they lowered the mainsail.

'This is where they must have let go the anchors,' he laughed while they bundled up the cotton sail. Anna was pointing to the right of the statue, to a strip of sand and shingle guarded by a large, conical rock. '*There*! Floating on the timbers,' she cried, 'they'd have been flung on to the little beach.' She turned to him, touched his arm. 'Do let's picnic there.'

Running in under jib, and lifting the keel, he grounded *Boojum* gently on the beach. They hauled her out of the water and, while Anna sorted out the rations, he collected driftwood for a fire. With the aid of the wrapping paper from the sandwiches, the sticks were soon spitting and crackling.

'Two bottles of "Blue",' John announced, while he extricated his monthly beer ration from his oilskin in *Boojum*'s bows. 'You don't know how you're privileged, Anna.'

She laid his black oilskin in the sun between the two rocks under the red seam in the cliff. He opened the bottles and, while washing his blackened hands, watched her spreading the sumptuous meal. She was so carefree and relaxed: how *could* he shatter her happiness? He'd wait until after they'd eaten and choose a suitable moment then to break his news. Perhaps, too, she would have stopped shivering from the cold discomfort caused by her wet trousers.

'Down the hatch!' Her teeth were chattering as she raised her bottle.

'Anything but that,' he chided. 'Cheers, Anna.' He could not meet those smiling eyes when she faced him. He felt so much tenderness, such love for her: yes, the craving was still there although he'd tried to quench it for so long . . . They munched their sandwiches, but he felt the tension while the shyness between them slowly dissolved. Though the sun was bright, there was little heat to it so, collecting more flotsam, he threw it on the embers until the fire was crackling again. He stood gazing down at her while she tidied up the picnic things. Then, lying back against the rock, she patted the oilskin alongside her.

'Lieutenant Carbis,' she teased. 'I do believe you're more scared of me than the enemy!' She swept off her headscarf and, shivering, hugged herself to keep warm. He joined her on the oilskin and stared seawards towards the cliffs on the mainland, where the gulls were squealing above the rocks.

'I'm glad you came, Anna,' he murmured. 'I didn't think you

would.' She was watching him with that half-amused look on her oval face.

'I wanted to see *you*.'

In the long silence, he heard the wavelets lapping the rocks and the skirling of the birds.

'Why me?' he asked, turning towards her.

She looked so serious, her dark brown eyes smouldering, intense.

'You're the *only* person,' she said softly. 'I can't tell anyone else yet.'

'You're not . . .' He found it difficult to put his doubts into words.

Her laugh was brutal: 'No. I'm not having a baby.' She whispered, touching his hand: 'I couldn't have made my decision, if I was.'

'It wouldn't be such a calamity,' he said, trying to be gentle. 'It happens even to the Maltese,' he bantered.

She was sitting up, facing him squarely. She was still trembling spasmodically from the cold of her clammy trousers. 'Look at me, John,' she insisted, taking his hand.

'I can't go through with it,' she said, her tiny jaw jutting. 'I'm breaking off the engagement; calling off the marriage.' She went on in a flat voice: 'I daren't tell my parents. But Lofty . . .' Her voice trailed to a whisper: 'When he comes in, tell him for me, *please* John.'

As he was steeling himself, she added: 'You're his friend; he'll take it from you. He will know, then, that I won't change my mind.'

He took her other hand, folded his around it. For a long moment he stared at her, recognized desperation flashing in her smouldering eyes. His heart went out to her.

'Anna, my dear. Listen to me . . .' But he couldn't go on. She was stiffening with antagonism. He stared into her resentful eyes, then rushed headlong to his heart-rending task:

'I've asked you to share today with me because I've got something to tell you, too.' A flash of doubt clouded her gaze. 'Anna,' he forced himself to continue, 'I shouldn't be telling you. It's still secret, you see.' She snatched her hands from him, pressed her fingertips to her lips.

'No,' she whispered. '*No*, John . . .' Her eyes were very round, staring fixedly at his.

'*P50*'s overdue, Anna.' He held her shoulders. 'Missing, presumed lost.'

She did not speak. The bushes on the cliff were whispering in the breeze above them; the gulls were wheeling and dipping, mewing above the rocks.

'But you *can* escape, can't you?' she asked. 'In your submarines.' She whispered: 'Prisoners of war?'

He shook his head. God! Why did he, John Carbis, have to inflict such pain?

'They're all dead,' he said, his words sounding brutal. 'We were next to them. Heard it all.' She flung herself into his arms and he whispered into her soft, black hair. 'There's no doubt, Anna, dear Anna. No doubt at all.'

The February sunlight was casting long shadows across the shingle and turning the turquoise water into the deepest blue. And as the sun began to dip below the main island, the birds began flapping in from the sea for the approaching night. He felt her taut little body trembling suddenly alongside his.

'You're cold,' he said. 'Put my sweater on.' Gently prising her thin arms from about him, he fetched his sweater which he'd left in *Boojum*. He handed it to her where she lay deep in thought. He began trying his hand at ducks and drakes.

'John,' she said. 'Come back to me.'

These were the first words she had spoken for more than an hour. She was sitting up, leaning against the rock, arms about her knees.

'Warmer now?' As he sat down beside her, he sensed her eyes upon him. She leaned sideways, her head against his chest.

'Put your arm around me.'

He felt her heart beating beneath his hand, as with the other, he stroked her hair. They sat in silence for he knew not how long. No hot tears, no uncontrolled crying now. Earlier her body had been wracked by spasms of dry sobbing. And when that had subsided she had curled into his body, taking comfort from his warmth. He'd waited for the shock to subside, let her talk when she wanted. She'd lain with her back to him, curled into him like a child, her eyes wide and staring towards the blue horizon where lay what remained of *P50*.

'Talk to me, John.' She wrapped his other arm around her.

'Can you bear it yet, the banal questioning?' he asked her gently. 'Why did you want to call off the marriage?' He tightened his arms momentarily. 'Don't tell me, if you'd rather not.'

Her thoughts were miles away. There was a long silence before she answered him.

'Not yet,' she said. Turning slowly, she regarded him squarely.

Lifting her hand and barely touching him, she traced the outline of his face with her fingertips. 'It's too soon . . . after Lofty. I'll tell you later.' She said softly: 'I've got to be back in Sliema tonight. I'm on duty at twelve tomorrow.'

'What about the buses?'

'None now. It's only a couple of hours' walk. It's what I planned.'

'What d'you mean?'

'I *had* to see *you*,' she said, stamping her foot. 'The rest could take care of itself. Anyway, I enjoy walking.'

'It's a lonely road after the blackout.' He felt she was being stupid, irresponsible. 'And there could be another raid tonight.'

'What d'you suggest, then?' She was appraising him, her eyes wide, challenging him. 'It's just as far to Mdina to my parents' home: I'd never get to the hospital on time.'

'I'll go with you, then. We can haul out *Boojum* at Oleander Villa.' He peered at her nurse's solid wrist-watch. 'If we push off now, I can have you at the de Marcos' by eight.' He began collecting together the impedimenta, rolling everything into his oilskin. 'I'll ask the caretaker not to wait up. They'll leave out some food, I'm sure. Anyway,' he added, 'I'll not be later than ten-thirty back at the villa.'

'Don't worry about supper,' Anna said. 'I'll find something.' She was smiling up at him. 'My Sir Galahad,' she said softly. With the sun now gone from their beach, they stowed the oilskin for'd in the dinghy, pushed off and hoisted the sails. It was calm between the island and the mainland.

'Look out for the rocks. We'll save a bit of time.'

It was fun rock-dodging and *Boojum* was soon through the narrow channel between the mainland and the island. When the dinghy reached open water, Anna, who was tending the fore-sheets, was gazing astern. As he steered for Bujebba, she nudged him with her elbow.

'Look.'

He glanced back at their island. The winter sun was dipping below the heights of the Victoria Lines: its last ray was piercing the night clouds like a searchlight beam, its flaming finger focused on that solitary statue standing high on the islet. The Apostle, his arms outstretched towards the Rome where he knew Death awaited him, was swamped in a golden light, transcending description.

John turned to retrieve his course. Anna was searching his face and tears were streaming down her cheeks.

CHAPTER TWENTY

Tomorrow, the Dreams

They had been on the road for over two hours, but Anna felt no tiredness as, her hand in his, they walked down the final stretch of road bordering the sea in St Julian's Bay. The stars had gradually emerged from the vast, indigo bowl above them; their reflections were sparkling like diamonds on the dark sea which stretched away into the blackness where crouched the enemy.

'There's Pembroke House,' he remarked and she had to force herself back to the moment.

'The Wingrave-Tenchs',' she said. ' "The Boss", Tonio calls him.' She tugged at John's hand, indicating the short-cut around the mounds of rubble.

'Hungry?'

'Famished,' he grinned. 'Always am.' He jerked his head towards the *cul-de-sac* leading to the de Marcos' house. 'Memories,' he said. 'I'll not forget my first visit here.'

He stood back, opening the gate for her. 'We'll let ourselves in through the kitchen,' she murmured while fumbling in her canvas bag for the key of the back door. He remained silent before her as she juggled with the lock.

'Give me a hand with the blackout,' she said. 'Then we can eat.' She started downstairs first, drawing the curtains and fixing the blackout screens. 'Peg's away this weekend in Gozo with her little Paul,' she explained hurriedly. She led the way upstairs and blacked-out Paul's bedroom, then that of the de Marcos.

'And Tonio?' John asked, holding up the large screen for her. She settled it in place, then moved to fix the last window, the one in her own bedroom. He was leaning against the doorway, watching her . . .

'He's in Dingli,' she said, too matter-of-fact. 'Taking part in an exercise with the army. He'll be back on Monday.' She spread wide her arms. 'All mine,' she said. 'Small, but it's home.' She took his hand and led him downstairs to the kitchen.

'That's better,' she said, flicking on the lights. 'Now for food.' She pointed to the crockery cupboard. 'Lay up while I fix supper.' She ballooned the cloth across the kitchen table.

'Baked beans,' she laughed. 'A treat for me. How about you?' She was watching him through lowered lids. 'Peg said I could use their bread ration.'

His half-smile was reassuring. 'It's a long time since our picnic. I could eat a horse,' he said.

'You probably will be, if you want soup.'

'Beans will be nice.' He shook his craggy head and they burst into laughter.

And so, sitting opposite him, she watched him eating. The conversation was one-sided, but her mood had changed as she prattled on, trying to draw him out. Was she shocking him? He wasn't shy, but seemed so cautious of his feelings . . .

'I've nothing to offer you to drink,' she apologized. 'You know how it is.' He reached for her hand across the table, covered it with his.

'Silly old thing. It's nice to be with you, that's all.' He looked so serious, as his thoughtful eyes held hers. His cheeks were sunken and there were hollows beneath his eyes – his pleasant, open face had a cadaverous look about it. He was glancing at his wrist-watch. 'Thanks,' he said. 'That was good.' He was folding the napkin she had given him.

'You don't have to go,' she said softly. 'Not yet.'

'It's six miles,' he said. 'A couple of hours' walk.'

She got up and held her hand out to him. 'I want to talk.' As she moved into the sitting room across the hall, she heard his chair scraping on the kitchen tiles. She switched on the table lamp and watched his lanky figure coming towards her.

'There's no coffee, John.' She stood, her hands clasped before her, embarrassed by his silence. Why *was* he making it so difficult?

'You said you'd tell me,' he said quietly. 'Can you now?'

'Why I'd decided to break off my engagement to Lofty?' Her heart was racing: if she couldn't tell him now . . .

He nodded. He was standing close, his eyes searching hers.

'Don't *you* know?' she whispered. He shook his head. 'Can't *you* guess?' She could hide her frustration no longer. 'I *love* you, John.'

She flung herself against him, encircled his body with her arms. 'Oh, John, John, I've tried to stop loving you since those very first days.' She pressed her head against his chest, poured out her heart to him, careless of what she said, the dam bursting. 'But I've known it inside me, so deep inside me, all this long, long time.'

His chin was rubbing the top of her head while he let her talk. She'd been overwhelmed by events. When they'd first met, his kisses and his passion had frightened her. Due to the de Marcos' erroneous first impression, her parents had bolstered Lofty's image, to the detriment of John's. She'd been so very young and incapable of resisting their pressure. And even when she'd agreed to go to England and become engaged to Lofty, she'd been unable to bury totally her deep longing for John. Could he imagine the force of Maltese tradition, the power of the family, the Church? At the last moment, only two days ago, and desperately alone, she made up her mind. But she *still* hadn't had the courage to tell her parents, with all the fuss of the wedding arrangements they were making. She felt his hands stroking her, rhythmically, up and down her back. When she ran out of words, he asked, murmuring into her dishevelled hair:

'I can't believe it. You *love* me? *Why*, Anna?'

'Oh, John . . . John,' she whispered, tightening her encircling arms. 'Does a woman ever know? Your gentleness and understanding, perhaps.'

He was pushing her from him, peering again into her eyes. 'You don't really know me.'

She shook her head. 'D'you remember the day you came to Mdina to see us? I didn't want you to meet Dad. It's hard on my mother, having to endure everyone's contempt.'

'But he's sick, Anna,' he said quietly. 'No normal man in his position hides himself away in a cellar for the duration.' He was hugging her against him, pressing her head against his chest. She could feel the pounding of his heart.

'You were kind to him,' she murmured. 'Few people are.'

'*That*'s why you love me?' His hands were stroking her, but differently now. 'Anna, Anna . . .'

'Yes?'

'I've never stopped loving you, Anna. Not since *Warspite*.'

'Why did you give up? Oh, John, *why*?'

'Lofty: your engagement changed everything. I tried to forget you.' Without another word, he tilted up her face and crushed his mouth on hers. When, aeons later, he held her apart from him, she looked up and whispered, 'D'you still have to go?'

He stood motionless, his brown eyes bright and fixed on hers.

'During the whole of our walk, I was hoping,' he said. 'But Lofty . . .'

She held her hand out to him. Her fingers hurt as he crushed them through his. He flicked out the light as she led him from the room towards the stairs.

'What time is it?'

He heard her whispered question, from somewhere far, far away; and as he tried to fathom where he was, he felt Anna's warmth beside him. The first aura of dawn was flooding the little room. Outside, he could hear the music of the waves across the rocks.

'What's it matter, beloved Anna?' he answered drowsily. 'Our lives lie ahead of us. We need to live every minute.'

'I'm a working girl, remember?' she whispered. 'Oh, John, we've so little time.' Her hair was tickling his nose. He turned her head, covered her mouth with his.

'You prickle,' she chided, propping herself on an elbow. He could feel the fingers of her free hand tracing his eyebrows, the length of his nose, his lips. He opened his eyes: her face was close to his, the fires dancing in her jet-black eyes. 'Darling, we've so little time . . .'

And as they abandoned themselves to their final loving, the certainty flashed through his mind that never again would they reach the summits of happiness they were giving each other during this cruelly short night. When at last she drew him to her breast, she said softly: 'Sleep, beloved. Just a little while.'

'Anna?' he murmured, feeling the soft roundness against his lips. 'Can you hear me?'

'Don't talk. I want this moment to last for ever.'

'Lofty,' he whispered. 'D'you feel guilty? It's so soon, isn't it?'

She answered vehemently. 'He's happy about us. I know it. We talked about it.' She added softly: 'He was such a . . . *joyous* person.' She paused, then went on: 'He often told me you were the only real friend he had. He'd be so glad, John.'

'Then we'll marry as soon as we can?' He tightened his arm around her. 'Sure?'

'Certain,' she said. 'Why wait, darling?'

'He loved you very much.' He turned from her and lay on his back, watching the patches of light rippling across the ceiling, the reflections of dawn caressing the glassy sea. She was nestling again into the crook of his arm. It had never been like this with Pam. He'd never known such peace. 'You talk in the present: that he *is* happy about us,' he said, turning on his side to face her. 'So you believe in a life hereafter, then?'

'I'm a Catholic, John.'

'I know. But do you *believe* that, if I'm killed, I'll *always* be there, waiting for you?' The touch of her fingers was delicious as they wandered over him. 'At the moment, *that*'s me,' he said, smiling at her in the half-light. 'But when I'm dead?'

'*You*'ll be waiting for me,' she whispered. 'I'll join you one day, whatever happens down here.'

'Raised from the dead?' He lay on his back, talking to himself. 'I think a lot about it. Depth-charging concentrates the mind.'

'Jesus' resurrection,' she asked. 'You accept that?'

'Of course; that's what makes a Christian.'

She went on, choosing her words: 'Then you must believe, if they kill your body, that you'll go on existing in a different form, as He promised us.' She whispered, 'Oh John . . . It's wonderful, isn't it, to be sharing this?'

'We're not the only ones, Anna. If you got inside all of us in *Urgent*, I'll bet that each one of us, in his own fashion, admits the same.' He paused, realized that instead of laughing at him, she was waiting for him to go on. 'I get fed up with cynics. Accept things like a trusting child: that's what He asked, wasn't it?'

'That's what He wants.' She kissed his cheek.

'When we're being hunted, I pray, oh Anna, I pray so hard. I want to live. Then I think about the German and Wop Christian praying too: either he or I has to die.' He turned again on his side to face her: 'It's too complicated, isn't it?'

' "Thy will be done",' she replied softly. 'That's all you need ask, John.' She kissed him again, then added: 'Our St Paul on that island: he should know. You remember, he wrote to the people of Corinth telling them that God works only for good, not evil.'

'Paul wrote that?' he queried. He'd never been much of a bible reader and he'd never talked like this to anyone before. 'That's a comfort, then.' He stroked her cheek with the side of his finger. 'You know, Anna, the greatest strength Britain has is its faith. Our national days of prayer really mean something.'

'Look at us in Malta,' she said. 'It's only our religion which has held us together. We all know that.' She added: 'And in England, too.'

'If we ever win this damned war, Anna, things'll never be the same. We'll have had a bellyful. The cynics'll have a field day.'

'The men and women who fought it will never change.'

'And when we're gone?'

She remained silent for a long time. 'Our children. It depends. We may be too engrossed in our puny problems to bother bringing them up properly.'

'Why should God bother about a nation which doesn't bother about Him? It's illogical.'

Her smile was like an indulgent mother's for her son:

'You're too simplistic, John. How can we, as you said, *begin* to understand? If there's just one *real* Christian in a nation, isn't that important?'

'No, not if you think of a nation as representing its people.'

'Like bees: with a corporate will?'

'All this flag-waving,' he continued bitterly. 'When this bloody lot's over, I'd burn them all. The world's too small for nationalism: look where it's got us.'

She was chuckling to herself. 'You ought to be a politician.'

'God forbid!'

She turned to him and, placing her hands about his head, pulled him towards her.

'Kiss me,' she whispered. 'I'll be on the battlements waving to you when you sail on Wednesday. Remember, darling, you'll never be alone again.'

'Be there, too,' he told her, pressing her close, 'when we return with our Jolly Roger flying.'

'John, oh my darling . . .' She was clinging to him in a final frenzy of loving; kissing, caressing, hugging him to her jewel of a body. The fire of her Latin blood set aflame his own, until together they found their heaven. He gazed down at her where she lay, utterly spent and at peace, a half-smile at the corners of her mouth, and slid from her bed. Picking up his things, he gently closed the door behind him, tip-toed down the stairs. He dressed in the kitchen, then silently left the house.

The sonorous ringing of the Angelus bell was floating up from St Julian's church as he walked down Grenfell Street. The wavelets were lapping the beach; from somewhere behind him the clapping of house-shutters being opened was welcoming the new day.

The clean smell of damp, musty road rose to his nostrils and his heart lifted. Over and over again he muttered to himself the words she had spoken to him after he'd reminded her: 'You'll never know how long I've got.'

'I'll always be there,' she'd said fiercely, 'waiting for you. God can't let it happen twice to me, can He?' She'd added softly: ' "But His will be done." '

And with her words singing, singing, singing in his heart, he turned his back on the brightening horizon. Ahead of him the dark clouds of night were retreating westwards; he set his face towards them and strode down the road. He should just make breakfast at Oleander Villa if he hurried.

CHAPTER TWENTY-ONE

The Slings and Arrows . . .

Urgent's captain was bent over the chart table, his officers around him. 'Any questions?' He straightened his back. Ross asked: 'If the vis. is bad, sir, and the officer of the watch on the bridge sights a U-boat, may he fire if you can't see it?'

'Fire on sight. All our submarines are through to Cape St Vito by now, so there's no chance of faulty identification.' He placed his finger on Marittimo. 'All U-boats are Africa-bound, anyway. They're just as likely to be rounding Marittimo at the same time as us. I repeat, the E-boats are *the* menace. They'll be listening off the Egadi Islands.' He nodded at his first lieutenant: 'Piccadilly's been nice and quiet, anyway. Stand by to surface, Number One. I'll get dressed,' and he left them for the wardroom.

'Shift to night lighting. Diving stations,' Carbis ordered.

So once again, they were poised to reach their billet. *Urgent* had sailed two days ago, bound for a train-wrecking patrol in Castellmare Bay, on the north coast of Sicily. Makes a change, thought Carbis, while he surveyed the scene which was now part of his life.

Men were scurrying to their stations. The Ursula suits rustled in the quietness as the officer of the watch, young Tonks, the lookouts and the signalman donned them awkwardly in the passage outside the wardroom. Down dropped the canvas skirt from the lower conning tower hatch; the final night bulb was fitted, the eerie, red glow shining on the greasy faces around him. The lower hatch clunked open and, slipping their binocular straps around their necks, the bridge team disappeared into the darkness of the tower. Hammer, navy blue polo-necked sweater enveloping his khaki shirt, binoculars dangling on his chest, dark spectacles on his nose, sat waiting on the wardroom settee.

'No HE, sir. All-round sweep completed,' the HSD reported.

Carbis stuck his head around the protective grille of the gyro panel:

'Ready to surface, sir. No HE.' Hammer rose and strolled into the control room. 'Periscope depth.'

Taking her up from deep, Carbis settled her at twenty-eight feet.

'Up periscope.' Hammer swung round swiftly, though in the darkness he could expect to see little. 'Damned bright moon,' he cursed.

'Surface.' The handles snapped shut and the gleaming tube slid downwards into its well.

'Blow One . . . blow Two,' Carbis ordered while Hammer climbed into the tower. Then *Urgent* was wallowing on the surface and rolling gently in the swell, while the bridge team searched the horizon. Down below the helmsman caught in his bucket the water gushing from the voice-pipe.

'Start the generators. Half ahead together,' the captain's muffled voice called. 'Start the zig-zag; mean course 330°.'

He's keeping outside the 100-fathom line then, thought Carbis: giving Marittimo a wide berth. *Urgent* should be rounding the island at 0200: so the alteration eastward would occur during Carbis' watch, the 0100–0300. He'd get in a good sleep first for, with this moon, they were bound to be put down by the lurking E-boats. The diesels roared into life; the fresh, keen air swept past him. He could sense the hands watching him as they extracted their 'ticklers', itching to light up their 'roll-me-owns'.

Hammer was keeping her trimmed right down, with minimum buoyancy: no risks tonight. *Urgent* was showing little more than her conning tower: up the path of this full moon even her tower would be standing up like a block of flats . . . 'Carry on smoking,' Carbis said, extracting his pouch and pipe from his pocket.

Matches flared in the red half-light, as Carbis watched Mott, the LTO, moving for'd with his hydrometer to record his battery readings. Ewan Davies, the leading stoker, was rolling aft, his stout figure bending double when he knelt to dip the tanks . . . it was re-assuring to watch the methodical ritual beginning another night. He'd remain here for a bit, waiting for things to settle down: this corner was the most hazardous of all to traverse on the surface, but in order to be sure of the charge, there was no option . . .

The small submarine surged ahead, zig-zagging and making-good eight knots; trimmed right down and almost invisible but with the roaring of her diesels drowning everything, she could dive in sixteen seconds. To starboard, the land mass of the western tip of Sicily loomed darkly against the luminous night sky, the sheer mountains providing a menacing backdrop. On the bridge, they would be strung-up taut, searching, searching: they *had* to sight the enemy first.

In the moonlight and with no wind, the surface would be like a silvery mirror, the pin-points of the reflected stars sparkling like jewels, mingling with the phosphorescence. The undulating swell would be scythed by the willowy lines of *Urgent*'s wake etching her tell-tale presence into the mercurial surface: an indelible clue for the waiting E-boats. In a few hours, the rocky chain of islets would rear slowly from the depths like turrets of Wagnerian castles. It was deep, very deep here and no place to lose control if savaged. And up there, ahead . . . Marittimo. Carbis doused his pipe; he turned towards the wardroom and made for his bunk.

Not a breath of wind shivered the glassy surface when John Carbis took over his watch from Tonks at one o'clock. The hand-over was carried out in undertones: the captain was dozing in his camp chair at the after-end of the bridge. 'Mind the eels don't bite,' Tonks concluded as he made for the upper lid. 'See you at breakfast.' Carbis started his all-round sweep, working from the port quarter and up the port side. The charge was 'floating', the diesels rumbling down below, the exhausts coughing in the water on each quarter.

The full moon was veiled by a strata of high cirrus now spreading completely over the night sky. The effect was strange: a semi-daylight, a haziness stretching round the whole horizon. It was impossible through glasses to distinguish sea from sky; and his heart missed a beat when on the starboard beam the sombre outline of Marittimo cut into his field of vision. Its Monte Falcone, over two thousand feet high, brooded darkly, where the hump of the whale-back should be, a silhouette indelibly etched into their minds now . . . and, a couple of smudges further down the starboard side, the islets of Levanzo and Favignana. There, in that haze, was the dangerous sector, where the E-boats lurked, listening on their hydrophones . . . the visibility *was* shutting down, a ghostly mist shivering along that part of the horizon. If it deteriorated further he'd shake Hammer.

He shifted his search to the port side . . . and his heart leaped into his mouth: several lines of phosphorescence were streaking across the steely surface. Tonks' damned eels *were* realistic: they could have been torpedo tracks, as they wove steadily up the port side. And then he recognized that jolt inside him which he had experienced thrice in the English Channel, that alarm bell ringing, the intuitive warning that something was wrong . . .

'Captain, sir,' he murmured as he leaned above the sleeping captain. 'Captain, sir: visibility is shutting down.'

Grunting, Hammer joined him at the bridge rail. The haze was like a cloak now, Marittimo barely visible as it slid gradually down the starboard side.

'Don't like it,' Hammer said. 'Stop the generators.'

Carbis passed the order down the voice-pipe. The diesels died; then there was only the *swish!* of the sea sluicing along the pressure-hull to break the stillness. 'That's better,' Hammer said. 'We shouldn't be so easy to pick up now.' He cocked his head to listen. 'We should hear them first.' The roar of an E-boat's engines starting up was something they could distinguish anywhere . . .

'All right, Number One?'

'I had twitch just now, sir,' Carbis murmured, his eyes aching as he continued peering down the starboard quarter. 'Those electric eels . . .'

Hammer grunted. He was staring ahead into the haze. 'I'll be glad to put bloody Marittimo behind us. Is the box right up?'

'Fully charged, sir.'

'Half-an-hour, then, grouped up. Then we should be clear of the patrols.'

'Vis. is very low on the starboard quarter, sir. Quarter of a mile, max . . .'

Hammer was muttering to himself as he started searching to port. 'Keep your eyes skinned, lookouts,' he reminded the hunched figures on either side. Carbis shifted his body to begin yet another sweep up the starboard quarter. The breeze from *Urgent*'s own way soughed past his ears; the sea hissed along the waterline. Like mercury was the sea tonight, plastic and volatile. He shifted the weight to his other foot and began to clean the lenses of his binoculars. He crouched again, staring, staring into the mercurial haze . . . Damn them! more of those phosphorescent eel tracks, off to starboard, just abaft the beam. He followed them, two seeming broader than the others . . . but as straight as ramrods. Then a third, identically the same . . . He stretched out his hand and shouted:

'Torpedoes, Green nine-o!' Automatically he jumped for the voice-pipe: 'Hard-a-port!' Hammer sprang to his side: *'Dive! Dive!*

Dive!' His hand closed around the klaxon 'push'.

While down below the klaxon blared throughout the boat, John Carbis stood momentarily transfixed by the tracks of bubbles speeding directly towards *Urgent*. It seemed an eternity before the submarine started to swing, the bubbles now only two hundred yards away . . . and the torpedoes must be *ahead* of those tracks. The jumping wire was beginning to crawl across the invisible horizon, but wretchedly slowly . . . 'God! Won't you *ever* move?' he whispered to himself as he sprang for the hatch. Faster now, her stern was starting to comb the tracks . . . the hideous bubbles were upon them, the first track passing ridiculously slowly up the starboard side; then the next . . . The sea was hissing and splashing around the bridge as he jumped for the dark hole, the lookouts already gone; Hammer, still at the voice-pipe, was leaning over the rail and conning. 'Midships, *meet her* . . . Steady.'

As Carbis dropped down the hatch, Hammer jumped after him.

'First clip on!'

In the darkness, in that awful second as the boat plunged into the depths, they heard the unmistakable whine and clatter of torpedoes growing louder at each second.

'Shut off from depth-charging,' Hammer yelled downwards. *'Go deep!'*

As Carbis fell through the lower hatch, tumbled out through the skirt, the roaring of torpedo propellers was all around them. He slid to his station between the gauges, took charge of the trim. Then the crescendo of the main motors flooded their world as, with a vicious bow-down angle, *Urgent* plunged to one hundred and twenty feet.

'Blow Q!'

The roar of the venting drowned even the racket of the torpedoes; Snagge's mouth was opening and shutting while he tried to make himself heard. She was already at sixty feet, but still no annihilating cataclysm.

'HE closing, Red one-four-o,' the HSD finally managed to report. 'Fast running diesels.'

'Shut main ballast Kingstons,' Carbis ordered. 'Pump on O.'

The noise of the attacking E-boat was all about them. 'Group *down*, stop port,' Hammer commanded. 'Open main vents.'

Thunk! thunk! The vents opened above them to release the trapped air. Bulkhead doors banged shut as the drumming of the E-boat raced up their port side.

'Hold tight!' Hammer shouted.

Waiting was the difficult bit for all of them now. Snagge slid off his ear-phones, men gripped the nearest hand-hold. No explosion yet, nothing save the chattering and tinkling of the E-boat flashing overhead. Then . . . two *clangs*! against the hull, well clear of their port side.

'Port ten,' Hammer said. 'I'll go right round and give them the slip.' Ross was pricking off his distances on the chart.

'Another hour at slow one, sir, and we can turn up around Marittimo.'

Snagge reported another boat joining in the hunt; but, showering charges over a wide area, the attackers were gradually slipping astern.

'They'll be whistling up the First Eleven,' Hammer said. The jarring raps against the hull grew fainter and an hour later *Urgent* surfaced, two miles north-west of the detested island. By the end of this day, the Trapani boys willing, she should be in her billet and entering Castellmare Bay.

Gunlayer Banger Brawdie was in his galley, heating up his hot plates for breakfast. 'It'll make a change, Pat,' he told O'Brien, 'to be firing "Bertha" again.'

'Down periscope.' John Carbis stood back, then crossed to the chart table to check the night orders. The last half-hour of his watch was drawing to its close: these past three days since the Marittimo incident had been boring in the extreme. The captain's night orders were precise: *Urgent* was not to attack any shipping until her train-wrecking operation was completed. She'd been patrolling up and down Castellmare Bay for two days, a mile off-shore; they'd used only the attack periscope and the time-table was now accurate: tonight's 2123 Palermo–Trapani express was *Urgent*'s intended victim: in under two hours' time. He returned to the periscope for the routine, swift look.

The viaduct showed prominently, light grey and slender, where it spanned the deep chasm. Its arches supported the railway line high across the road from Terrasini to Trappeto and ran within a hundred yards of the coast which plunged vertically into the sea. With a hundred feet of water running right up to the beach, the spot was ideal for *Urgent*'s gun attack.

Brawdie had been sharing the periscope with the captain during the afternoon and could pick out his point of aim with his eyes shut.

Urgent's battery was well up and, after the action, the submarine would retire from the bay to the deep field to surface and recharge. Carbis continued his routine checking around the horizon.

There was Cape Rama with its tower, the rocky coast behind it plunging into the sea, as did most of this coast as far as Cape St Vito. To the west, the sun was hanging like a crimson orb above the horizon; nothing in sight except the patrolling Cant which had been bumbling up and down all day. There was evidently some A/s activity, because Snagge had picked up the HE of a destroyer and an E-boat earlier this afternoon: routine during the past two days, and probably caused by *Urgent*'s near-miss off Marittimo. And there, to the south, the town of Balestrate was perched on its rocky cliffs, the square belfry conveniently placed for Ross's fixes.

'Down periscope.' Carbis turned to find Hammer standing beside him.

'Well, John, I'll bottom her: no point in hanging about now that we're all set.' He glanced through the periscope, then slammed the handles shut with finality. 'Take her down on the watch as we did yesterday. Nice and sandy.' He stood back: 'Okay. Bottom her and shut Kingstons.'

While Carbis planed *Urgent* down, Hammer continued: 'Diving stations at nine o'clock. Issue an extra tot with supper.'

John Carbis remained in the control room while the rest of the officers tackled O'Brien's supper. Brawdie had other matters on his mind than cooking, while he supervised the shells being stacked along the passage-way and heaped in the corner of the control room. The gunlayer had, for two days, been waiting for this moment.

Urgent lay comfortably on the bottom: there was no swell in this unusually calm weather, in spite of Castellmare Bay being open to the northerlies. Carbis sat himself down on the captain's chair and, with the five others, waited for the time to pass. It was this tension before action which tugged worst at the nerves . . . but tonight he was feeling a new emotion, a serenity he had never before known.

During this past, hectic week, whenever he could find a quiet moment to himself, the image of Anna focused in his mind. Time and again he relived those eighteen hours which they'd shared. Her pale, oval face drifted before him, her red lips parted in invitation, her eyes shining with excitement and happiness. And that night, that most glorious, golden moment of his life . . . he relived each second, savouring every detail. And her last words to him – 'I'll always be waiting for you' – were like the gleam from a lighthouse on a dark night. Perhaps they *could* marry soon, because there *were* signs that the tide was turning.

Only last week, four days before sailing, the Russians had finally flung the Germans from Stalingrad. The Eighth Army was chasing Rommel back to the Mareth line in Tunisia; and our first supply ship had entered Tripoli which the Inshore Squadron had finally opened up. The RAF's Wellington torpedo bombers, Beauforts and Beaufighters were creating havoc with the Axis convoys, many attacks being co-ordinated with boats from the Tenth. We were averaging the loss of one submarine with each week that passed, a heavy toll: to compensate, last week the Tenth had sunk sixteen ships, totalling 19,000 tons – and *Unseen* had just sent a 1,500-ton ship to the bottom: Tubby Crawford and his men were off again soon for Calabria.

Things *were* improving – and he supposed, too, that he was feeling happier within himself because of this new-found respect which he felt for his captain: Hawke was a superb captain and at last first lieutenant and CO were sharing an essential bond of trust and affection. It was good, very good . . . another week to go and, after a few days on the St Vito billet, they'd be homeward bound . . . his heart leapt with that ache he'd never really known before. To be loved by Anna: God, he was lucky! He glanced towards the clock: five minutes to diving stations. He folded up the camp stool and crossed to the wardroom where his captain was waiting for him.

'2025, sir,' he reported. 'All-round sweep completed. No HE.'

'Ready, Banger?'

Brawdie grinned up at the cox'n. 'Sure, Swain. Single ticket only for the Trapani Express tonight.' Wescombe picked his way past the 3-inch ammunition stacked neatly down the length of the passage-way, while the gunlayer continued to count the rounds they'd got up from the magazine. Twenty-four brass cylinders with their grey HE shells and impact fuses . . . he patted the last one affectionately. He checked that his crew were ready in their dark sweaters, then threaded his way aft to the control room. The Old Man was leaning over the chart table and Jimmy was talking to the subbie, Brawdie's new gunnery officer.

'Gun's crew ready, sir,' he reported to Tonks. 'Twenty-four rounds ranged along the passage-way.'

The captain turned: 'Good luck, Guns,' he said quietly. 'It's your night, this time.'

'Thanks, sir.' He grinned in embarrassment while the others made way for him under the tower.

'Diving stations,' the Old Man ordered. 'Open the lower lid; gun's crew in the tower.'

Brawdie followed 'Bunts' Kipps, the signalman, into the clammy darkness, then stood aside above the lower hatch to allow the captain space on the upper ladder. Through the hatch he listened to the methodical drill being carried on as Jimmy unstuck *Urgent* from the sea-bed. He felt her taking on a bow-up angle and then he knew that at last his moment was imminent. This was a controlled surfacing, not a 'gun-action' affair when *Urgent* would leap to the top. She was too close to the beach and needed to break surface silently above where she'd bottomed . . . He could hear the captain climbing up, so it must be 2115.

Eight minutes to go before the Palermo–Trapani express, bulging with German troops for Rommel, emerged from the tunnel. The Old Man and Ross had worked it out to the last second . . . and now Hawke was above him on the ladder and holding on to Bunts' ankles. Banger climbed up the rungs until his chin was level with Hawke's calves; below him, he felt the others pressing behind him, Swinley, the trainer, Fergie, the loader, and Stoker Greg Gooch, the new range-setter. Close on their heels and waiting on the control-room ladder would be Tonks.

'Surface!' The skipper's voice hailed downwards in the darkness. 'Blow One and Two main ballast.'

The air was screaming along the lines. He felt the angle steepening. Then Jimmy blew his whistle down below.

'Open up!' the skipper called out. Bunts threw the clips and the air whooshed past his ears. Banger followed the scrambling bodies through the upper lid and then he was vaulting over the starboard bridge rail. Down the rungs, the slippery deck still awash along the toe-rail to the gun's guard rails. Slick was the drill: in no time 'Bertha' was free and the ammo was clattering down the chutes.

'Not so much bloody noise,' Hawke whispered hoarsely from above.

Brawdie could see it clearly, the dark hole in the mountainside which was the exit of the tunnel, the span of stone wall leading on to the beginning of the viaduct. He wound down his layer's handwheel until the cross-wire of his sight was centred on the tunnel exit. 'Good-o, Swin,' he muttered across the breech to his trainer. 'All set?'

'Trainer on,' Swinley murmured. The gunlayer called up hoarsely to the gunnery officer above him: 'Gun's crew ready, sir. On target.'

'Two minutes to go. Load,' Tonks ordered. Fergie rammed home the first round; the breech slammed shut. We've got it just right, Brawdie mused happily, the moon's still behind the mountains; *Urgent's* in the shadow and trimmed right down. All he could hear was the sea swirling softly along the after-part of the fore-casing to drench their feet . . . The gentle swishing of the swell lapping the beach, two hundred yards off . . .

'Stand by to open fire,' Tonks muttered from the bridge . . . then Brawdie saw the faint orange glow growing brighter in the black orifice of the tunnel. 'Remember, Swin,' he whispered hoarsely across to the trainer, 'aim just ahead of the engine; ease back when the carriages are on the viaduct.'

'Roger.'

Brawdie's heart was pounding, pounding; he wet his lower lip with his tongue. He could hear the express' whistle tooting louder, louder and then there was the gob of steam and smoke billowing from the tunnel . . .

'*Open fire! Local control* . . .' Tonks shouted.

There was the cab of the engine, bang on his cross-wire.

'Trainer ON . . .'

He squeezed his firing trigger. The gun crashed. The barrel recoiled, slid forwards: Fergie slammed in the next round. Nothing yet . . . *nothing* . . . then, an orange flash on the crown of the parapet, yards ahead of the engine. He heard its whistle wailing.

'*Left* ONE!' he yelled. Gooch applied the correction.

The trainer wrenched at his wheel and then Banger's sight centred again on the orange glow from the cab: it looked like a Hornby train, with its external pipes curling all over its boiler. As he squeezed the trigger again, he heard the squeal of brakes, saw the sparks on the steel rails. The *crash!* of his gun again; the recoil; and then he saw the second round bursting a yard below the parapet. The engine and its string of carriages were rumbling on the viaduct now, pounding along, perched like a toy, hundreds of feet above the gorge. '*UP one* . . .' Gooch wound one unit of correction on his dial.

'*Trainer ON.*'

Crash! He fired again. A brilliant flash on the top edge of the boiler.

'*Rapid fire!*' from Tonks.

The rounds were ramming home fast, faster . . . and as he squeezed his trigger, time and time again he began to lose sight of his spotting. The express was half-way across. *Crash!* Then *crash!* again . . . the shells spluttering like sparklers where they found their marks, first on the steam-smothered engine, then working slowly along the carriages. The engine was slowing, halting . . . The bursts were now missing ahead.

'*Left TWO . . .*'

The next round burst squarely on the cab. Flames were licking all over the engine. Then, like a Western film, it toppled slowly, so slowly, over the far side of the viaduct. He heard a cheer from the bridge behind him, but he was too shocked by the appalling sight to register any feeling. Poor bastards . . . The flaming engine and its tenders had disappeared, to drag several carriages with them. The remainder of the train, two thirds along its length, was dangling like a necklace over the viaduct. A whistle was blowing behind him . . .

'*Check, check, check!*' As he lifted his hand from the firing lever, he was blinded by a vivid blue-white light. He covered his face, squinted through his fingers to discover the source . . . then realized with horror that *Urgent* was bathed in the beam of a searchlight originating from Cape Rama.

'*Clear the gun! Dive, dive, dive!*' And as he leapt clear to follow his crew up the conning tower, the pencil beam was swinging back and forth along the submarine's length.

'*Get a move on!*' Hawke bellowed. There was a fluttering sound above Banger's head, a crimson and orange flash, a stench of cordite. A cone of water spouted on the port quarter. As he reached the bridge rail, the sea was swirling up the conning tower to drown him. Another spout kicked upwards over the starboard bow: the blast whipped across his face . . . and as he tumbled towards the opening of the upper hatch, he glimpsed the captain standing above him. Behind Hawke, Brawdie saw the E-boats, two of them leaping towards *Urgent*, less than five hundred yards away, their bow waves gleaming white, their red ensigns with the crooked crosses streaming in the wind.

'*GO DEEP!*'

The captain's call from the tower echoed downwards to the control room, the instant after the klaxon had stopped braying. McVicker's hands were flickering over the diving panel, wrenching at the main vent levers. Men were tumbling from the lower lid, picking themselves up, disappearing to their diving stations. Carbis stood feet astride, murmuring his commands to his planesmen.

'*First clip on!* Shut off from depth-charging,' Hawke yelled. At least the boat was watertight, and he, the captain, was safe . . . Carbis took her down, grouped up and full ahead on both motors, the helmsman steadying her on 300° to take *Urgent* clear of the bay.

55 . . . 60 feet . . .

'Blow Q.' The submarine was twelve degrees, bow-down, and was gaining depth nicely. The cacophony of the E-boats' fast-running diesels was drowned by the roaring of Q venting inboard.

Watertight doors were slamming shut, the captain was struggling to keep his balance between the periscopes, Tonks was extricating himself from his Ursula jacket . . . when the first two explosions blasted the depths. Above the tinkling of shattered glass, Carbis ordered: 'Shut main ballast Kingstons,' as the pointers on the gauges in front were sliding past seventy-five feet.

The emergency lights flickered on and then the clatter of propellers above them faded. 'Group down. Stop starboard. Silent routine,' Hammer commanded.

'Eighty feet, sir,' Carbis called out.

'Unfriendly lot, those E-boats,' Hammer announced. 'We'll make for the deep field, Number One.'

'Four Kingston is jammed open, sir. Can't shut it.' The Stoker PO was wrenching with all his force at the big handwheel. 'It's stuck, sir.' He stared at Carbis, his eyes wide.

Then the second pattern split open the sea very close to the submarine – and directly beneath her. Carbis felt the deck flexing beneath his feet; he saw the ship's side springing towards him momentarily; he gasped as the air was knocked from his lungs. Cork spattered from the deckhead, glass from the gauges crunched beneath their feet . . . *Urgent* was being scooped upwards by a giant's hand, swooping towards the surface with a twenty-degree bow-up angle.

'Can't hold her, sir,' Carbis said. '*May I speed up?*'

'Yes.'

'Group up, full ahead together,' Carbis rapped at the telegraph operator. 'Hard-a-dive on both planes,' and he watched anxiously as the planesmen spun their brass-handled wheels clockwise.

But the boat continued to soar upwards, out of control . . . 55 . . .

48 . . . 40.

'Flood Q,' Hammer shouted. 'We can't break surface now, Number One, for God's sake . . .'

'Vent Q inboard,' Carbis ordered. Q had its immediate effect, the pointers slowing their swinging across the dials; but another pattern then blasted their world. Though the emergency lights stayed on, both planesmen called out: 'After . . . fore-planes jammed . . .' Wescombe added, for the first time a note of anxiety in his voice: 'At hard-a-dive, sir.' There was fear in his eyes when he turned towards Carbis.

Without warning, their world was transformed into pandemonium. *Urgent* was porpoising, her stern now cocked upwards as she started to plunge to the deeps.

'Stop together. Group down!' Hammer shouted above the din. 'Both planes, in hand.' She was plunging rapidly . . . 60, 65, 75, 88 . . . 95 . . . down, down and out of control. Men were sliding down the corticene deck past Carbis; he clung to the ladder rungs to keep his feet: 'Shut Q inboard vent . . . Blow Q.'

'Shut main vents,' Hawke added. The HP air screamed along the line, the vents clunked shut above them . . . then, at the instant when *Urgent*'s plunge downwards was coming under control, two more depth-charges exploded, very close but immediately under her stern. Her after-ends jerked even more steeply upwards, men were flung to the deck. *Urgent* plunged on downwards, down, down with the bubbles against the stops of the inclinometers. Must be over thirty degrees, flashed through Carbis' mind as he jammed his back against the ladder.

'*Fore-planes in hand*,' the white-faced telephone operator reported above the pandemonium.

The after-phone howled. Tarr shouted, his eyes wide with fear:

'The mainline valve's lifted, sir. Water's flooding the after-ends.'

There was a rumbling noise from the far side of the for'd control room door. The phone screeched: the 3-inch ammunition had broken adrift, was crashing against the fore-ends door and jamming the passageway.

Fell, the second cox'n, was wrenching at his handwheel: '*Fore-planes in hand*! Hard-a-rise . . .'

He was too late. Though Wescombe had shut off the shallow gauges, the deep gauge was already showing one hundred and forty-five feet.

'I've got her, First Lieutenant,' the captain shouted from the deck. 'Blow Bow Buoyancy. Blow One main ballast.'

The air shrieked again to the tanks in the eyes of the boat, screaming, it seemed, for an eternity . . . At one hundred and eighty-five feet a violent shock shuddered through the length of the hull. Gear was torn from its seating, men hurled together in heaps.

'*Stop blowing*! Stop port.' In the silence, the last emergency light flickered out. The control room was in darkness. Carbis could hear only the gasping of men. Then, above him, the whisper of propellers revolving sluggishly, languidly, as if their hunters had all the time in the world . . .

The time was 2207. *Urgent*'s bows were stuck fast on the bottom, at a bow-down angle of twenty-seven degrees. Torches flickered; the emergency lighting came on. Then, working as quietly as they could, a semblance of order was restored in each compartment. Hammer ordered the opening of all watertight doors, except for the after-ends which, as far as they could guess, was still flooding. Snagge began his all-round HE sweep, while they waited for the reports to come in. Leaving Tonks in the control room, Carbis and Ross joined the captain in the wardroom. They said little as they waited for the cox'n and Plumb, the Chief ERA, to join them.

'Well, gentlemen,' Hammer began, 'we've some decisions to take which we'd better decide together.' He glanced at Ross: 'Where are we, Pilot?'

'One-point-six miles south-west of Cape Rama, I reckon, sir. Our bows are in about two hundred feet of water.'

'Our stern?' Hammer asked his first lieutenant.

'About one hundred and seventy feet, sir. We've settled at twenty-five degrees bow-down.' Carbis watched them, his comrades now discussing their bid for survival as if the whole thing was normal routine: but he knew, as they all did, that only one course remained. He felt a serenity which he could not explain as he watched them reaching the inevitable decision.

'The moon, Pilot?'

'Should be just clearing the mountain peaks, sir.' Carbis was not the only man to glance at the clock: 2207. Much had happened in thirty-three minutes.

The third hand stuck his head round the corner of the gyro panel: 'The HSD reports HE from three destroyers approaching rapidly, sir, on a bearing of three-three-o.' There was no need for amplification: the faint, insidious *tick . . . tick . . .* was bouncing all about them.

Hammer glanced at the chief: 'Even if we bale out, Chief, there's no guarantee that we'll break free. How much HP air have I got left?'

'The reservoir's almost empty, sir. You blew a lot on our way down.'

'The after-planes are still hard-a-dive,' the cox'n reminded them. 'They had to get out quickly from the after-ends.'

Carbis heard, for the first time, the coughing from the control room. As Bill Dale stuck his head round the corner, his normally impassive face now convulsed by choking, John smelt the fumes himself; the Kingston which had been jammed open by the explosion was admitting water at this depth and pressure into number two battery compartment. The chlorine must be seeping through the deck plates. The spluttering was continuous now in the control room.

'That settles it,' the captain said, without raising his voice. 'I take it we're all agreed?'

'No option, sir.' The chief was speaking for all of them as they spread handkerchiefs across their faces.

'We'll have to be slippy about it,' Hammer said. 'Pass the word about what I have to say.' He glanced at each of them in turn: 'Open all doors. Put on DSEA sets, each compartment under the charge of its senior rating. Remain in your compartments until ordered. Muster in the control room when I call you.' He paused for a second, then fixed his piercing blue eyes on the cox'n:

'Things'll happen fast, if I can break free. I'll not start until we're all ready, so take it steadily. Bale out through the conning tower: the signalman will open the upper lid on the whistle for "Gun Action" drill.' Carbis was watching his captain. Hammer has never had a finer moment, he thought.

'Panic means oblivion for us all,' the captain continued. There was even a gleam of amusement in Hawke's eyes when he added finally: 'We've come a long way together. Thanks a lot.' He nodded up at the deckhead. 'Stick together when you reach the surface. And no heroics. Survive for another day. See you "in the bag".' He chuckled quietly as they shook hands. 'At least we'll be spared O'Brien's scran.'

CHAPTER TWENTY-TWO

. . . of Outrageous Fortune

Carbis stood between the gauges, the DSEA set on his chest, tapes tied, mouthpiece prepared to bite between his lips.

'Ready to surface, sir,' he announced quietly, breathing easier now that the chief was compressing atmospheric air through the ventilation directly into the HP reservoir: but for a very few minutes, because when the atmospheric pressure became a vacuum lungs would collapse . . .

'Ship's company all dressed in DSEA sets, sir,' the cox'n reported.

'Open the lower lid,' Hawke commanded. 'Signalman in the tower.'

They were ignoring the asdic pulses, the purring of slow-running propellers while, above, *Urgent*'s hunters relentlessly drew tight the net. Snagge had had to be commanded to abandon his asdic cabinet. He stood, gazing down at it sadly, looking like a disconsolate clown, in his DSEA outfit.

'Leave the skirt up,' Hammer said. 'Makes it easier.'

'Lower lid open,' Kipps reported.

'Up you go, then,' Hammer said. 'Open the upper lid on the whistle . . . and good luck.'

'Thanks, sir,' and the signalman clambered up into the darkness.

'Cox'n, take charge of the tower, please. First lot in, *now*. Second batch stand by here, at the for'd end of the control room. Watch out for the broken glass.'

When the six men had vanished into the conning tower, the next batch mustered in silence around the helmsman's wheel, the fore-endsmen and the engine-room crew all lumped together.

Hammer glanced at his first lieutenant: 'Ready?'

'All set, sir. Main vents checked shut.'

'You are to precede me,' the captain said. 'You're *not* to wait for me should anything go wrong. You are to take charge on the surface.' He spoke harshly: 'Understood?'

'Yes, sir. Understood.'

'The control-room crew will leave last,' Hammer ended. '*Now*, blokes, good luck . . .' He fiddled with the final adjustments of his escape set. Steady, calm and confident; his men, silent, watching him . . .

Tick – tick . . . the steady beat of slow-revving propellers . . .

'Blow Bow Buoyancy,' Hawke commanded the outside ERA. 'Blow One, blow Two main ballast.'

McVicker's hands spun open the HP air valves. The lines hissed and screamed . . . a slight trembling the length of her, that was all.

'Stop blowing.' Hammer glanced at the chief who was slowly shaking his head: 'Almost empty, sir.'

Hammer's jaw jutted: '*This* is it, then. Motor-room crew, stand by to abandon the switchboard. Ready aft?'

Mott's and Nunn's voices echoed through the tomblike engine room: 'Standing by, sir.'

Carbis could not prevent the backs of his legs from trembling uncontrollably: their last chance . . .

'*Group up* . . .' He could hear the clacking of the switches being thrown.

'*Full ASTERN together*,' Hawke shouted.

Gradually the purring of the armatures howled to a crescendo as two thousand amps surged through the main motors. She was quivering the length of her stalwart hull which had withstood so much. The pointers of the depth gauge did not move. She was stuck.

'Blow Bow Buoyancy. Blow One, blow Two main ballast.' The captain's commands crackled like pistol shots in the tense silence . . . nothing, not even a quiver on the pointers.

Oh God! Was she moving? The air was screaming again along the lines to the for'd ballast tanks, the noise dying away as the reservoir emptied. She shook suddenly, trembled again. And then they were flung to the deck as the bows, drawing free from the bottom by the surge of astern power, kicked upwards.

'*Stop blowing!*' Hammer called above the din.

When they saw the pointer of the deep-gauge quivering, beginning to move, they knew that they still had a chance. To reach the surface was all that mattered now . . . To hell with the enemy and his reputation for machine-gunning survivors! To breathe the air, to see the sunlight . . . 150 feet, 130 . . . swooping up, the bubbles sliding to the centre of the crescent inclinometer tubes, then rushing for'd as she took on a violent bow-up angle.

'One hundred feet, sir.' Carbis twitched at the shallow-gauge cock as he regained his feet. 70, 65, 50 . . .

'*Stand by*!' Hammer yelled, 'Ready, John?' Carbis stuck the whistle into his mouth. Men were grabbing every projection they could find; the broken glass was slithering across the corticene; the pale light from the emergency lights bathed the control room in ghostly unreality . . . 45 feet, 30 . . .

'*Open up*!'

Carbis blew the whistle with all the power of his lungs. Air whooshed past his head. Water splashed downwards. *Urgent* reared momentarily, then slammed down on to her bows.

The second group was clambering into the tower . . . Silently, one after the other . . . Fourteen, fifteen, sixteen . . . Hammer was bawling into McVicker's ear. Wescombe was counting the hands moving steadily past him for the ladder. 'Twenty-three, twenty-four . . .'

Hawke nodded at McVicker, then waited by himself at the panel. Carbis heard a sound like raindrops pattering above him, when Wescombe reported; 'All hands cleared from for'd and aft, sir.'

'Carry on, control-room crew,' Carbis ordered.

Helmsman, telegraphsman, Stoker PO, Outside ERA, Fell and lastly Wescombe himself, shinned up the ladder. Disappeared.

Hawke's hands were poised over the diving panel: '*Up you go, John.*' Carbis heard the main vent levers clacking open as he scrambled upward into the darkness. The vents were thudding as he reached the step of the lower hatch. He felt her bow-down angle increasing and, when half-way up the tower, paused to listen for his captain.

For God's sake, what was holding him?

Down below in the darkness there was a scrabbling; then Hammer's hoarse cursing as he hauled himself through the lower hatch. Carbis scrambled on upwards towards that aura of half-light through which the cox'n's heels were kicking. As he groped for the lip of the upper lid, water was splashing all about him. He paused to grab the clawing hand beneath him, then hauled Hammer upwards.

The bridge was awash. As the water swirled across the lip of the upper hatch he tugged with all his force at Hammer who was caught up on some projection. Kicking frenziedly, struggling to keep afloat while the boat sank beneath him, Carbis yanked with a final heave . . . and Hawke was free, spluttering beside him. Then, as they supported each other, Wescombe splashing beside them where the periscope standards frothed above their heads, Carbis saw the bullets. A hail of spurting splashes was kicking up straight for them.

He ducked below the surface. Felt Hammer slumping backwards, suddenly limp. And when John came up for air, all he could see was the dark hull of a destroyer blanking the whole of his vision. He gulped air. Turned. Saw Hammer floating in his DSEA set, horribly dead. Blood was pouring from the head and staining even darker the surface of the sea.

He heard the E-boat roaring past, its red Nazi ensign flapping proudly, its machine-gunner grinning. He ducked once more; and when again he surfaced, he saw that the Italian destroyer had eased herself between the murderous E-boat and the survivors. Scrambling nets were hanging from the destroyer's side; dark-skinned Italians were leaning across her guard rails; heaving-lines were splashing across the heads of the swimmers in the water.

He heard the TI's voice, calm, encouraging his messmates. Davies was supporting Tonks who was pouring blood from his neck. Carbis turned towards Hammer: all that could be seen of him was the yellow hump of his DSEA set being swept towards the destroyer's stern by the swirl of her propellers. Of *Urgent* there was no trace, save a threshing, frothing, boiling sea.

A heaving-line burnt across Carbis' neck. Grabbing the monkey's-fist, he was dragged underwater; then swinging towards the scrambling-net . . . a wall of grey plating, encrusted with weed and barnacles along the waterline; a line of rivets . . . and he was reaching upwards for the hands stretching down to pluck him from the frothing sea. The rope of the scrambling-net scoured his shins and his groin; seconds later, he stumbled on to the warm plating of the destroyer's upper deck.

An officer was gabbling Italian, white teeth gleaming in his swarthy, grinning face. But Carbis did not heed nor see his captor; lying prostrate, gasping for air and coughing water from his lungs, there flashed in clear-cut detail the vision of a girl: her black hair was framing her pale, almond-shaped face. Her smouldering, dark eyes were laughing as she held out her arms towards him. Her lips parted: she was whispering, but he could not catch the words.

Epilogue

He wasn't *old*: middle-aged perhaps, with his white hair, but he'd been greying since the age of twenty-three. It's watching all these exuberant youngsters which makes me feel my age, John Carbis thought, as he twitched up the collar of his coat. It was cold here, even in the lee of the passengers' bridge up in the bows of the cross-Channel ferry. He suddenly felt exhilarated as he sighted the first occulting group from the Needles lighthouse, broad on the ferry's port bow. But there was pain, too, with the memories pricking his heart. He must be suffering from the bitter-sweet malady that came with age: nostalgia.

He should have resisted the Segunas' invitation for a short stay in Mdina; the whole Maltese visit had been too unsettling. He had insisted on returning by sea: another stupid decision, particularly with the ferry calling at Trapani . . . And Mr John Carbis stuffed his hands deeper into his jacket pockets as the north-easter cut through his bones.

From the Sicilian ferry he'd even sighted Castellmare Bay, an experience he could have done without. After escaping with Doug Ross from the 'bag', when finally he reached England he had called on Hammer's parents. They had retired to Haywards Heath from Ulster. Almost *fifty* years ago? Ridiculous . . .

The flashes from St Catherine's were brighter; the Nab's light was just showing. A man with a loud voice was huddled with his girl behind the central glass wind-dodgers. 'Over there,' the yachtsman announced: 'The Needles' entrance. Bloody in a hooley.'

Mr Carbis smiled in the darkness: how would the fellow have got on in 1940? No lights, no radar. Darkened ships; five nights on end, 'watch-on, stop-on'; seventeen-hour nights . . . He wouldn't want to know; why should he? It was all too long ago, irrelevant for today's computerized world.

Over to the westward, two miles south of St Albans, his little chasseur still lay in thirty feet of water, a steel coffin for her twenty-two men. And on this side of the Needles' light, in Freshwater Bay, the destroyer *Acheron* still lies: setting out for the nightly anti-German invasion patrol, she was mined during that rotten December night of 1940, with the loss of most of her company.

He did not realize until years afterwards why he had been pitch-forked so abruptly into submarines for that special commanding officers' scheme: if the disastrous losses during the Spring of 1942 were to continue, where were trained submariners to come from – cos, officers and men, to man the boats which were starting to roll from the yards? So they'd press-ganged even Carbis . . .

What had become of those fine men so full of humour, full of human faults; so endowed with the stubborn courage to endure? They had reason to feel proud of their calling; of being the élite of the Service, because that was what they were. Age was beginning to claim them; at the memorable annual *Dolphin* gathering of the 'Old Comrades', numbers were dwindling; cruel diseases, physical and mental, were taking their toll.

What did they think now, these proud survivors, as they watched the futile and wretched divisions in the nation for which they and their dead friends had fought? Carbis' morbid thoughts were cut short when a couple in anoraks, with West German colours on their sleeves, propped themselves next to him against the glass windows.

'*Guten Abend,*' the young man said, his tone courteous and friendly. 'White Island, *ja?*' He was pointing towards the lights of Sandown and the faint, grey cliff showing up ahead.

'We call it the Isle of Wight,' Carbis said. 'You can just see the lights of Portsmouth, behind.'

'Thank you, sir.' The German was pointing to the sprinkling of lights on the horizon while he explained the coastline to his girl. 'You know this place good, sir?' the young man continued.

'Yes,' Carbis said. 'Pretty well.'

He smiled in the darkness . . . Off Culver, there, he'd been involved in that bad night of '41 when a couple of German destroyers had wiped up the off-shore patrols between Culver and Portland; and, a mile to starboard, just south of the Nab, he himself had downed a 109: the ferry could be steaming at this moment over the Messer-schmitt's watery grave . . . the skeleton in its cockpit could just qualify as this young man's grandfather . . .

Carbis was confused by his mixed emotions, incapable any longer of trying to fathom the muddled complexities of today's computerized, media-controlled, robot thinking. It was so much more difficult for today's youth which had infinite choice. It had been simple enough in '42: to kill as many of this chap's forebears as they could, to finish the bloody war . . . peace for all time, they said. For a few months his generation had believed it.

'You've come for a holiday?' Carbis asked.

'*Ja*,' the German replied. 'We stay with English friends of my *Gross mutter*. In Hammersmith, London.' He paused, but seemed eager to explain: 'The husband was in your *marine*, sir.'

'So was I,' Carbis said. 'A long time ago.'

'You *were*, sir? He was on a British destroyer in that terrible war.' He hesitated, then continued shyly. 'He sank an *Unterseeboote* in the Mediterranean. He took prisoner my *Gross fader* who was *Kapitan*. After the war they became friends and stayed in each other's homes. But *Gross fader* is dead: four years since.'

The wind was buffeting against the superstructure, the only sound in the long silence. Then Carbis said:

'There's hope, then. It's up to your generation now.'

'Sorry, sir,' and he shook his large, blond head. 'I do not understand.'

'Doesn't matter,' Carbis said. 'I'm glad you told me about your grand-father.' He turned towards the couple: 'I must leave you to collect my things.' The German extended his hand in the darkness:

'*Auf Wiedersehen*,' he said. 'It is good to talk to you, sir.'

'Good-bye,' Carbis said, grasping the proffered hand. 'Good for me, too. Enjoy your holiday.'

He began walking aft along the deck, as the ship started surging to her new course around Bembridge Ledge. Off the bow, the orange lights of Southsea were stringing like pearls along the coast. He leaned across the rail, tried to pick out the entrance to Portsmouth Harbour.

Wylie's Tower should be there; and opposite, Fort Blockhouse where it had all begun for him. The ninety-nine-foot-high Escape Tower was a landmark now; HMS *Dolphin* was still the *Alma-Mater* of modern submariners. Her young men were still the élite, splendid as ever: silently, without fuss, day-in, day-out, they were patrolling the oceans so that free men and women could sleep at nights.

While the crowds milled round the Submarine Museum, thereby contributing their admission fees to help the families who needed help, the first of the new class of submarines were sliding in and out of

Haslar Creek. These were the new *U*s of the *Upholder* class which were heralding in the new millennium. The Tenth had come home after nearly fifty years.

So, it had been worth it, then? Though the world was still dangerous, it *had* progressed in many ways, hadn't it? There *was* meaning to it all: the duty done without question; the sacrifice; the sadness and the despair had not been pointless.

Anna – my dearest Anna . . . she'd stuck by him through all those terrible months following *Urgent*'s loss, never giving up hope. She'd never failed him, had stood by him through all the hassle of life, the trials and the tribulations . . . and in half-an-hour's time their Paulina would be waiting for him at the Customs in the Ferry Terminal.

Without Paulina life would be so much bleaker. He could picture her waving to him at the Nothing-to-Declare barrier: milky-white, almond-shaped face; those mischievous, dark eyes laughing at him when she flung her arms around him . . . her image still tugged at his heart-strings. Paulina (and each day he thanked God for it) was the very re-incarnation, if ever there was one, of her mother.